PUT OUT THE LIGHT

PUT OUT
THE LIGHT

Ann Quinton

This first world edition published in Great Britain 2000 by
SEVERN HOUSE PUBLISHERS LTD of
9–15 High Street, Sutton, Surrey SM1 1DF.
This first world edition published in the U.S.A. 2000 by
SEVERN HOUSE PUBLISHERS INC of
595 Madison Avenue, New York, N.Y. 10022.

British Library Cataloguing in Publication Data

Quinton,   Ann
   Put out the light
   1.Cults - Great Britain - Fiction
   2.Detective and mystery stories
   I. Title
   823.9'14 [F]

   ISBN 0-7278-5523-9

Typeset by Hewer Text Ltd.
Edinburgh, Scotland
Printed and bound in Great Britain by
MPG Books Ltd, Bodmin, Cornwall.

Acknowledgements

I should like to thank the many people who helped me with the research for this book, in particular Simon Grew, Renata Moriconi and Jeremy Trowell.

Put out the light, and then put out the light:
If I quench thee, thou flaming minister,
I can again thy former light restore,
Should I repent me: but once put out thy light.

Othello, Act 4, Scene 2

One

"Your sister is missing."

Clare Holroyd leaned forward and gave the man sitting opposite her an accusing stare.

"She's not my sister."

"Your *step*sister then."

"She's not my stepsister."

"That's typical of you, Nick. I'm half out of my mind with worry and you sit there splitting hairs. Surely you feel some responsibility towards her – she's always looked up to you, thought you were the bee's knees, though God knows why!"

Nick Holroyd gave a wry shake of his head. "Suppose you tell me what this is all about. Ellen's eighteen, legally and mentally old enough to manage her own affairs and quite capable of looking after herself. You can't keep her tied to your apron strings for ever, you know."

"You don't understand." The woman jumped to her feet and moved towards the sideboard on which was displayed a large collection of bottles. "How about a drink?"

"Not for me –" he looked pointedly at the clock – "but I'd love a coffee. Go and make us both a coffee and then tell me what is worrying you."

With a longing look at the alcohol she went out of the room and Nick Holroyd eased back into the vulgar, overstuffed sofa and wondered just what was behind his stepmother's summons and in just what she was trying to involve him. He had had very little contact with her in recent years and it wasn't until after his career move to Dorset that he had remembered that Clare and Ellen had settled here some years previously. Not such a good move on his part perhaps but for all her faults Clare was kind-hearted and had guts.

His parents had divorced when he was four and his father had immediately re-married; a woman almost identical in looks to his first wife, though half her age and very different in character. His mother had been intellectually superior to his father, reserved and a snob; Clare was pea-brained, gregarious and brassy. When his mother had died a few years later of a sudden brain hae-morrhage he had gone to live with his father and Clare and stayed with them until he had left home in his teens to pursue his career in the police force. Not long after this his father had been killed in a car crash and a couple of years later Clare had produced a daughter, Ellen, as the result of some liaison.

As far as Nick knew, Clare had never married Ellen's father and this mystery man had long disappeared from the scene leaving Clare to bring up her daughter on her own. Well, she'd been a dreadful mother to him, mused Nick. Not in the tradi-tional stepmother mould but rather from her total lack of mothering skills. He had been alternately smothered by over-powering affection and completely ignored. If she had behaved in the same way to her own daughter then it was no wonder Ellen had upped sticks and left home as soon as she was able. It was only surprising that she hadn't done so before.

His reverie was interrupted by the return of Clare bearing a tray of coffee. She put it down on the table, indicated a mug and lit up a cigarette.

"How long has she been missing?" he asked.

"Three weeks."

"And you've had no contact with her?"

"Of course I haven't. Why do you think I'm asking you for help."

"I don't know what you think I can do. She's of age and there's nothing to stop her leaving home if she wants."

"You're a policeman, aren't you? Isn't this what you do?"

"Trace missing persons? We have to be sure first that they *are* missing and may have come to some harm. We can't waste police resources setting the whole machine in motion every time a teenager decides to give Mummy a fright. Have you any idea what's involved in trying to find a missing person?"

"Oh, I know where she is."

"You *know* where she is?" Nick looked incredulously at his stepmother. "Then what is this all about?"

"She's living with that queer religious sect over at Moulton Abbas. Moonies or some such."

"I didn't know the Unification Church was active in these parts."

" 'The Unification Church' " she mimicked, grinding out her cigarette. "Sometimes, Nick, you're too clever for your own boots. I don't suppose they *are* Moonies but they're just as weird. Call themselves The Children of Light or some such name. They've got her in their clutches and have brainwashed her. She doesn't want anything to do with her poor old mother now."

"I thought you said you'd had no contact with her?"

"Not since she's moved out –" Clare spoke patiently as if explaining to a five-year-old – "but before that, when she started getting involved, she was on about this group of people who really cared about the state of the world and how they were working to make things better for the poor and underprivileged."

"Sounds a good idea to me."

"Don't you believe it! There's only one person getting anything out of this and that's the so-called leader of the group. According to Ellen he can do no wrong. He's mesmerised them all and as far as she is concerned the sun shines out of his . . . well, you know what I mean." Clare Holroyd lit up another cigarette. "He needs investigating and she needs to be brought to her senses."

"How did she get involved?"

"Through some young fellow she met at college."

Ellen, Nick recalled, was doing a course in Performing Arts at the local college. A strange choice, he had thought, as Ellen had always appeared to be timid and self-effacing, a complete contrast to her more flashy mother. Perhaps this had been Clare's idea to bring her out of her shell.

3

"So there's a boyfriend in the offing?"

"Ellen has never been interested in boys." Clare's voice and expression were a nice mixture of pride and bafflement.

Nick put down his empty mug and regarded his stepmother with amused tolerance. "Look, I know you're worried about her but if she chooses to go off and live in a commune or whatever there's not really anything you can do about it. Look on it as part of the process of growing up. It's just a phase she's going through and she'll soon come to her senses. It's her way of rebelling and the more you rubbish it to her the more appealing it will seem."

"Chance would be a fine thing," said Clare tartly. "As far as I'm concerned she's completely vanished. She could be murdered for all I know!"

"Come on, Clare, get real; you don't really believe that."

"You just don't care, do you? A young, innocent girl, part of your family even if you won't admit it, and you couldn't care less!"

"There's really nothing the police can do in the circumstances. No crime has been committed, she went of her own free will and . . ."

"The police don't own you body and soul, do they?" she interrupted him. "You're talking like their PR man. If Mr Plod can't get involved surely you can have a snoop round this cult and find out what has happened to her? I thought your current woman was into religion?"

Now, how on earth had she found out about that? thought Nick as he drove back to Casterford. His friendship with Rachel was not common knowledge and if there was one thing that was certain it was the fact that she was *not* his woman – unfortunately. His transfer to Dorset had been prompted as much by his pursuit of physiotherapist and lay reader Rachel Morland as by personal ambition. God only knows they were an ill-matched pair; Rachel, the widow of a Church of England priest and actively involved with the religious community, and he, a divorcé with a bad reputation with women. They had met – or rather clashed would be the better word – when both were living in East Anglia. He had been working on a case involving a serial killer in

4

which Rachel had been caught up and had almost lost her life. It had been the attraction of opposites, he supposed. Against their wills, they had admitted to the flaring of passion between them but she had fled to Dorset to start a new life and he had followed, hoping to build on and improve the shaky start to their relationship. Well, he hadn't got very far. A strictly platonic friendship existed between them that bewildered and tormented him. How his ex-colleagues would jeer if they knew how singularly unsuccessful he was being in pulling this bird. But that was just the point; he didn't want a quick conquest. Rachel meant far more to him than that and he knew he had to proceed carefully or he would lose her altogether.

How Clare had got to hear about he and Rachel he couldn't imagine but at least she had made a valid point. Rachel might well be able to help in sorting out his wayward stepsister.

For early May the heat was intense; an early taste of summer that had carried off the last of the spring-flowering bulbs and was already dulling the acid green of the burgeoning foliage. People drifted round the town centre in their shirtsleeves and summer dresses, forsaking the sunshine for the shady side of the streets. In Faulkener's Walk, where the new shopping arcade met the colonnaded arches of the old Benedictine priory, a small crowd was gathered. This was a favourite spot for street entertainers but the girl busking today was very different from the usual flamboyant performers. For a start she was playing classical music on a flute and although the Baroque tune spilling into the air was vaguely familiar, Bach would not have recognised the tempo and phrasing. She was tall and thin and dressed in a long blue shift that reached her ankles. Her hair was a pale curtain that billowed and spun round her shoulders as she swayed and glided on bare feet to the lilting tune she was piping.

Rachel Morland had been hurrying through the mall, intent on finishing some last-minute shopping but she stopped entranced and joined the onlookers. The girl looked as if she had stepped out of a medieval frieze. One half expected to see tapestry flowers scattered round her feet and unicorns prancing behind her in the shadows. Instead, she was joined by another girl who held a strange carved drum on which she accompanied the recorder player with insistent beating that rose and fell as she gyrated round the little circle formed by the onlookers.

This girl was very different in appearance to her fellow busker. She had a mop of tightly curled black hair and as she swung past, Rachel could see that she was considerably older. For all her frenetic movements there was a blankness in her face as if she were a zombie and not in complete control of her actions. At intervals she would break off from her drumming and mingle with the spectators, thrusting a velvet cap at them as if daring them not to contribute. Her importuning seemed to work, if the chink of coins was anything to go by. Rachel fumbled in her handbag for some change, then pushed her way back through the crowd unaware that she has just met up with two people who were to play a large part in her life during the coming months. She was also unaware of the signal that passed between the two women and was picked up by the figure huddled on the ground with his dog at the foot of a column further along the arcade.

Lonny was an unprepossessing youth of indeterminate age with a pale, unhealthy skin, liberally tattooed. He wore studs in both nostrils and an array round each ear, and his hair was tied back in a skimpy ponytail. In his crouched position his dog looked almost as large as he. It was some sort of cross breed with bull mastiff in its ancestry and it kept guard over the begging bowl on the ground in front of them. No one would dare to filch from the meagre collection of coins it held; it was a moot point whether anyone would actually dare approach close enough to add to them. At the signal, Lonny heaved himself to his feet with the aid of a crutch. Through the holes in his tattered jeans one leg appeared to be heavily bandaged. He gathered up his belongings and limped away down the mall, his dog padding beside him. Behind him, the two female entertainers had also disappeared.

The girl stumbled up the bank and tottered into the road. Dazzled by the lights of an oncoming vehicle she threw up her hands to protect her eyes and reeled out into its path. There

6

was a screech of brakes and the car spun sideways ending up on the grass verge.

"Bloody idiot!" snarled the driver, flinging open his door and swinging out. "Pissed as a newt! What the hell do you think you're doing? I could have killed you!"

The girl slumped against the bonnet, shaking and convulsed and the man's wife scrambled out.

"She's hurt, Derek, not drunk." She put an arm round the girl. "What happened? Was it a hit and run driver?"

The girl shook her head and tears oozed down her mud-stained face. "I've been . . . been . . . raped . . ." Her voice was a hoarse whisper. ". . . he jumped me . . . down there . . ." She opened her eyes and gestured wildly towards the dark fringe of trees marching parallel to the embankment. "He . . . he tried to kill me . . . strangle me . . ."

The husband and wife exchanged horrified glances.

"Oh my God! You don't think it's the Wessex Rapist, do you?" The man looked towards where she had pointed and the woman spoke hurriedly:

"Quick, we must get her to the hospital."

"He may still be out there . . ."

"Well, you're not dealing with it, leave it to the police. Help me get her into the car."

"Not the police, not the hospital. I just want to go home," the girl pleaded as she huddled on the back seat tightly gripping the woman's hands.

"You need medical attention, dear, we'll take you to Casualty."

"No . . . I can't face that. My doctor . . ."

"Who is that?"

"Dr Clarke. At Barton Road Clinic."

"There'll be no one there at this time of the evening."

"She lives there . . . above the surgery . . ." The girl shut her eyes again and slumped back against the upholstery and the couple had a whispered consultation.

"Perhaps that would be best. I think this Dr Clarke is a woman."

"Right, we'll go and see if we can raise her but the police must be told. Not that they've had much success so far in catching this monster!"

"Ssssh . . . We'll take you round to Barton Road, dear, and let's hope Dr Clarke is at home, but you'll have to talk to the police – this man must be stopped."

Jane Clarke said the same thing a short while later as she comforted the girl in her surgery.

"I know this has been a terrible experience, Sarah, but we can't let this man get away with it. The police will want to talk to you and you'll have to be examined. You understand what I'm saying, don't you? There'll be forensic evidence to be gathered."

"I can't bear anyone to touch me."

"I know, it's the last thing you want but can you be very, very brave?"

"Can you . . .?"

"I don't know, but I'll do what I can. You want this fiend put away so that he can't do it again, don't you?"

"I never want to see or think about him again!"

Jane Clarke wrapped a blanket around the girl and went to make some phone calls.

"The fourth one in as many months and we still haven't a clue as to his identity or where he hangs out." Superintendent Powell paced the floor, snapping his fingers. "Who is the victim this time?"

"A Sarah Gleed. She's a student at the college. She was returning home to her lodgings after a Student Union meeting and she took a short cut through that piece of waste land near the old railway cutting at Pilbury." DS Keith Adams had just returned from the hospital with WPC Fiona Walker and was reporting on the information they had gathered.

"Can't she read or hear?" demanded Tom Powell. "The papers and media have been full of nothing else since the first one. What did she think she was doing walking on her own through a deserted area at that time of night with a rapist on the loose?"

"The others all happened on the other side of the town. She

probably didn't think. She'd just had a row with her boyfriend, had missed the last bus and was desperate to get home," said Fiona Walker.

"Could he . . .?"

"No. She left him drinking in the bar with half the Student Union. She says a car followed her along Fitzwilliam Street, going very slowly. She thought it was a kerb crawler which is why she took off across the waste land. She heard the car door slam and was aware of footsteps coming after her which is when she panicked and started to run. He caught up with her in the trees and dragged her into the old disused railway tunnel."

"Did she get a good look at him? Can she give us a description?"

"No, only that he was wearing a black hood and gloves as before. She put up a fight though and that's when he got really nasty. He got his hands round her throat and was trying to throttle her. She reckons if she hadn't gone limp and let him have his way he would have killed her."

"I don't like this one little bit." Powell resumed his pacing of the floor. "With each successive attack he has become more violent. At first he was just after sexual kicks, now he seems to want to inflict physical punishment. I'm afraid the next time it happens, if we don't manage to catch him first, he'll go too far and she'll end up dead. How is his latest victim?"

"Very distressed, sir," Fiona Walker said shortly, wondering why he had to ask such a question. "Her instincts are to crawl into a hole and hide but she has been very cooperative. We've got a good DNA sample from the rapist."

"Which would be useful if we had someone to match it against. We seem to know no more about him now than we did after the first attack."

"We know he has transport," said Adams, "and this fits in with him not concentrating on one particular area but covering the whole of Casterford and district."

"Which hardly makes our job any easier."

"He's an opportunist, not a stalker," put in Fiona.

"Yes, Constable Walker?"

"These are random attacks," she said firmly, determined to be heard out. "He couldn't have known that Sarah Gleed was going to have a row with her boyfriend and decide to walk home alone. He's just cruising the area and grabbing the chance when it offers itself."

"Which makes our task more difficult. If he were targeting a particular section of the local community it could be warned and protected. As it is, the entire female population is at risk and that could lead to mass hysteria . . ."

"Not everyone," she dared to interrupt. "Only those within a particular age group."

"So he likes them young and pretty. Tell me something new."

"We just don't know what type of man we're looking for." DS Adams drummed his fingers on his notebook. "He could be your archetypal frustrated loner who can't manage a normal relationship with someone of the opposite sex. On the other hand, he could be a married man with a family, whose wife has no idea he is leading a secret life.

"I'm drafting more men on to Collins's team. Where *is* Mark anyway?"

"His mother has just died, up north. He's organising the funeral."

"Oh yes, of course. Well, this man has got to be caught before he claims his next victim. If he follows the same pattern as before it will be four weeks before his next attack."

"There were only three weeks between the last rape and this one."

"So, his urge is growing and he's giving in to it because he knows we're helpless and he can get away with it. He must be stopped."

Two

The phone rang as Rachel Morland was coming in from the garden. She kicked off her old shoes and plunged inside the cottage, shedding gardening gloves on her way through the back lobby, and snatched up the receiver.

"Hello?"

"I've got a job for you."

"I'm very well, thank you, and you?"

There was a pause at the other end of the line, then Nick Holroyd sounding sheepish replied, "Sorry, Rachel, you're OK, aren't you? I knew you'd probably be in at this time of day and . . ."

"You couldn't be bothered with the social niceties. Quite right. At least you know where *your* priorities lie."

"Look, I'm sorry, let's start again, shall we? Are you doing anything tomorrow?"

"Why?"

"Don't sound so suspicious. I'm asking you out."

"For your benefit or for mine?"

"You don't trust me, do you?"

"Should I?"

Nick sighed audibly down the phone. "You've obviously had a bad day. Forget it's me. Forget I'm a policeman. Pretend you're a young girl and your favourite boyfriend is ringing for a date."

"Even my imagination can't stretch that far!" Rachel settled back on the hall chair and relented. "I'll give you the benefit of the doubt, and to answer your question, I'm free after morning service. What had you in mind?"

"We must make the most of this weather. I don't know about

11

you but I'm fed up with being cooped up in an office. I thought about a trip to the Isle of Purbeck; lunch in Corfe and then perhaps a walk along the cliffs near Durdle Door."

"Sounds inviting. What do I have to do to earn this little treat?"

"Rachel! Forget what I said. It's just that something has come up – a little family problem – that I thought you might be able to help me with. It's not important, I'll put you in the picture tomorrow."

"I didn't know you *had* any family." She was intrigued in spite of herself.

"There's plenty about me you don't know. There are depths to my character you have never dreamed of. Peel away the many layers and discover the *real* me."

"Like an onion? I'd just be left with streaming eyes and a bad smell." She chuckled. "Actually, I think you're a very devious person who is very careful not to expose your true feelings."

"Except to you."

There was a silence at the other end and Nick silently cursed himself.

"Rachel? You're still there . . .?"

"Yes."

"What time shall I pick you up tomorrow? Shall I meet you out of church?"

"No, I'll come home and change after the service. I should be ready by about twelve o'clock."

"Fine. Well, I'll let you get on – what are you doing, incidentally?"

"Gardening."

"Gardening?"

"As in cutting the grass and hoeing the borders."

"Of course, you've got quite a large plot there, haven't you. You must let me lend a hand some time."

"I wouldn't dare let you loose amongst my precious flowers but I'll remember the offer when the hedge needs cutting or there is some digging to be done."

"I'm a dab hand with a spade."

"Where did you get your practice – digging up bodies?"

*   *   *

The next day, seated in the crowded restaurant area of one of Corfe's pubs, Nick Holroyd looked about him ruefully.

"Perhaps this wasn't such a good idea after all. I didn't realise it would be so busy."

"A Sunday, fine weather, local beauty spot and a lot of holidaymakers about already."

"Yes. At least we got served reasonably quickly. Is it all right?" Nick had chosen the roast with all the trimmings, whilst Rachel had opted for the seafood lasagne.

"Yes, it's fine. Very good actually, though rather a large portion."

"You don't have to worry about your figure. Are you going to manage a pudding?"

"Not for me, thanks, but I'd love a coffee."

"I'll go and get them."

She watched his fair head threading through the customers jostling round the bar, then turned her attention to the scene outside the nearby window. The garden was as full as the interior, with families crowded round the wooden bench tables and children running riot on the scrubby lawns. Beyond, was a stand of trees shimmering in the midday heat and behind this the ruins of Corfe Castle stood sentinel, the jagged tower a black finger against the cerulean sky.

Nick returned, balancing two coffees carefully in one hand as he negotiated the packed tables. Whilst they were sipping them loud disco music burst from the loudspeaker above their heads and Rachel winced.

"Come on, let's get out of here," he said. "It's as hot inside as out. The sooner we get to the coast the better, we may find a sea breeze."

They found crowded roads and every car-park in the vicinity of Lulworth Cove full, but eventually they managed to park, and set off along the coastal path. It appeared that half the population of Dorset had the same idea: the Downs and cliff paths were dotted with walkers, both serious hikers and families out for an afternoon stroll. By stepping out they overtook most of the stragglers and, after struggling up a particularly steep incline, Nick called a halt.

"Let's have a rest. I'm not as fit as I thought I was." He flung himself down on the ground and Rachel joined him, stretching out on the springy grass and closing her eyes. The sun beat against her eyelids and there was a background hum of bees, distant seagulls and the lazy drone of a small plane.

"What is that I can smell – like coconut?" Nick's voice roused her as she was drifting off.

"Gorse. It *does* smell like coconut, doesn't it? It's at it's peak now but you can usually find some out in bloom at any time during the year. Thomas Hardy – he lived in these parts you know – said something about 'When the gorse is not in bloom, kissing is out of fashion.' "

"Is that an invitation?"

"Behave yourself." She sat up and clasped her arms round her bent knees. "Tell me about your family problem and what I can do to help."

"Have I told you about my stepmother?"

"No, I thought your parents were dead."

"They are, my real parents." He rolled over on to his stomach and plucked at grass stalks and clover as he explained about Clare and Ellen.

"I'm not quite sure what you think I can do," she said, when he had finished.

"Well, you see, Clare's getting into a state – quite needlessly I'm sure – and I thought you could investigate this cult and put her mind at rest."

"Investigate? I'm not one of your police officers!"

"I know, I know, but I thought as you're half ordained it would give you an entrée into this religious sect."

"I'm not half ordained. I'm a licensed lay reader and although I have shelved the idea of becoming a priest for the time being it is still a possibility in the future. It's on hold, so to speak. It won't go away."

"I know. I admire you for it. I just wish . . ."

"What?"

"That I could understand . . . share your views about religion . . ."

14

"Don't worry, I haven't given up. I'm still working on you."
She smiled at him and he grinned back.

"Anyway, didn't you mention that you were going around participating in different forms of religious worship?"

"Yes, I'm very much in favour of ecumenicalism. I've taken part in Methodist, Roman Catholic and Unitarian services and also the Society of Friends – Quakers; that was very moving. But this sect is hardly an orthodox schism of Christianity, is it?"

"I don't know. Clare seemed to think they could be Moonies."

"Then you would have something to worry about. But I should think that is most unlikely. 'Children of Light' is a very ambiguous name. It could have a Christian meaning, the light of Jesus' teaching perhaps? Or they could be pagans, worshipping the sun."

"Have you heard anything about them?"

"Actually I have, but not in the sense you mean. The community runs a farm, or a smallholding, and they sell herbal remedies, organic produce and free-range eggs – that sort of thing. They sometimes have a stall at the local market and you can also go over to their place at Moulton Abbas and get supplies."

"There you are. You can go and buy some eggs, get talking and insinuate yourself into their set-up."

"I don't think it would be as simple as that, but supposing I do – how am I going to recognise Ellen? I can't go asking for her by name, can I?"

"If they are above board I don't see why you couldn't mention that you know of her; friend of a friend, etc., but I leave the logistics to you. As for recognising her, she's tall and fair-haired and, believe it or not, she's supposed to bear some resemblance to me although we aren't related."

"Poor girl."

"I shan't rise to that. But enough of my problems, how is the new job going?"

"I'm enjoying it but my clientele is very different. Living in a city before, with large manufacturing industries, I tended a great many work-related injuries. Here, there are more elderly and

15

retired people so much of my time is spent dealing with the geriatrics. Of course, there are also the injuries and strains connected with farming and the rural occupations. How about you?"

"It *is* very different. I suppose in a way it is good to get away from the inner-city syndrome. After all, I was born and bred in the country and although I am part of the town constabulary, it certainly feels more rural. Not that there isn't just as much crime in this part of the country, and some of it particularly nasty."

"You mean the Wessex Rapist?"

"Yes. He claimed another victim last night."

"Oh, Nick, how awful. Are the police any closer to catching him?"

"Between me and you – no, but we will get him. I promise you."

"Are you involved in the case?"

"Not directly."

Nick looked out across the sea surging many feet below them and screwed up his eyes in the brilliant light. A smile tugged at his mouth as he reflected on how his presence had been received in this Force. He had arrived with his reputation having come on before him; a reputation as a good detective though impetuous and a trouble-maker, who had once stepped out of line and been punished for it but was now reinstated.

"What are you smiling at?"

He chewed on a blade of grass and squinted at her.

"I don't think they quite know what to do with me. At the moment I'm working on a larceny case. There has been a rash of burglaries in the past few months, ranging from snatch and grabs from individual victims to break-ins at well-heeled residences and country estates. Not vast amounts of money or valuables have been involved, just electrical goods, portable antiques, wage packets – that kind of thing. They appear to be the work of the same gang though it is difficult to see how they are connected. But to get back to our rapist – don't take any risks, will you? Until we get more of a line on him every woman needs to take the greatest care."

"Don't worry. Every woman on the staff of the hospital is aware of the danger and is extra vigilant."

"That cottage of yours is very isolated."

"Rubbish, it's in the centre of the village. Anyway, all the attacks have been in Casterford itself, haven't they?"

"So far, but our man seems to be extending his territory. I think you need protection, someone to live with you at that cottage."

"Don't push it, Nick." She jumped to her feet and smoothed down her skirt. "Let's walk some more. We're both going to get heatstroke if we sit here with the sun beating down on us."

"You can't say I don't try."

"Too true. Mission defeated."

She started off along the track and with a shrug he followed her.

The young woman blinked as she entered the car-park; the sudden transition from brilliant sunshine to cavernous gloom almost blinding her. As she trod down the ramp to the lower level she paused and shifted the weight of the large box she was carrying from one arm to the other. She hadn't realised how heavy it would be. She really ought to have had it delivered but that would have meant nearly a week's delay and she wanted to try it out today. Weeks of saving and going without proper lunches so that she could buy the latest state-of-the-art music centre had been rewarded. The one she had set her heart on had been marked down just for this one week and she had managed the new asking price.

Walking along the serried ranks of parked cars she was vaguely aware of footsteps echoing behind her but she took no notice. She spotted her Fiesta tucked in between a Range Rover and an ancient Volkswagon and set down her package on the ground whilst she fumbled in her handbag for her car keys. One day she might be able to afford a car with a remote control locking system, though not if she splashed out on equipment like this. Her father would complain that she had squandered her money and what was wrong with the perfectly good music centre they already had? He didn't seem to understand that she wanted her own system in her own room where she could entertain her friends without subjecting them to the chaos of family life as lived by her younger tearaway twin brothers.

At least she had central locking in this car, she thought as she turned the key in the driver's door. Should she put her precious purchase on the back seat or in the boot? She decided the boot would be safer and lifted up the lid, rooting amongst the jumbled contents to make a space. She didn't notice the shadow as someone slipped past momentarily blocking the light from the nearby fluorescent wall strip, or the click of a door handle. With her new purchase safely stowed in the boot she got into the car and fired the engine. She backed out of her parking space, engaged first gear and headed for the exit ramp. The car had hardly started moving when a slight noise immediately behind her head startled her so much that she stalled the engine.

She felt something cold and sharp pressing into the nape of her neck and as she tried to scream a hand came over her shoulder and hard fingers clamped her mouth tightly.

"Shut it if you want to stay healthy," a voice whispered harshly in her ear. "I've got a knife so don't try any tricks." Paralysed with fright she froze in her seat.

"Start the engine. Go on – do what I say." With shaking fingers she did as she was bid and the voice hissed further instructions.

"Get going. No, not that way. You're not going home, darling. Go down to the bottom level."

It was even darker down there. Little used, if people could avoid it, most of the spaces were allocated to season ticket holders. There was no one about at that time of day and with dreadful certainty she knew that she was in the hands of the Wessex Rapist. So petrified that she was shaking all over, her foot slipped off the accelerator pedal and the car stalled again.

"I said no tricks. Drive over to the far corner, behind that pillar."

She obeyed, knowing that she was utterly helpless. He was going to rape her and there was nothing she could do. If she tried to escape or scream for help he would use the knife on her. A quick glance in the mirror had revealed a dark shape wearing some sort of a hood over his head with slits through which his eyes gleamed. The rapist wore a hood, it had said so in the papers. She couldn't believe this was happening to her. She and all her friends were very careful not to venture out alone at night in lonely areas believing there was safety in numbers, yet here she was, in the middle of the afternoon in a public car-park, at the mercy of the man who had already attacked and raped several women.

"Switch off the engine and get out." The instructions were accompanied by a prod of the knife and as she complied he scrambled out behind her, cutting off what little light there was as he loomed over her.

"Unlock the boot."

She did so and he lifted out the boxed music centre and stood it on the ground.

"Now let's have your handbag." As she handed it over she noticed that he was wearing gloves. He rifled through the contents, extracting the few notes and coins left in her purse.

"Not much here, is there? I suppose you've spent it all on your goodies. Get back in the car. Go on – in the driving seat." He gave her a little push and she collapsed inside. "Put your hands *there*." He held them together and snapped on a pair of hand-cuffs, fastening them to the steering wheel. He slammed the door shut and she was dimly aware of retreating footsteps and then silence.

She leant her hand on her manacled hands and wept with relief. He wasn't the rapist, he was a thief. She had been robbed, not ravished. It was several moments later before she realised that she could manoeuvre her hands and press the horn to summon help.

A little while later a startled council worker came to her rescue.

"Whoever is behind these robberies, whether it's a gang or one person masterminding them, there's one thing for sure. He or they don't operate like our rapist. They're not smash and grab, take a chance affairs. They're all carefully planned and the victim is watched and followed before the snatch is made." Nick Holroyd was discussing the situation with his sergeant, Tim Court. "Or, if it's a house done over, they've had it under surveillance and know exactly when the owner's absent and what to take."

"With this latest one our laddie took an almighty risk. She buys the stuff in Gurney's, the largest store in town, parades down the High Street with it and goes back to the multi-storey car-park. How did he get her on her own?"

"Well, to some extent he's an opportunist. He must have seen her buy it and followed her in the hope that he could nick it. If there had been people around in the car-park he would have given up the attempt."

"She can't even give us a description. Just that he was tall and wearing a hood. Poor kid thought it was the rapist."

"Where did he get the handcuffs from?"

"They weren't real. The sort you get from a joke shop. She could have busted free if she had really tried but she was too terrified to think straight." Tim Court hitched his behind on to the edge of the desk and swung his legs to and fro, and Nick was once more astounded at what enormous feet he had. Clad in trainers sprouting extended tongues, heel shields and a mass of grubby laces they looked like nothing so much as a pair of beached trawlers. "You still think the house robberies are down to the same operator?" he continued, scratching the back of his knee with one scruffy foot.

"Yes. Not because of the MO but because of what they whip. All small stuff that can't easily be traced and which there's a good market for. Take that raid at Ulvermere Manor last week. There's some very valuable pictures there and priceless ceramics but they left those strictly alone. Just went for small antiques, a canteen of cutlery and two televisions – and a microwave."

"I reckon it could be an inside job, one of the domestic staff."

"Don't forget there was a Spring Fair held in the grounds the week before. A lot of people visited the place and it would have been easy for someone to get into the house and have a snoop around. There's a pattern to these stately home scams. They all happen just after the place has been open to the public for a day or a weekend. There was Harnley House a couple of months ago; opened in aid of the Red Cross and done over a few days later. An ideal opportunity for someone to get inside and case the joint, and only small stuff was taken again, but enough of it to make a worthwhile haul. I reckon we've got a Fagin in our midst. Someone organising a gang of petty thieves, who must be a very successful fence."

"Why don't people get their property marked? Then at least there is a chance of us tracing it if it turns up later.

"They don't think it's ever going to happen to them. Can't you lean on your informers? I haven't been here long enough to build up a network of moles but someone must have heard something or know what's going on."

"Maybe it's going abroad. They're shifting it straight across to the Continent and not trying to get rid of it over here."

"If that's the case it is going to be even more difficult to trace."

There was a knock at the door and a young constable poked his head inside.

"There's been another robbery reported, sir. Happened late yesterday afternoon at a jeweller's shop in Eastgate."

"Happened yesterday and it's only just been reported?"

"Yes. It's owned by an old chap in his seventies with a duff heart. He'd just been adding up his takings in the till when this masked man threatened him and snatched the lot. The old boy was game. He chased out into the alley after him and had an angina attack. He somehow managed to get himself back into the shop – he lives above it on his own – and took his medication, but he felt so ill – and, according to him, thought he was going to peg out – that he didn't do anything about the theft until this morning. Then he discovered the thief had also taken a tray of rings and some silverware."

"Counting out the till receipts in full view of every passer-by? I don't believe this!"

"Apparently he did it every day at about the same time."

21

"There you are, someone had been monitoring his movements over a period of time. What did I tell you?"

"What time was that girl robbed in the car-park yesterday – four o'clock wasn't it? About the same time that this one was taking place so it can't have been the same person."

"I tell you, it's a highly organised gang," said Holroyd gloomily. "Is the old man OK?"

"Yes, he seems to have recovered and he may have given us a lead. Before he was taken bad he had followed the thief out of the alley into a side road – Bucks Lane – and saw him get into a blue van and drive off."

"I suppose it's too much to hope that he got the registration number?"

"Yes. All he could say was that he thought it was a Bedford van and it looked old."

"Not much to go on but we'll put out a call and hope that we may be able to trace it."

Rachel had decided to discuss the Children of Light with the vicar of the church at which she helped to officiate before approaching them herself. Peter Stevenson was a dynamic young man who had in his charge the parish of St James and the churches of the surrounding villages. He had a very modern outlook and was succeeding in drawing in the young families and teenagers despite the ageing population of the area. He was vastly different from the vicar of her last parish who had been spiritual and well-meaning but a bad communicator. Peter Stevenson was irreverent and go-getting and, with his long hair and beard, could have modelled for 'The Light of the World' if you ignored the wicked twinkle in his eyes.

He played the guitar, and for good measure the drums, and one was more likely to meet children scampering up and down the aisles and teenagers making their own music in his services than pious silences. Nick, who had been persuaded to attend one of his services, had dismissed him as one of the clappy-happy brigade, but Rachel was sure that if he got to know Peter he would change his mind.

To her surprise, when she tackled Peter about the Children of Light he seemed to be familiar with them.

"But are they *Christians*?" she asked puzzled when he admitted to having met the leader.

"Not as you and I think and practise Christianity but loosely speaking you could say yes. I suppose you could call them secessionists. They have sifted out what appeals to them from the basic Christian principles and ignored the rest. I don't approve of this bending of the rules to suit one's needs but I believe they do a lot of charity work with the needy and homeless. Why this sudden interest in them? You're not going to desert us, are you?"

She explained that the young relative of a friend of hers had apparently joined the sect.

"Yes, I can see that would be worrying" said Peter Stevenson. "Young people are very impressionable at that age and can be sucked into all kinds of weird cults but I don't think you have too much to fear about this one on the whole. They appear to be pretty harmless and it's better than drugs and many of the things they get mixed up with these days. However, I think their leader, or guru, needs watching."

"What do you mean?"

"He's a very charismatic character but I have my doubts as to whether he is really sincere. I think he could be on a big ego trip and enjoys having these youngsters hanging on to his words."

"Are you saying he only picks young people to be his followers and you suspect his motives?"

"No, it is a mixed community and I understand he is married and runs it with his wife's help. Would you believe his name is Gabriel?"

"You're having me on?"

"I'm not. I shouldn't think for one moment it's his real name but that is what he is known by."

"Well, let's hope he is a real Gabriel and not a Lucifer. How does he recruit people? Is it by word of mouth or do they advertise?"

"I really don't know. Perhaps I should have made it my business to find out more about them."

"I need to visit the place to find out if Ellen *is* there and is alright. Is there any way I can approach them officially?"

"You mean on behalf of the C of E?" He considered this. "I don't see why you couldn't go and issue an invitation for their community to attend the big ecumenical service we're holding at St Botolph's in a few weeks time. We've got most denominations represented."

"Do you think it would meet with the Bishop's approval?"

"Probably not, but we don't have to tell him."

Three

Rachel did not manage to visit Moulton Abbas until the following weekend. The Children of Light occupied the old Moulton Manor estate which was situated on the outskirts of the village. It consisted of a rather beautiful house built in cream stone and a farm with numerous outbuildings plus a substantial acreage. She decided to leave her car in the centre of the village and walk to the manor, thinking she would get a better view of the set-up if she approached on foot.

It was another hot day and she wrinkled up her nose as she strolled along the road. The hawthorn blossom which frothed over the hedgerow was past its best and now resembled dirty suds and smelt of decaying meat. Soon it would be overtaken by elderflowers in the floral calendar. Already a few large creamy saucers of bloom were pushing their way through the tangle of branches and these would soon be joined by the first dog roses and honeysuckle. Moulton Abbas itself was a picturesque village which featured frequently in travel brochures, and she wondered what the inhabitants thought of the controversial community in their midst.

She walked up a slight incline past the recreation ground, and the roof of the manor came into view, rising above a clump of black, sculptured yews, the tall elegant chimneys free from television aerials. She had read up about it in a local history book and knew that the main structure was Stuart though parts of it were much earlier and the magnificent barn dated from the fourteenth century. It would take serious money to buy a property like this and she had discovered that the Children of Light had only been in residence for about three years so by her reckoning the organisation was not short of a penny.

As she drew near the driveway a man and woman came out of the honeypot lodge that guarded the entrance and walked through the open gates towards her. The man was dressed in jeans and a T-shirt and the woman was wearing a long green dress that flowed around her as she moved. Rachel was reminded of the young woman busking in Casterford and realised that probably she and her companion had been members of the Children of Light. No sooner had she absorbed this thought when another one struck her. Maybe that girl had actually been Nick's stepsister. She fitted the description he had given her – tall and fair. Rachel wondered how he would react to learning that Ellen was a street entertainer. Was it legal, did one have to have a licence to perform in this way? It was akin to begging and she was sure that was illegal and anyone found begging was smartly moved on by the police.

She hesitated as the couple drew abreast and the woman spoke to her.

"Can we help you? You look lost."

Rachel resisted the urge to say "take me to your leader".

"I'm visiting the community; are you members?"

"Yes. Does Gabriel know you're coming?"

"No. Do I need an appointment?"

The woman smiled. "Oh no, we live very informally here. Gabriel is always pleased to welcome callers but sometimes he's rather elusive; he's a very busy person. I'll walk down with you and try and find him."

"That's kind of you but there's no need. You were on your way out."

"It's no trouble." She turned to her companion. "You go on ahead, Martin. I'll catch you up later."

The man squeezed her shoulder and set off towards the village. He hadn't spoken a single word during the encounter and Rachel wondered if he might be dumb. She walked down the drive beside the woman who, at close quarters, looked older than she had first appeared. Rachel reckoned she was in her late-twenties but there was a childlike innocence in her face and she wore her dark hair braided into a simple plait which hung down her back.

"Have you lived here long?" asked Rachel, hoping to discover something about the community before she met up with its guru.

"I don't think I really lived until I came here," the woman answered enigmatically. "Have you come to join us?"

Rachel explained that she was already a committed Christian and held a lay position in the Church of England.

"Ah, an HBS."

"A what?"

"A hide-bound sectarian. That's what Gabriel calls those who follow the old insular religious orders and haven't been enlightened."

"And Gabriel has been enlightened?" She tried to keep the sarcasm out of her voice.

"Yes. God has spoken to him and shown him the Truth. All the old prejudices and rituals are like veils masking the truth. He has torn them aside and revealed the real heart of the matter."

"Which is what?"

"We are here to help our fellow men. To give to the needy and underprivileged and persuade the wealthy to be more charitable. The divide between the rich and the poor is obscene."

"Well, I go along with that."

"The organised religions are self-centred. They invest in their hierarchy and buildings rather than people. They do not address the problems of today."

Wow, wouldn't Peter like to get his teeth into this one, thought Rachel, resisting the temptation to get drawn into an argument. Instead, she said lightly: "Gabriel certainly seems to have converted you. I must say your ideals are very worthy but how do you put them into practice?"

"What do you mean?"

"To have an objective is one thing; to put it into practice is another. We're talking money here not ideals. How exactly does your community help the poorer factions of society?"

"We support many charities . . ."

"Where does your money come from?"

The woman was immediately on the defensive.

"We are almost entirely self-supporting. What we don't need we sell – cheese, eggs, vegetables, honey, flowers. We also produce herbal remedies and have some very skilled craftsmen who make the beautiful objects we sell in our craft shop. Some of us are also entertainers who perform for a fee."

"You mean buskers," said Rachel brutally.

"Yes. What is wrong with that? It is using the gifts God gave us."

"Very admirable, I'm sure, but we're not talking big money here, are we?"

"Well, of course, when we join the community we bring a dowry with us."

"A *dowry*?" Now this *would* interest Nick, thought Rachel. It sounded very suspect and she wondered if Ellen had money of her own.

"Whatever we can afford," the woman continued. "There are no hard and fast rules. We just contribute as much as we can – like the novices used to do in the olden days when they entered a religious house."

"Is that so?"

"Oh dear, I'm making it all sound so mercenary, aren't I?" She smiled at Rachel and suddenly looked much younger and more carefree. "Money is important but there are many more ways in which we help people – counselling, giving emotional support and care, prayer . . ."

"It sounds as if your community is providing a very useful service. Your Gabriel must be quite something; I can't wait to meet him."

"He is and he's over there."

Rachel had been so engrossed in the conversation that she had hardly noticed where they were going. Now she realised that the fields and parkland had been left behind and they were walking past a large kitchen garden that was backed by a high wall in the same mellow cream stone as the house. She followed the woman's pointed finger and saw a man straightening up from some task in the far corner of the garden. He had a shock of white hair and she immediately had to adjust her preconceived ideas about Gabriel. She had imagined that he would be a far younger man with the stature and presence to influence gullible, would-be adherents, not an old man hunched over his vegetable patch. However, as he walked towards them she changed her mind again. Gabriel was not an old man. Beneath the thatch of white hair his face was ageless. Very dark, deep-set eyes beneath well-marked brows looked out of a lightly tanned, unlined countenance. He could be any age from thirty to seventy and Rachel felt both intrigued and strangely repulsed. Was he a phoney intent on parting people from their money or was he a genuine man of God, albeit an unorthodox one? He was wearing a short linen tunic, of the kind associated with Russian peasants, belted at the waist over jeans. On his feet were not the open sandals or bare feet she expected but a pair of very smart trainers. He didn't speak but raised his eyebrows at Rachel's companion who hastened to explain their presence.

"Gabriel, you have a visitor. This is . . . I'm sorry I don't know your name . . ." she said to Rachel.

"I'm Rachel Morland. I'm a lay reader at St James's in Barminster."

"And have you come to save us or to satisfy your curiosity?" He had a deep, resonant voice and he smiled as he spoke.

"I've come to issue an invitation." She explained about the ecumenical service that had been arranged. "I believe you have met our priest-in-charge?"

"I believe I have. A young man falling over himself to be trendy in the hope of attracting the wayward youth of our society."

"Isn't that rather a case of the pot calling the kettle black?"

"Touché, Miss Morland – or should it be Ms?"

"It's Mrs actually."

"Well, Mrs Morland, I think our community has far more to offer society, but then I'm prejudiced, aren't I? Anyway, now you are here let me give you a tour of the place."

He turned to the woman who had accompanied Rachel and

who had been listening to the conversation with a rather bemused expression on her face. "You go off on your errand, Penny, I'll take charge of Mrs Morland."

He put his hand lightly on Rachel's elbow and steered her past a row of raspberry canes. She felt an almost overwhelming desire to snatch her arm away from his contact but told herself not to be so sensitive. She was here to learn as much as she could about the Children of Light, and to antagonise Gabriel was not going to help matters. Besides, she was sure that he knew exactly how she felt and was secretly amused at her reaction.

"Has your community lived here long?" she asked as they moved towards the first of the outbuildings.

"Three years come July. But I thought you would have known that. I'm sure our movements are closely monitored by the establishment."

"I'm a newcomer here myself."

"And where did you come from?"

"East Anglia, though from the Midlands originally."

"East Anglia has a mixed reputation. I believe it has many picturesque areas but that parts of it are very bleak and inhospitable."

"You mustn't believe all you read. It is not all rural and undeveloped. There are some beautiful towns and villages and I lived in a thriving city."

"So what brought you down here? Your husband's job? Is he connected with the Church of England?"

"I'm a widow. I've recently taken up a post at Casterford General as senior physiotherapist."

"You are young to be a widow. I expect in your grief you turned to religion for solace?"

Rachel did not disabuse him. She felt the conversation was getting out of hand and instead of learning about him and his community he was eliciting her life history.

"Is the Children of Light a recently established community or did you already exist before you moved into Moulton Abbas?"

"God called me here to Dorset."

"And before?"

"I was about God's business."

He was being deliberately obtuse, she was sure, but she ignored it and changed the subject.

"I know very little about farming but you seem to be making a go of it here." She looked around her at the trim fences and hedges enclosing the green rolling acres and well-kept farm buildings anchored round the magnificent tithe barn like tugs round a liner.

"This is very fertile land and the soil yields up its goodness to those who treat it well."

"I take it you're talking organic farming here? No fertilisers or pesticides?"

"Those are dirty words around here. We practise husbandry as it should be practised and as a result we are pretty well self-sufficient."

"But not quite. You have electricity and are connected up to the national grid." She had heard the quiet hum of machinery coming from a nearby shed and noticed the overhead wires.

"We have a fully mechanised milking parlour, yes, but the goats are milked by hand and we use very little machinery in our cheese and butter production. We don't exploit the land but we are not ashamed to take what we need from the commercial world outside our little kingdom."

For commercial read 'real' thought Rachel cynically, but she had to admit to being impressed as she was shown round the cowsheds, the sheep pens, the pigsties and the hen houses. No factory farming here. The animals seemed as happy and contented as the people tending them. Gabriel introduced her to one or two of these, others she observed in passing and although most of them were young, in their twenties or even younger, there were several quite elderly people, all of them men. Many of the women were wearing simple, long shifts like the ones she had already remarked, which she was sure were home spun and hand woven, but the men mostly wore jeans and T-shirts.

"Where is your church? I presume you have a place of worship?"

"We have a chapel attached to the house. It is the heart of our fellowship. The original chapel, built in Stuart times, was not big enough for our needs so we have a custom built one. You shall see it, but first come and explore our craft centre."

He led the way past the tithe barn, which resounded with the noise of hammering and sawing, towards another smaller, wood-framed building.

"We have our workshops in the big barn," he explained, "but use this smaller one to display our range of crafts and produce. We open to the public several days each month and run a mail-order service."

The building had been radically altered since its days as a storage barn. One whole wall consisted almost entirely of windows and there were skylights in the roof making the interior light and sunny. Bunches of herbs and dried flowers were tied to the old beams and the floor space was divided into units, each displaying its own variety of goods. Gabriel stood aside and watched as Rachel walked slowly round looking at the things on display. There were toys, both soft and hand-carved wooden ones, quilts and wall-hangings, pottery and sculpture and wood-turned artifacts, candles and dried flower arrangements and a large variety of creams and lotions and potions, all neatly labelled and packaged. This was no amateur offering, thought Rachel, the whole thing was run on a professional basis.

"I'm impressed," she said, returning to Gabriel's side, "you have some very accomplished people living in your community. Do you choose them for the skills they can bring to your enterprise?"

"Certainly not." Gabriel looked shocked. "We are a religious community and everyone is welcome who accepts the Word. I have found, though, that a spiritual dimension seems to heighten artistic awareness in people. Maybe you would like to purchase something?"

"To be honest, I could spend a small fortune here. Perhaps I can come back another day when you are officially open. Do you have a herbalist in your group?"

"You are interested in alternative medicine?" he countered.

"As one connected to the medical profession I have to admit

that these fringe therapies cannot be entirely dismissed. More and more people are turning to natural remedies such as homoeopathy and reflexology and it seems to work for some of them, though I'm not sure that it isn't the placebo effect. I think, to answer your question, that there is a place for it in traditional medical practice."

"An enlightened woman. You must meet my wife, she is the specialist in this side of things. I think I can hear her outside now."

He ushered her out of the craft centre and Rachel noted that he didn't even shut the door behind them, let alone lock it. Security obviously didn't figure high on the agenda at Moulton Manor but perhaps Gabriel considered they were isolated and remote enough from the asphalt jungle not to warrant any concern along those lines. Outside, the dazzling sunshine nearly blinded her and she blinked and screwed up her eyes, not at first noticing the woman lumbering towards them. When she did she was astonished by the sheer bulk of her. Gabriel's wife was enormous. She was almost as tall as he and built like a giantess though it was difficult to ascertain just how fat she was beneath the flowing caftan she wore. She had a mass of black hair liberally streaked with white which was piled loosely on top of her head and secured with cascading combs and her earrings were like miniature chandeliers. In comparison, her little pudgy hands and stumpy feet peeping out from beneath the vividly patterned material looked small and out of proportion to the rest of her. She panted towards them, a beaming smile wreathed in the folds of her double chins whilst her thick-lashed, rather beautiful hazel eyes summed them up shrewdly.

"We have a visitor, dear. Rachel . . . you don't mind if I call you that do you? We are very informal here . . . this is my wife, Gaia."

Rachel did a double-take at the name but shook the hand that was offered.

"How lovely to meet you, my dear. Are you a recruit?" The question was directed as much to her husband as Rachel and he answered.

33

"Alas no, Rachel is already spoken for but we can but hope." Rachel again explained the reason for her visit and the woman chuckled.

"Well, we can't ignore the hand of friendship extended to us. Half the local population thinks we are the spawn of the devil, the other half that we are mealy-mouthed do-gooders. Perhaps you can put them right. Has Gabriel been showing you round?"

"Yes, you have a lovely place here. It must take a deal of organisation and hard work."

"Yes, we all work to the common good and the Lord looks after us. Have you been in the house yet?"

"Rachel is keen to see our place of worship," said Gabriel smoothly. "I am about to take her inside. Shall you join us?"

"You must excuse me, I am needed in the greenhouses. This is a busy time for potting-on and some of our helpers are more enthusiastic than experienced," she explained to Rachel. "Why don't you join us for our evening meal? We always sit down to eat and pray at six o'clock"

"I'm afraid I have to get back but I should like a quick tour of the house before I go."

"Come this way and I'll take you through the back entrance," said Gabriel. "We very rarely use the front doorway."

"Goodbye, my dear." Gaia tweaked a lock of hair back into position. "I'm sure we'll see you here again. I can always detect a sympathetic soul."

Now, what did she mean by that? thought Rachel as she followed Gabriel across a gravelled courtyard; and how to broach the subject of Ellen?

Gabriel took her through a maze of passages off which opened a warren of rooms. This had been the old servants' quarters and now housed an up-to-date laundry besides two cavernous kitchens and various storerooms. It had an institutional flavour about it – Rachel guessed that it had been radically altered from its original layout and Gabriel confirmed this when she mentioned it to him.

"I know what you mean; it looks better from the outside. I'm afraid parts of the interior have been completely gutted and altered. This was done in the days before there were such tight planning controls on listed buildings. It was built by Francis Witchingham in 1664 and his descendants lived here until the early part of this century when the family died out. It stood empty for many years and then was taken over by the RAF during World War II. In the 1950s it became a private girls' school and we stepped in when that ceased functioning and it was put on the market a few years ago."

There were people working in the kitchens but Gabriel whisked her past so quickly that she only glimpsed them. As they approached the end of the stone-flagged corridor a black and white cat streaked out of a half-open door closely followed by an enormous dog in noisy pursuit. Rachel hurriedly flattened herself against the wall and the dog thundered past just flicking her with the tip of its bull-whip tail. Gabriel scowled and poked his head round the door.

"I told you that dog was not to be brought into the house. This place is supposed to be a sanctuary not bedlam. Get him outside at once and keep him there!"

There was a mumbled reply from whoever was in the room and Gabriel turned back to Rachel.

"I'm sorry about that, are you all right?"

"Yes. You don't like dogs?"

"They are fine in their place and that is not in the domestic quarters where food is being prepared. Our dining hall is through here." He pushed open the door at the end of the corridor and Rachel found herself in a beautifully panelled room with a high-vaulted ceiling and lancet windows. It was dominated by an enormous refectory table that ran the length of the room and was laid out for a meal. Wooden benches formed the seating down the sides of the table but an ornate throne-like chair stood at one end. On the wall behind this hung a large cross carved out of dark wood.

"Do you all eat together?"

" 'The family that eats and prays together, stays together,' " quoted Gabriel. "There is always food available in the kitchens during the day. I try and insist on a full gathering for our evening meal."

35

"How many of you are there living here?"

"We vary between forty-five and sixty. At the moment there are fifty-two of us."

"And you all live in this house?"

"There are dormitories for the young folk – all strictly segregated according to sex you understand . . ." he twinkled at her, ". . . and single rooms for our more mature members and our families."

"You have families living here?" Rachel was surprised as she had seen no evidence of children about the place.

"Most certainly. We have four families with a complement of eleven children between them. Our children are very precious to us. The young ones will be in the nursery now having their quiet hour. We'll look in on them when you have seen the chapel."

The chapel had been tacked on to the main hall and looked rather like a giant conservatory. Approaching it from inside the house it looked quite impressive, with the sun reflecting off the burnished candlesticks and carvings, and highlighting the magnificent wall-hanging that covered the wall behind the raised dais and made a backcloth to the cross that stood on a simple altar; however, from the outside it must look like an excrescence, thought Rachel, and she wondered how Gabriel had managed to run this one past the planning authorities. The smell of incense was very strong and she wrinkled up her nose.

"Shall we pray?"

Gabriel swept up the central aisle and knelt dramatically in front of the altar. Feeling distinctly uncomfortable, Rachel dropped to her knees by a pew.

"Lord, look down on your humble servants and hear our prayer. Bless our sister Rachel and show her enlightenment and smile on our efforts carried out in your name." Gabriel lowered his outflung arms and continued to pray inaudibly but Rachel found herself unable to reciprocate. The feeling of peace and sanctity that she always knew in a consecrated building failed to materialise. She felt instead that she was on a stage set taking part in a theatrical experience, not a religious one. She could not pray and instead she let her attention wander. The sun flooding into the chapel enveloped Gabriel in a golden aureole and his white hair gleamed like a halo. She knew he had positioned himself in just that place to achieve this phenomenon and was sure he had done so many times before to better impress his followers. As she said to Peter Stevenson afterwards, she had never been prayed over in such a manner before and had never felt so unspiritual as a result of it.

Gabriel reached the end of his devotions. He bowed down and touched his forehead on the step, then got up and came back down the aisle and sat beside her in the pew.

"What do you think of our chapel?"

"You have created an attractive setting."

"Do you feel the presence of God?"

"I think I must reserve judgement on that."

"It's the answer I should have expected. You are following the usual stance of the Church of England: sitting on the fence."

"I really don't think my opinion is important to you, is it? I am speaking personally, not as a mouthpiece for my Church."

"Oh, I am sure of that, Rachel, and now perhaps you'll tell me why you are really here."

She tried not to let the shock show on her face. Was it so obvious that her visit had an ulterior motive? He was regarding her with an inscrutable expression in his dark eyes but she felt she was being judged and found wanting. Whoever, whatever Gabriel was, she mustn't underestimate his intelligence. His was a forceful, dominant character, but whether that force was for good or evil she did not know . . . yet.

"I came here in good faith with an invitation from my vicar to your community," she said lightly.

"I believe you, but that was just an excuse, wasn't it?"

"You are an astute person, Gabriel, I had better be honest with you. You are quite right, there is another reason for my visit. I think you have a young girl living here who is a relation of a friend of mine. Her family are concerned for her."

"Whom would you be talking about?"

"Ellen Holroyd."

"Ah yes, Ellen. A very gifted young woman. I think she will be a great asset to our community. Why are her family concerned?"

37

"She has cut herself off without a word, dropped out of college . . . wouldn't you say that was cause for concern?"

"These young people like to make dramatic gestures. She has been a willing convert to our way of life and eagerly embraces our aims. I cannot see why that should be so worrying."

Rachel chose her words carefully. "Her mother is a single parent who has devoted her life to bringing up her only child. When that child disappeared she was obviously distraught."

"But Ellen has not disappeared. She is here learning to be a better person and a useful member of a spiritual fellowship. I can assure you she has not been lured away for any nefarious purpose." He chuckled. "How did you say you came to be involved with her family?"

"I didn't," said Rachel shortly, knowing that he was laughing at her. "I understood that she was involved with a boyfriend?"

"I think you are talking of Daniel. I believe he originally introduced her to us. Now, there *is* an intelligent, level-headed young man. One I should not be ashamed to call my own son."

"You have children of your own?"

"Alas, the Lord has not seen fit to bless me. You need have no worries about the friendship between Ellen and Daniel. I know the young of today live in a very different moral climate but we do not encourage loose living here."

"Nevertheless I should like to see Ellen."

"To try and talk her out of her commitment to the Children of Light? I think you will find that impossible."

"Nevertheless, I should like to see her."

"Then we had better go and find her." Gabriel consulted the digital watch which somehow looked incongruous on his wrist. "She should be in the nursery. She is very good with the children and they all adore her."

He got to his feet, stepped out of the pew and genuflected in the direction of the altar before moving back towards the door. He held it open for her and she went through, carefully avoiding any contact with him.

This time he took her through a different part of the house, up a grand staircase that led off the central hall, along a corridor and up another, narrower staircase. On the way they passed an open door through which Rachel glimpsed a range of computer hardware and someone working at a VDU.

"At least you are keeping abreast of modern technology," she said lightly.

"We ignore it at our peril."

There was the sound of children's voices drifting back along the corridor from a door at the far end; squeals of excitement followed by the murmur of an adult voice. Gabriel threw open the door and she found herself looking at a cosy domestic scene. There were half a dozen children, ranging in age from about two to six, sitting on the floor in a circle round a young woman who was reading to them. They were engrossed in the tale and only gradually became aware of the interruption; then one of them, a little boy scarcely more than a toddler, whimpered and scrambled to his feet and ran to hide behind the young woman. She looked up and Rachel immediately recognised her. It *was* the young woman who had been playing the flute in Casterford. So she *was* Nick's stepsister. The girl closed the book and got to her feet looking enquiringly at them.

"Ellen, a friend has come to see you."

She stared suspiciously at Rachel. "I don't know you."

"I'm a Church of England lay reader and a friend of your stepbrother."

"Nick has sent you to spy on me!"

"Isn't it time the children got ready to eat," interposed Gabriel smoothly.

"Yes . . . of course . . ." She turned to another girl who Rachel had not at first noticed. "Take them through and wash their hands, Libby, I'll be with you in a minute."

The girl scooped the youngest child off the floor and the others trooped after her as she went through a door at the far end of the room. As soon as they had gone Ellen said abruptly:

"What do you want?"

"Your stepbrother is concerned about you."

"Then it's for the first time in his life! Nick has shown precious little interest in me before, why the big brother act now?"

"He and your mother are worried about your well-being. You left home suddenly, without a word to your mother and naturally she is upset and worried."

"That's not true! I told her where I was going but she didn't want to know! She wants to run my life, stop me from really living . . ."

"She only has your welfare at heart."

"My mother has never had an altruistic thought in her life!" She brushed a long strand of blonde hair back from her face and glared at Rachel. "Who are you anyway – Nick's latest girlfriend? You won't last long, they never do!"

Gabriel moved forward and put an arm round her shoulders.

"Rachel has come here as an intermediary. Whatever has gone wrong between you and your relations it is not fair to take it out on her. You are not following the Golden Way."

Ellen seemed to slump visibly at these words. She made a gesture towards Rachel. "I'm sorry, that was appallingly rude, wasn't it? Gabriel, forgive me, I do try."

"The path to enlightenment is not easy. Shall you give Rachel a message for your family?"

"There is really nothing to say . . ."

"I shall tell your stepbrother that you are fit and well," said Rachel firmly, "and that you will make contact in the near future."

"I don't . . ." Ellen looked distracted. ". . . I must see to the children . . ."

"Off you go," said Gabriel, "and I shall see Rachel on her way. I'm sure she has had her fill of our community this afternoon."

He did not speak again until they had left the house behind and were walking back across the courtyard towards the driveway; then he took both her hands in his and smiled at her. "I hope you are now convinced that we are not Satanists or pagans."

"I didn't ever think you were."

"Ellen is in many ways very immature for her age. She is discovering herself."

"I should have said she was more trying to lose herself."

40

Four

Nick Holroyd was shunting papers around on his desk and feeling thoroughly frustrated. Another burglary had taken place and like the ones that had gone before it had been executed neatly and efficiently, leaving the police with mud on their faces and little to go on in nailing the perpetrators. This time it had been a garden shed ransacked of the new gardening equipment that had only been stored there the previous afternoon. Someone had watched it arriving and being lovingly placed in the ramshackle shed at the bottom of the garden and had returned under cover of darkness, broken the flimsy lock and removed the contents. A new lawnmower, strimmer and electric hedge-cutter had been taken together with an extension lead and two bags of potting compost.

There was a pattern to these robberies though he was damned if he could suss it out. He flung down his pen and ran his hands through his hair, ruffling it into a blond crest like a cockatoo. Oh, for a nice juicy homicide to get his teeth into. Instead, he had been sidelined on to a pedestrian case like this whilst his colleagues in CID got the more exciting options. He had yet to prove himself to the powers-that-be and in the meantime he was going nowhere fast. Shit! He glanced at his watch and decided to go up to the canteen and get something to eat. A plate of chloresterol-laden junk food might just kick-start him, though in this heat he could even consider the salad option.

As he rattled his tray past the till and exchanged words with the woman ringing up his meal he noticed Keith Adams sitting by himself in a corner of the canteen. Like himself, Keith was also a newcomer to the Wessex CID, having transferred from Lancashire at about the same time as he had moved down to

41

Dorset. Being two outsiders they had naturally gravitated together and struck up a casual friendship. Keith was a reticent character not at all forthcoming about his previous life but Nick understood that he had been married and the partnership had broken up acrimoniously with much bad feeling on both sides. He was now working as part of DI Mark Collins's team investigating the serial rapist and Nick envied him the case.

He picked up his tray and sauntered over to where Keith Adams was sitting.

"Skiving again? I thought with your boss away you'd be up to your eyes."

"He's back and I am."

Adams pushed some plates aside and made room for Nick who flung himself down on a chair and looked distastefully at his overcooked shepherd's pie which was already congealing round the edges.

"How's it going? Any nearer making an arrest?" he asked as he pushed the food around with his fork.

"Like heck we are. We know no more about him now than we did after the first one. You feel so bloody useless, just sitting around waiting for him to do it again. You just hope he doesn't get the chance. With all the publicity about, everyone should be on their guard but there'll always be some young thing who thinks it doesn't apply to her and takes a stupid risk."

"How's the delectable Fiona?"

"She's good. Knows her job and manages to gain the confidence of the victims."

Fiona Walker was trained in rape trauma and had been drafted on to the team to counsel and help deal with the psychological scars inflicted on the unfortunate women.

"She's having trouble with the super, though," continued Adams, "he's really getting up her nose."

"Is it personal or that he just doesn't like women on the team?"

"In his opinion, he's *the* greatest champion of women's rights but he talks down to her all the time; suffers from the 'little woman indoors' syndrome. I feel really sorry for his wife."

"From what I've seen of her Fiona can hold her own."

"She certainly speaks up for herself." Adams tilted back his chair and glinted at Nick through narrowed eyes. "She wants to be a decoy."

"A stalking horse, eh? A risky business."

"Yeah. If our laddie followed a pattern or operated in the same area at the same time of the month it might be possible to set something up but he's all over the place. He's obviously got wheels and the whole of the Casterford district is his stamping ground. We could arrange a trap in one part of the town with Fiona as the bait and a big police presence laid on and find he's knocked off some poor girl three or four miles away. Until we've got more idea what motivates him that's a right no-go. Anyway, how are things with you?"

"Petty robberies and petty results. In other words I'm stymied. Every week more stuff is walking off but it's not going through the usual channels. As far as we can tell from our snouts the known fences are not handling it. Someone has got a nice little scam going and taking the piss out of us. It's a good job we're not paid according to our clear-up rate or we'd both be on the breadline." Nick noticed his sergeant, Tim Court, bearing down on them. "Uh ha, here comes trouble."

"Thought I might find you here," said Court, slamming to a halt by their table. "We've got a line on that blue Bedford van that was used in that raid on the jeweller in Eastgate."

"Don't tell me the old boy has remembered the registration number?"

"No. It was nicked. We've had someone report the loss of a similar van – taken from a smallholding out Moulton way last Tuesday."

"And the owner has only just reported it missing?"

"It belongs to that commune over at Moulton Abbas. The person who normally drives it around thought it was being used by another member of the group. They've only just cottoned on to the fact that it's disappeared. Of course, it may not be the same van."

"Rather a coincidence if it isn't," said Nick, who had snapped to attention at the mention of the Children of Light. "Who has reported it missing?"

"Their guru or whatever he calls himself. Refused to give us a proper name – goes under the moniker of Gabriel. Do you want me to get someone to check it out?"

"No, I'll deal with this one," he said, to the surprise of Tim Court, "but first, I have another call to make."

Back in his office Nick dialled the number of the physiotherapy department at Casterford General and managed to catch Rachel between patients.

"I was going to ring you," she said, when Nick had identified himself. "I've been over to Moulton Hall and I've seen your stepsister."

"Ah, good, that's what I was going to ask you. Look, can we meet up? I'll come over to the hospital."

"What, now? You may have the afternoon off but I've got appointments booked until well after five o'clock."

"How about this evening? We can go out for a meal after we've talked."

"You mean I've got to sing for my supper?"

"Rachel, don't be like that! I *want* to see you. You know perfectly well I'd spend every evening *and* night with you if I had my way. It's you who's holding out on me!"

"I'm only teasing. Suppose you come to my place for a meal? I've been given some fish by one of my patients – freshly caught from the sea last night – and there's far too much for just me."

"That's an invitation I can't refuse. What time?"

"Make it after seven. That will give me time to get home and make some preparations."

"Fine. I'll bring some wine. See you later."

Nick put down the receiver and punched the air. The day was looking up. He'd got Rachel to himself for a whole evening; that couldn't be bad. He just hoped nothing came up to stop him keeping the date.

Jason Cunningham edged the car into the mainstream traffic and manoeuvred round a couple of cyclists. The car was an old Ford Escort, prone to carburettor trouble and belching out carbon monoxide fumes. He spoke to the woman beside him.

"That was a good afternoon's work if I say so myself. The juggling went really well and the crowds loved my act."

"It's you they love, Jason." Gina Bonetti pushed a swathe of black hair back from her forehead and spoke enviously. "All those young girls gawping at you with open mouths. They were eating out of your hand. You could have dropped every damn ball and they wouldn't have noticed."

It was true, thought Jason complacently, the girls flocked to him, fascinated by his looks and his silver tongue. He glanced at the woman beside him. Surely Gina didn't fancy him too? She was too old and besides, she was a real weirdo. They made a good team but that was as far as it went. He got his kicks other ways and performing in public like this meant he got to look the field over and mark one out for later.

"How much money did we make? Have you counted it?" There was no reply from Gina. She was staring out of the side window, her attention riveted on a pram being pushed along by a young mother.

"Wakey, wakey, I asked you a question." He changed gear and the engine spluttered and recovered.

"That's my baby! Look! Over there!" She clutched his arm and he shook her off impatiently.

"Give over. Don't talk such rubbish!"

"It *is* my baby, I know it is!"

"For Christ's sake, you *know* it's not your baby. You've gone walkabout again!"

Gina Bonetti subsided with a whimper but a few minutes later she spoke again.

"They took my baby. Have I told you about it?"

"Frequently," said Jason wearily. "You're fantasising again. You know perfectly well there was no baby and nobody took it. Now, suppose you just count the takings and stop blathering nonsense."

He had succeeded in diverting her and whilst she sorted out the coins, muttering under her breath, he wondered just what had set her off this time. In his opinion she was more suited to the loony bin than their commune, though Gabriel seemed able to work

45

wonders with her. He always managed to calm her down when she got in one of her states and most of the time she appeared more or less normal if eccentric. A few minutes later she grabbed his arm again.

"Look! There's Lonny. Stop!"

Jason slammed on the brakes and the car stalled. There was an almighty bang as the car behind them ploughed into their rear. Gina cried out as they were shunted forward and a cascade of skittles and balls rained over their shoulders.

The evening sky was a delicate aquamarine, deepening to ultramarine in the east where a single star hung suspended over the folds of Weldon Hills. One didn't get the vast skies and spectacular cloud formations here that were such a feature of East Anglia, mused Rachel, but this view took some beating. She and Nick had eaten their meal and brought their coffee outside to enjoy the still balmy evening and the lingering daylight. The garden was of moderate size, laid out mostly in lawns dissected by two herbaceous borders, and linked to the cottage by the patio area on which they now sat. The cottage had been let out as a holiday home for many years but Rachel now had a long lease on it and was toying with the idea of buying it at some time in the future.

She glanced over at Nick. He was sprawled on a sun lounger, one hand trailing on the ground, the other clutching his coffee cup which was tilting at a precarious angle. His hair flopped over his forehead and he gave the impression of being half asleep, but Rachel knew better.

"Aren't you going to ask me how I got on at Moulton Hall?"

"I think I've been containing myself with admirable restraint." He squinted at her through slit eyes and grinned. "I can see you are dying to tell me."

"First, more coffee?"

"Not for me. That was a super meal but the time has come to move on to other things. Lay it on the line, lady."

"I hardly know where to begin." Rachel wrinkled up her nose and paused in thought.

"General impression and then go on to specifics."

"Right. It's an impressive set-up; well-kept and apparently flourishing. One tends to think of communes and alternative communities as having a struggle to live off the land and life stripped to the bare necessities but that isn't so with the Children of Light. They are not short of money. Maybe Gabriel is a wealthy man in his own right."

"So, Gabriel?"

"I don't quite know what to make of Gabriel. I can't make up my mind about him. On the surface he appears to be genuine; a man with a mission who thinks he has been called by God. He has a group of followers who are devoted to him and it all seems fairly harmless . . ."

"But . . .?"

"I just have a gut feeling," she confessed, twisting a finger through one of the crisp curls that framed her face and teasing it out into a corkscrew, "that there is a hidden agenda. It's all sweetness and light and most of the people I met seemed too good to be true – almost as if they had been programmed to behave in a certain way – like zombies."

"We're not talking drugs here, are we?" Nick was all attention.

"No, I don't think it is anything like that. I should say it is more likely they've been mesmerised . . . brainwashed by Gabriel. A notable exception was your stepsister. She was quite belligerent at first and then there was the kerfuffle with the dog – that certainly spoilt his atmosphere of peace and calm. That dog . . . it rang a bell at the time . . . I've been trying to think why it seemed familiar . . . I've just remembered . . ."

"I presume you *are* going to tell me what you're talking about?"

Rachel explained about the episode of the dog chasing a cat down the corridors of Moulton Hall. "I'm sure I'd seen it before. It was the same dog that was with that beggar in Faulkener's Walk last week. A young chap, crippled in some way. He was sitting in a doorway with this enormous dog by his side; looked like the Hound of the Baskervilles."

"I think I know who you mean, a scruffy young lout who hangs around the town centre. We've been inclined to turn a blind eye, just move him on, but he risks a hefty fine if he persists in begging and causing an obstruction. I didn't realise that he lived in the commune. It looks as if Gabriel is collecting all the down and outs."

"Do you include your stepsister in that number? Did you know she goes busking?"

"Good God! I wonder if she's got a licence and if Clare knows about it. I'm glad you met her."

"Yes. Gabriel very graciously introduced us. I'm afraid she wasn't so gracious. She accused you of sending me as a spy which I suppose is perfectly true. I've never met her before so I don't know if she has altered much since being there, but she seemed in good health and spirits. I think she spends a good deal of her time helping with the children."

"Clare is upset about her dropping out of college."

"Is music part of the Performing Arts course? She plays the flute brilliantly, Nick. I'm not a musical expert but she really has got a gift, she ought to be professionally trained."

"I'll suggest it to Clare when Ellen comes to her senses. I don't think she'll throw in her lot permanently with the Children of Light. I think it was the boyfriend who lured her in. He's the one with the influence over her, not this Gabriel."

"I haven't told you yet about Gabriel's wife."

"So he *has* got a wife – and you've seen her?"

"And how. She has to be seen to be believed. Her name is Gaia."

"Gaia? That's a strange name, haven't come across it before."

Seeing that the name was lost on Nick she hastened to explain. "Gaia is the earth goddess. Mother earth – mother goddess – what you will, and Gabriel's wife is every cliché you've ever heard about earth mother types rolled into one." She described the woman to him and how they had met.

"That can't be her real name?"

"Probably no more real than Gabriel's is but I tell you something, Nick: for all her bonhomie and folksy behaviour I reckon she's a very shrewd character. I shouldn't be surprised if she is the business brain behind the venture."

"Perhaps I'll get lucky and see her too when I go there tomorrow."

"You're going to Moulton Manor? How come?"

"That's surprised you, hasn't it? I'm going on official business." He explained about the blue van and how Gabriel had reported it missing.

"So my visit wasn't necessary?" said Rachel, looking rather peeved.

"Yes, it was. You've given me good background information about the place. I know what I'm looking at now."

"You *are* worried about Ellen, aren't you?"

"Not so much worried as curious. I don't think she'll come to any harm but I'm intrigued about the whole set-up there. It's giving me something to think about besides this wretched case I'm on."

"How is it going? Not too well I take it."

"Don't ask. I'm trying to forget it for this evening." He flashed her a rueful smile. "You're shivering."

"It has turned cold all of a sudden, hasn't it? And it is getting damp. We'd better go inside."

Back in the cottage Rachel collected a cardigan and made another pot of coffee. She was very aware of Nick's eyes following her, watching her every movement, and of the way she was reacting to this scrutiny. The evening wouldn't end with a goodnight peck on the doorstep if he had his way and she felt panic flooding through her. She realised she would be fighting against her own instincts as well as him and was afraid her body would betray her.

When he put down his coffee cup a little while later and stood up she jumped to her feet with almost indecent haste and hurried to fetch his jacket from the hall. He stopped her with an arm on her shoulder.

"You don't really want me to go, do you?"

"Nick, it's getting late . . ."

"It's never too late for this."

He pulled her into his arms and kissed her. For a few seconds their lips and bodies fused and she was drowning in the embrace. She broke free and tried to push him away.

"No, please no . . ."

"You want it as much as I do, you know you do."

"No, I'm not ready . . ."

"When will you be ready? It's been a long while since Christopher died; don't tell me you're not ready." This time the kiss was even more devastating. His hands were exploring, caressing and his body hard against hers. She wrenched away, sobbing and gasping.

"No, Nick, no . . ."

"Don't *do* this to me, Rachel! You're killing me!"

"I'm so mixed up. *Please* be patient . . ."

He pushed her away so violently that she collided with a chair sending it crashing to the floor. The noise brought them to their senses. Breathing heavily, Nick righted the chair and shouldered himself into his jacket whilst she leant against the table and watched him.

"I'm not going to say I'm sorry, because I'm not," he said finally, clenching his fists and slamming them into his pockets. "I think it's time you decided just what you *do* want. We can't go on like this."

"Nick . . ."

"I'm a man – not one of the plaster saints on display in your church. Why do you think it is wrong?"

"Wrong?"

"Yes, wrong! You're fighting yourself as well as me. Why is it so wrong in your book to carry a relationship through to its natural conclusion?"

"I'm not into casual sex. You've always known that."

"*Casual* sex!" he exploded. "If I was after casual sex I wouldn't be hanging around *you*. I love you, woman! Can't you understand? And to me, love and sex are the same thing!"

"I don't think they are to me," she said sadly. "We're on different wavelengths. If I said yes I know I would enjoy it – I'm not denying that – but afterwards I wouldn't be able to forgive myself or you. Love to me is not just about sex, it's about respect, commitment . . ."

"But I *am* com— Oh Hell! This is getting us nowhere. I'd better go before I say or do something I'd really be sorry for!"

He strode into the hall and she followed him.

"Perhaps we should stop seeing each other?"

"Perhaps we should. Is that what you want, Rachel?"

"No, but I'll understand if you want to end our relationship."

"But we haven't *got* a relationship, have we? Not as it is understood in today's parlance. What is it they say – never act with animals or children? They also want to add – never get involved with a woman of the cloth!"

She unlocked the front door and stood aside for him.

"I'm sorry it's ended like this. I've enjoyed the evening."

"So have I and it's not ended. You can't get rid of me as easily as that. Thank you for the meal and I'll be in touch."

He brushed past her and strode down the path without a backward glance. She closed the door and sunk on to the hall settle, hearing the car engine fire and the roar as he accelerated up the lane. Sometime later she was still there, turning over in her mind the question he had asked. What *did* she want? She wanted Nick, but not on his terms, and what her terms were she hadn't yet defined. She sighed and wandered back towards the dining room where she came face to face with the dirty crockery and remains of the meal. Very deliberately she closed the door on the scene and went upstairs to bed.

The rapist struck again that night and this time his victim was a nurse. A multiple pile-up on the A35 had resulted in three fatalities and twenty injuries, several of them critical. Accident and Emergency and Intensive Care were stretched beyond capacity and a call went out to all off-duty medical staff. Anita Devenish answered the call. She had been out celebrating that night with her husband and a group of friends and when the call came thorough on her mobile she had not long been in bed. Beside her, her husband, Andy, snored lightly, out to the world.

She sighed and struggled into her uniform, putting on her shoes in the hall and trying not to make a noise as she shut the front door behind her. Fortunately her car was nearest the end of the drive. She unlocked it, threw her bag on the back seat, climbed behind the wheel and pulled the starter. Nothing happened, the engine was completely dead and with sinking heart she realised that she had left her lights on. She had elected to drive home from the pub as she had been well under the limit, but in the effort to get a slightly tipsy Andy into the house without disturbing the neighbours she had forgotten to check the lights.

She hit the steering wheel in frustration and pondered what to do. In the end she decided it would be quicker to walk rather than try and wake Andy and manhandle her car out of the way so that his could be used. Likewise the business of calling a taxi. By the time she got one out at this hour of the night she could be almost there, they lived less than a mile from the hospital. She tied the belt of her coat, grabbed her case and set off, wondering just what would be awaiting her at the other end. She never made it.

He pounced when she was within sight of the hospital buildings, taking her completely by surprise as he grabbed her and pulled her into the garden of a nearby derelict house. Anita Devenish was no timid adolescent; she was tough and fit and she fought desperately. This infuriated her captor who got his hands round her throat and nearly throttled her before raping her and leaving her half-unconscious. Some time later she managed to drag herself back to the pavement where she was spotted by a cruising patrol car and rushed to hospital, another statistic of that night.

The following morning Nick Holroyd checked with Traffic Control that the blue Bedford van had not been found abandoned anywhere, before setting off for Moulton Hall. Sergeant Bob Forsdyke had just reported for duty and was looking grey and haggard.

"God man! – you look as if you've had a night on the tiles!"

"I have, but not in the way you think. We were called to that smash-up."

"Oh Christ! The pile-up on the motorway! It sounded horrific."

"Nightmarish. If only some of these drink-drivers and speed merchants could witness a bad crash they'd never offend again. Mind you, the firemen and medics bear the real brunt of these accidents – they're the real heroes."

"At least you don't seem to get the joyriding around here that you get in the inner cities."

"Don't you believe it. The local youth may not be streetwise in that sense but they run a good line in old bangers; vehicles that should never be on the roads. How some of them ever get through the MOT mystifies me. I had a good example yesterday – the first accident we logged. A beat-up old Escort gave up the ghost suddenly in the middle of the High Street – caused a lovely concertina pile-up."

"Anyone hurt in that one?"

"Amazingly only superficial injuries. The passenger in the Escort had whiplash injuries and the occupants of the other cars had minor scratches and bruises but the driver of the Escort got off scot-free. A right cocky little bastard he was. Came from that weird religious community out at Moulton Abbas."

"Really? That's who this Bedford van belongs to."

"I reckon they may be running some suspect vehicles."

"Who *were* the two in the Escort?" Nick was suddenly worried that maybe Ellen had been involved.

"Half a mo." Forsdyke thumbed through his notes. "The woman was a Gina Bonetti. In quite a state she was; kept on about a baby. At first we were afraid a kid might have been thrown out and we'd missed it but apparently she's off her trolley and the driver told us to ignore her ramblings. His name is Jason Cunningham and he gave his occupation as juggler and male model, if you please."

"Male model?"

"As in life-classes at the College Art Department. Can't see myself how *that* ties in with a religious community."

"You've got a dirty mind. Anyway, I must go."

"Thought you'd be in on the briefing." Forsdyke jerked his head in the direction of the CID department.

"What briefing?"

"The Wessex Rapist."

"I'm not on that case."

"I heard they were pulling in everybody after what happened last night." Forsdyke saw Nick's expression. "Good God! Don't you know? There was another rape. This place was like a mad-house during the night – where were you hiding yourself?"

Gina Bonetti had been taken to hospital after the accident and X-rayed. No bones were broken but she complained of some pain in her neck and shoulder, and whiplash injury was diagnosed. She was kept in overnight for observation and the next morning sent to Physiotherapy to be assessed for a course of treatment. Thus it was that Rachel Morland found herself with a new patient whom she immediately recognised as the woman street entertainer who had accompanied Ellen Holroyd. She was wheeled into the physiotherapy department wearing a surgical collar and sporting signs of two emergent black eyes.

Rachel moved her into a cubicle and started taking down personal details.

"Can I have your full name please."

"Gina Bonetti."

"Is that Miss or Mrs?"

"Ms."

"Ms Gina Bonetti," she wrote down. "That sounds Italian. Are you Italian? Or perhaps your husband is?"

"I'm not married," said the woman shortly. "My father was Italian."

With her black hair and dark eyes she certainly looked Italianate, thought Rachel scribbling down the rest of her particulars. When she had finished she gently removed the surgical collar and examined her patient.

"How did it happen? Car accident?"

"The car I was in stopped suddenly and the one behind smashed into us."

"Typical scenario for whiplash injury. Does it hurt here?"

"Yes." Gina winced as Rachel's fingers explored her neck and shoulders.

"Any pins and needles down your arm?"

"A bit."

"Have they given you any painkillers?"

"Yes. I didn't want them," said Gina mutinously. "Chemicals poison our bodies. I will get something to help when I get home."

"One of Gaia's herbal remedies?"

"You know Gaia?"

"We have met. This is going to be painful for quite some time. Don't scorn traditional analgesics."

"It's only a stiff neck, it will soon be all right."

"Believe you me, you can feel the effects of an injury like this for a very long while if you're not extremely careful. You are too sore for me to do much today but I think we'll try some ice treatment to ease the swelling and pain and a little ultrasound. Next time we'll do some soft tissue massage and when you're feeling easier we'll work out a programme of exercises which you must do regularly."

"How are you going to get back to Moulton Manor?" she asked a little while later when she had finished the treatment. "Have you got transport laid on?"

"I will phone through and someone will come and collect me."

"If you give me the number I'll do it for you. You lay there and rest." Rachel went to her office and made the call. She didn't know who answered at the other end but it was agreed that someone would come for Gina. She went back to her patient.

"Someone will be here in about half an hour. Will you be all right?"

"Yes." Gina twisted round to look at Rachel and gasped in pain.

"*That*'s something you mustn't do. We'll put the collar back on. You must wear that for a few days at least and you must take things easy."

"I'll be careful." Gina plucked at Rachel's jacket. "Have *you* seen my baby?"

"Seen who?"

"My baby. Have you seen my baby?"

"Your baby?" Rachel was startled. "You have a baby?"

"They took my baby away . . ." Gina's voice trailed away and she closed her eyes.

"There was a baby with you in the car? Was he injured?"

"No one will tell we where my baby is . . ."

Rachel was bewildered. Had there been a baby involved in the accident and was it being treated in another part of the hospital? Or was Gina Bonetti suffering from delayed concussion? She was lying there now with her eyes tightly closed and Rachel thought she might have fallen asleep. She tiptoed out of the cubicle and made another phone call, this one to the Sister of the ward where Gina had spent the night. She was told that there had certainly been no baby in the crash and that Gina Bonetti was probably suffering from delayed shock.

"In my opinion she needs psychiatric treatment more than she needs physio," said the voice crisply down the line. "A very muddled persona. If that's what living in a commune does for you, give me the nuclear family any time!"

Rachel thanked her and put down the phone. It certainly sounded as if Gina Bonetti needed help – was she getting it at Moulton Manor or was the environment feeding her neurosis? She decided this was one more snippet of information she must pass on to Nick as and when she next saw him. She wondered who would come to pick up Gina. Would it be Gabriel? She was alarmed at how disturbed she felt at the thought of seeing him again.

Although she was busy with other patients she kept a look out for new arrivals and was rewarded when a Land Rover drew up outside disgorging Ellen Holroyd and a tall red-haired youth. She hurried out to intercept them and when Ellen saw her a look of almost comic surprise flashed across her face as she took in the uniform.

"What are *you* doing here? I thought you were a *priest*." She managed to make it sound like the last word in depravity.

"I'm a full-time physiotherapist and a part-time lay cleric. And this is . . .?" She indicated the youth at Ellen's side and wondered if this was the boyfriend.

"Dan," said Ellen shortly. "How is Gina? Is she going to be all right?"

"She's got a nasty whiplash injury which is going to take some time to heal. She's going to need regular physio sessions and she must do the exercises I shall give her. She's not very cooperative at the moment."

"That's Gina. You stay here, Dan, and I'll go and get her."

The two women went into the building and Rachel led Ellen into her office.

"Before you collect her can I just have a few words with you?"

"What's this about then? It's no use you trying to interfere with the way I'm running my life!"

"Are you always as aggressive as this?"

Ellen looked rather shamefaced. "I'm sorry. It's just that I'm fed up with other people trying to run my life and tell me what to do all the time. Now *I'm* making the decisions."

"Fine. This is not about you. Your friend Gina seems . . . rather disturbed . . ."

"Don't tell me she's on about her baby again."

"Well, yes. *Has* she lost a child?"

"No, it's all in the mind. She's got a fixation about babies. I think perhaps she had a miscarriage at some time and it's preyed on her mind."

"Perhaps a cot death?"

"No, I'm sure she's never had a baby. She doesn't even *like* children. She helps me sometimes in the nursery and there's no . . . rapport there. She doesn't know what to do with them, never cuddles or comforts them and looks annoyed if they cry. If she ever found this mythical baby she's always on about she wouldn't know what to do with it."

"Something in her past has traumatised her. You don't have to be a psychiatrist to know that. She needs help."

"Gabriel is healing her," said Ellen dismissively.

"Well, let's hope he is successful. Before you go let me consult our register and fix up her next appointment."

Shortly afterwards Ellen and Gina Bonetti went out to the Land Rover and were driven off. There had been no more talk of babies, missing or otherwise, from Gina, and Rachel began to wonder if she had imagined the whole thing as she went to deal with her next patient.

Five

Gabriel was busy in his office when he heard the car approaching. He left his desk and went to the window in time to see the red Mondeo pulling up outside the front portico with a crunch of gravel. He frowned and the frown deepened as he watched the man climb out of the car and look about him with interest. He wasn't in uniform but Gabriel knew that he was a policeman. He could always tell.

He turned back to his desk and picked up the internal phone, punching in the extension number of the old dairy where he knew his wife would be busy distilling herbs.

"Gaia? We have a visitor. One of the boys in blue, I think, though he's not in uniform. It would be a good idea if you went and met him first." He put down the phone and went back to the window, standing to one side so that he could see out but not be observed doing so. The man was tall and fair-haired, dressed in jeans and a maroon blouson jacket, and seemed in no hurry to announce his presence. He locked the car, pocketed the control and strolled over to the front door. Gabriel heard the door knocker but knew that no one would answer it from within the house.

The man knocked again and then moved back into Gabriel's vision, gazing up at the front façade until he was diverted by the arrival of Gaia, who plodded round the corner of the house and called out to him. Gabriel waited to see the man's reaction. Most strangers, on meeting Gaia for the first time, showed visible surprise if not embarrassment. This man seemed completely unaffected by the sight of his wife bearing down on him like a galleon in full sail. Gabriel decided it was time he put in an appearance.

"Gabriel, this is a detective inspector from the police come to see us." Gaia bustled the visitor towards him as he walked out of the house.

"Good morning, officer, nothing wrong I hope? I trust none of my flock has been transgressing?"

"I'm here in response to your visit to HQ yesterday. You reported that a Bedford van had been stolen."

Nick Holroyd felt the same initial recoil at coming face to face with Gabriel that Rachel had felt but he kept his features deadpan and spoke woodenly.

"Ah, the van, yes. Has it been recovered?"

"Not yet. We believe it could have been used in connection with a robbery. If so, it will probably turn up abandoned somewhere. Perhaps you can give me some more details about when and where it went missing."

"Certainly, but let's go inside out of the sun. This heat is quite extraordinary; a blessing for the crops but one hopes the good Lord will favour us with some rain soon."

"Goodbye, Inspector, I'll leave you in my husband's hands." Gaia waddled off and Nick followed her husband through a side door into the main building and up a flight of stairs. The building appeared deserted apart from them. He saw no one else and there was no sound of any other human activity.

Once inside Gabriel's office Nick made a great play of taking down notes in answer to his questions. Gabriel had very little to add to the statement he had made at the station the previous day, but Nick prolonged the interview in the hope of learning something more about the man and his community. The ploy backfired on him.

"Well, I'm afraid that's all I can tell you, Inspector . . . I'm afraid I didn't catch your name . . .?"

"Detective Inspector Holroyd."

"Holroyd? That's not a common name." Something moved behind Gabriel's dark, enigmatic eyes and he regarded Nick with renewed interest. "It so happens that one of our sisters here has the same name. Quite a coincidence – except that I don't believe in coincidences; do you, Inspector?"

Nick decided to come clean.

"Ellen Holroyd is my stepsister."

"Ah, you have solved a mystery for me. I have been wondering why our missing van should warrant the attention of a CID officer, a detective *inspector*, no less. Now it begins to make sense." He smiled, a smile completely devoid of humour, and Nick thought irrelevantly, Now I know how Red Riding Hood felt when she came face to face with the wolf.

"I am in charge of a case in which the theft of your van has a direct bearing. Now that we've dealt with that we can concentrate on Ellen. I should like to see her."

"I'm afraid you've come at the wrong time. Ellen is not here."

"She has left you?"

"Not in the sense you mean. She has gone into Casterford to collect someone from the hospital. Another of our members was involved in a road accident yesterday and was hospitalised overnight."

"I hope it wasn't the pile-up on the A35?"

"No, that was a terrible business. We had a special service this morning to pray for the survivors. But I digress – this was a minor accident earlier in the day. The car she was in broke down . . ." Gabriel shrugged.

"You seem to be having bad luck with your vehicles at the moment," said Nick, recognising that this must be the accident he had recently been told about. "It must be difficult living out here if you have no transport."

"We have other vehicles," said Gabriel vaguely. "My young people need to be mobile so that they can put their talents to good use and support our cause."

"I take it you are referring to the increasing number of characters who seem to be turning up on every street corner engaged in rather dubious activities. I think the authorities may well be very interested in that."

"Are you threatening me, Inspector?"

"Your aims may be laudable but how you set out to achieve them may be infringing the law. I hope you are aware that street entertainers have to have a street trader licence? And that doesn't sanction begging."

"Alms and charity are taboo words these days, aren't they? It's every man for himself and leave it to the welfare state." Gabriel neatly side-stepped the question and continued: "But the welfare state falls down continuously and I have been chosen to help those poor unfortunates who slip through the net, and to aid our brothers and sisters in other parts of the world who are struggling against poverty and adversity."

"Who has chosen you?"

"God." Gabriel drew himself up and pronounced it gravely. "I am God's chosen instrument."

Well, I asked for that, thought Nick. "Have you been ordained?"

"Ordained – what is that?" Gabriel dismissed it disdainfully and changed tack. "We are straying from the subject of Ellen. Ellen seems to be attracting a great deal of attention from outside these days. I presume the charming Mrs Morland is a protégée of yours?"

Nick parried this by mounting his own attack.

"You seem to have gathered up many of the local waifs and strays; Ellen is not one of them. She has a family who are very anxious on her behalf."

"I don't understand this worry. We are a religious community striving to help others. We are not some weird sect. No one is coerced. They join us of their own free will as Ellen did. She is free to come and go as she pleases but I think you will find that she has no wish to return to your world where values are twisted and Mammon reigns."

Nick decided the time had come to beat a tactful retreat. He snapped his notebook shut and tucked his pen away in a pocket.

"Well, I shall try and assure her mother that Ellen is OK. Thank you for your time. If we have any news of your van we shall be in touch. May I suggest you take more care of your vehicles in the future? If we had known earlier about the theft we might have had more success in tracing it."

With this parting shot Nick took himself off aware that his

visit had achieved little and that his feelings about Gabriel were as ambiguous as Rachel's had been.

In the time that she had been dealing with rape and the aftermath of sexual incidents, Fiona Walker had experienced many different reactions from the victims. In most cases there was a reluctance to talk about it at all, which was understandable. The only way some women could cope was by trying to suppress all memory of the attack, pretend it hadn't happened. Many had a feeling of shame, as if the violation had somehow been their fault; that because they had not been able to prevent it taking place they had acquiesced in their fate. Physical and mental stress often resulted in suicidal tendencies and these could often surface many months after the actual rape had taken place. Anita Devenish's response was unlike anything she had met before. She was angry. Deeply, intensely angry.

She lay propped up in the hospital bed, the bruising and weals on her neck covered by a dressing but her face displaying grazes and an ugly contusion over her left cheekbone, and her eyes snapped with fury as she struggled to answer the policewoman's questions.

"Can you give me any description? How tall was he?"

"A lot taller than me, at least five foot ten," croaked Anita.

"He was wearing a hood but could you see what colour his eyes were?"

"He jumped me from behind, didn't he? It was dark and this hood thing was right over his face . . ." She had a paroxysm of coughing. When she had recovered she moved her head restlessly against the pillow and glared at Fiona.

"I was a sitting duck. And after all the care we'd been taking. All the nursing staff were very aware that there was a rapist out there and we took precautions. Then I get called out in the night and I'm so eager to do my bit I forget all about it . . ." Her vocal chords failed her and Fiona handed her a glass of water.

"Don't blame yourself. You just happened to be in the wrong place at the wrong time. Did you hear a car? Could he have been following you by car?"

"I didn't notice . . . I wasn't aware of anybody around. It was so sudden . . . so out of the blue . . ."

"Is there anything at all that you can remember? Any little thing that might give us a clue to his identity?"

Anita Devenish screwed up her eyes and frowned. "Well, I was second best."

"Second best? What do you mean?"

"That's what he said, or intimated."

"He *spoke* to you?" Fiona leaned forward very alert. In the previous attacks the Wessex Rapist had been notably silent and this had somehow seemed to add to the terror of his attacks. His victims had struggled with a silent adversary who had overwhelmed and raped them without uttering a word.

"What did he say? Can you remember his exact words?" Anita searched her memory.

"Something about I wasn't his usual type but I'd have to do . . ."

Well, that figured, thought Fiona. The earlier victims had been younger and pretty. Not even her best friend would call Anita Devenish a raving beauty and she was short and stocky in build.

"What about his voice? Young? Old? Educated? Had he got an accent?"

"Oh God, I don't know . . ." Her voice rasped and got fainter. "He didn't sound *old* and he certainly hadn't got a local accent . . . I'm sure I would have noticed if he had. It was just an . . . an ordinary kind of voice . . ."

"Would you recognise it if you heard it again?"

"Yes . . . No . . . I'm not sure."

Fiona Walker tried a tactful approach to her next question.

"I know you fought hard and he nearly strangled you." She consulted her notes. "You were semi-conscious when he entered you. Did he come?"

"He came all right. You got your seminal samples, didn't you?"

This was one tough cookie, decided Fiona, but when she came off her high and reaction set in she'd crash.

"We've been considering the possibility that he has sexual hang-ups; can't perform in a normal relationship."

"He can get it up all right. He's certainly not dysfunctional in that respect!" Her voice cracked and a surprise tear slid down her cheek.

Fiona patted her hand. "I know this is difficult for you. How do you feel?"

"Vile, but I'm not going to let it beat me. I shouldn't be here. I'm taking up a valuable bed and they're very short-staffed . . ."

"You must follow medical advice, that's not my domain."

"I'm on the receiving end for a change." She gave a wry smile and winced. "I don't like it."

"I'm not going to bother you any further for the moment," said the policewoman, stowing her notebook and pen away in her handbag and getting to her feet. "But if you remember anything, no matter how insignificant you may think it, please let me know. And you know counselling is available to you."

"It's not me who is going to need the counselling," said Anita Devenish bitterly. "It's my husband."

Clare Holroyd was the manager of a boutique in Casterford selling expensive clothes and accessories that teetered on the brink between glamour and vulgarity. If you wanted a glitzy evening top or diamanté sandals you went to Feathers. If your tastes ran to county tweeds and cashmere you did not. That morning she was sorting out a new delivery of swimsuits and nursing the start of a migraine.

"You all right, Clare? You look a bit peaky." Chloe, her assistant, poked her head into the back room where Clare was working.

"I've got one of my heads coming on and this heat doesn't help." Clare pressed her fingers lightly against her temples and closed her eyes. "It's so *humid*. I can't breathe."

"You want to take your pills before it takes hold. Prevention is better than cure. I'll get you some water."

Clare rummaged in her handbag for her pill bottle. She couldn't find it and had upended her bag and strewn the contents over the table by the time Chloe returned clutching a glass of water.

"Oh no," groaned Clare. "I've just remembered. I finished the old ones and got a new prescription made up. I left them in my bedside cabinet intending to top up my handbag bottle but I forgot."

"Why don't you go home? I can hold the fort here. It's early closing and we're not exactly overrun with customers. You'd think this weather would bring people into the shop after summer clothes but the whole centre is like a ghost town."

"They're probably all headed for the coast. I think I'll take your advice; get home whilst I can still see straight and before I start being sick."

"That's right. Go home and have a rest. I'll lock up here at one o'clock and see that everything is OK."

Clare stuffed the contents of her handbag back again, put on a pair of dark glasses and went out to her car which was parked in an alley-way at the back of the shop. She backed out, wincing at the sunlight reflecting off the bleached pavements, and drove cautiously through the town. By the time she reached the road where she lived lights were flashing across her vision and she felt decidedly nauseous. She left the car in the road, feeling incapable of negotiating the narrow gateway and tottered up the path, fumbling her key in the lock. Once inside the house she dumped her handbag in the kitchen, kicked off her shoes, collected a glass from the cupboard and made her way upstairs clinging to the bannister. All she wanted was her pills and a lie-down in the dark.

She had actually taken her migraine tablets and pulled the bedroom curtains shut before she realised that there was someone else in the house. There was the sound of a drawer being closed and it came from one of the back bedrooms. There's a burglar doing me over! was her immediate thought. I can't cope with this – I'm going to be sick! She clasped her hand across her mouth and listened. Yes, there was definitely someone in Ellen's bedroom – what was she going to do?

She wanted to curl up on the bed and ignore the situation but she knew she must try and get to the phone and ring the police. She tiptoed out on to the landing. The door to Ellen's bedroom stood half open and as she tried to creep past she risked a peep inside. Ellen was standing by the dressing table going through the drawers.

"My God, Ellen! You gave me a scare. I thought you were a burglar!"

Ellen looked up guiltily. "What are you doing here, Ma, at this time of day? Are you OK?"

"One of my migraines . . . I came home for my pills. So you've come back."

"No, I've just come to collect some things."

"So you come sneaking into the house when you think I'll not be here. I've been worried to death about you. I've missed you so much and you don't even want to see me!"

"Because I knew you'd make a scene like you're doing now."

"I'm not making a scene! Oh God! My head! What have I done to deserve this!"

"You see? You're turning it into a melodrama. Like you always do."

Clare sank on to the bed and stared at her daughter piteously.

"You've changed. You used to be such a gentle, docile girl, always happy to take my advice. Where have I gone wrong? Why have I got such an ungrateful child!"

"I'm not a child any more, that's just the point. You've smothered me all my life, never let me do my own thing. Well, I've grown up at last. I'm my own woman now – I'm in control."

"You are? If you ask me you're under the thumb of that . . . that man. Your guru or whatever you call him and the rest of them . . . You're obsessed by them!"

"For Heaven's sake, Ma! What do you think we do? Murder babies, take part in Black Masses?"

"Now who's being melodramatic!"

"We're talking about God. G-O-D. Have you ever given him a thought in your entire life – apart from taking his name in vain!"

"There's no need to shout, Ellen. My head is bad enough as it is."

"Sorry. Look, why don't you go and lie down. You look awful."

"Thanks very much! You just want me out of the way. What did you come home for anyway? You haven't brought a case."

"I just came for some of my personal belongings."

"Your passbook, your savings book." Clare had just taken in what Ellen was holding. "What do you want them for? What are you going to do with them?"

"It's *my* money and I decide what I spend it on."

"You're going to give it to them," wailed Clare. "How could you be so gullible!"

"I know what I'm doing and it's no business of yours."

"No business of mine? When I think of how I've scrimped and scraped and gone without so that you could have a decent lifestyle – and now you're going to fritter it away . . ."

"Come on, Ma, be honest for a change. You're still narked because Granny left her money to me instead of you."

"Not at all. I'm glad she thought of you but she must be turning in her grave now. I don't know what Nick will say when he knows what you're doing."

"Nick can go screw himself."

"Ellen!"

"And he can stop sending his girlfriend to spy on me. She forgot her bell, book and candle."

"I don't know what you're talking about."

"I think you do."

Ellen put the documents she was holding in her handbag and moved towards the door. Clare stared at her in dismay.

"You're not going? Stay and have something to eat. I'll make some coffee . . ."

"No thanks, Ma. And you mustn't drink coffee in your state."

"No, you're right. I feel like hell."

"Let's get you to bed." Ellen propelled her mother out of the door and into her own bedroom.

"Are you going to undress?"

"No. I'll just lie on top of the bed."

"I'll get a compress for you."

Clare subsided on to the bed and Ellen went into the bathroom and came back with a damp flannel which she laid over her mother's temples and eyes.

"How is that?"

"Mmm. Lovely. I don't mean to nag, Ellen, but I do worry about you."

"There's no need. I've got my own life to lead."

"But what do you *do*? You've given up college . . ." Clare moved her head on the pillow and the flannel slipped, exposing one eye that stared up at Ellen, giving her the look of a rakish pirate.

"I'm putting what I've learnt there to good use. I'm earning my living."

"I don't know how or to what purpose."

"I told you before. Our aim is to help people who are worse off than ourselves. To give what we acquire to the really needy."

"Now you're going to start talking about the re-distribution of wealth again," moaned Clare. "It's all right in theory but how do you put it into practice?"

Ellen bent down and whispered something in her ear, a sudden mischievous grin on her face.

"I don't know what you're talking about . . ."

"Don't worry your head about it, Ma. I've got to go. Will you be all right?"

Clare clutched her hand. "You'll keep in touch, won't you? I *do* miss you . . ."

"Stop worrying and try and have a sleep. Bye." Ellen disengaged her hand and stole out of the room, gently shutting the door behind her.

Superintendent Tom Powell steepled his fingers, rested his chin on them and gazed balefully at the three officers ranged on the other side of his desk.

"Didn't the house-to-house net any results?"

"The other attacks all took place in the evening between eight o'clock and midnight. This was the first one to happen in the small hours," said DI Mark Collins. "Practically everyone we interviewed was supposedly tucked up in bed."

"I don't think that I believe that."

"One bloke . . ." Collins consulted his notes, ". . . a John Greengrass who lives at number 23 Holbeach Close – that's the road that joins Ivry Street where the attack took place – got up for a leak at about one thirty and heard a car passing. He reckons it was a diesel, said it was noisy."

"And I don't suppose he looked out of the window and got a sighting?"

"No, sir. Apart from that, nothing."

"Except for the party in Temple Road," put in Keith Adams.

"Party?"

"Temple Road backs on to Ivry Street. There was a party going on in Number 8A until after three in the morning. The house is split into two flats and rented out to students from the college. Apparently there was hell of a din going on, with very loud music. The woman who lives in the nearest house was in a right state about it. She reckons half the population of that road could have been murdered in their beds and no one would have noticed."

"I suppose she didn't get as far as an official complaint? No, pity. If she had done we might have had a patrol car in the area. Have all the people who were at the party been interviewed?"

"Yes, sir, and we drew a complete blank. Most of them were too hungover to remember anything about the night before."

"Has the nurse been able to give us any sort of description?"

"No, sir," said Fiona Walker. "He got her from behind and it was pitch dark – the street lighting had gone off."

"She fought back, didn't she? Could she have marked him?"

"He's probably got some bruises but he was covered up. Hood over head and shoulders and wearing gloves. No bare flesh so no scratches or abrasions."

"What about fibres?"

"Yes, some fibres were recovered from her clothes. Forensics think they match up with the ones found on previous victims and they're running checks on them."

"And we got another DNA sample this time?"

"Yes, sir. Again they think it matches with the ones taken from the earlier victims and they're doing tests to verify it."

"So, we have a DNA fingerprint and fibres from his clothing. All we want is a suspect to match them against. Someone must know who he is or be harbouring him."

"He spoke to Anita Devenish, the latest victim. All she could say about his voice was that she thought he was young. Could it possibly be someone from the college – one of the students who was at that party? Can't we get DNA samples from them?"

"The youths at the party or all the students at the college? There would be an outcry from the Civil Rights people if we targeted one section of the population."

"Then the entire male population of Casterford?" said Keith Adams. "It would be a horrendous task, let alone very costly, but it's been done before."

"And we know how that went wrong. We don't know that he lives in Casterford. He could live in some village or rural community miles away and come into Casterford when he gets horny because he's more likely to find a victim here."

The superintendent capped and uncapped his pen and rolled it from hand to hand. "For want of any better lead I think we must focus on the male students. I don't think we have enough evidence to press for DNA testing yet but I want them all interviewed and those who were at the party re-interviewed. Also prioritise the ones who knew about the party taking place even if they didn't attend."

"That's going to be well-nigh impossible. You know how these things snowball. Someone learns that there's a party in the offing and word gets round and you get gatecrashers from all over."

"It may not be so difficult in this case," put in Fiona Walker. "Everyone at that party was from the Art faculty. For some reason they seem to hold themselves aloof from the main body of students. Whether they think they are superior or just too way out to mix I don't know but I'm pretty sure no one who wasn't an art student would have got an invite or known anything about it."

"Right, concentrate on the male students from the Art School to start with; if you get no joy from them you'll have to widen the scope to take in the other faculties."

Taking this as dismissal, the three officers filed out of Tom Powell's office and returned to CID.

"Well, what are you waiting for?" demanded Mark Collins of Adams and Walker. "You heard what the chief said. Back you go to the college and this time check out any of those at the party who had wheels."

Jason Cunningham draped the dressing-gown round his naked body and strolled out of the cubby-hole into the studio. Most of the students were already there, sorting out their tools and turntables or wedging clay. A fine film of dust coated most surfaces and the original floor colouring had long been lost beneath a covering of grey-white sediment. There was an overwhelming odour of damp clay mingled with the smell of oil, hot wax and slip and glazes.

"How do you want me?" he asked Ben Frewer, the tutor, who was bending wire for armatures.

"I think we'll have you astride the chair." Frewer was tall and cadaverously thin. He wore a grubby smock and faded jeans and his long, grey hair was knotted back in a ponytail. Jason discarded his dressing-gown and mounted the podium, swinging a leg over the chair and Frewer joined him.

"That's right. We won't excite the lasses today by exposing your manhood. You nearly lost it last time."

"Christ! I didn't think anyone had noticed!"

"Grasp the back of the chair with your hands and rest your chin on them." The tutor manoeuvred Jason's shoulders.

"Bloody hell, man – how did you do that?" He gestured to the large bruise which covered the top of Jason's right arm and was in its full purple, green and yellow glory. "It's a good thing we're doing 3D here and aren't into colour."

"I was in a car accident."

"Well, I suppose it could be worse and you could be sporting a plaster cast. Lean forward a little more and stick your bum out."

"I've always had my doubts about you."

"You've got a one-track mind. Sex never comes into a life-class – or it didn't until you became one of our models."

Ben Frewer stepped down from the podium and clapped his hands.

"Come on everybody, get stuck in. We'll work for thirty minutes – you can hold it for that, Jason? Good. Then we'll have a short break. Concentrate on the basic shape – the way the spine curves and the angle of the legs – and leave the details to later."

The class settled down. There were twelve students, evenly divided between male and female. Two of the women and one of the men were mature students, the rest of them around Jason's age. He had been quite disconcerted when he had first started life modelling to discover how little he was regarded by the sea of eyes devouring, measuring, analysing his body. He was not a person to them, just a collection of bones and muscle and sinew; a joint of meat on a butcher's slab. They discussed and probed his physique dispassionately and were completely devoid of any embarrassment. He considered this a challenge and concentrated his powers on making the young, female students aware of him. One of his ways of doing this was to single out one of the girls and stare at her intently. Sooner or later she would become aware of his gaze – though it was often later rather than sooner, so dedicated were these art students – and then he would send silent messages in the quirk of an eyebrow or subtle body language.

It was a great game to him and helped to relieve the boredom of posing still and silent for long periods of time. One of the girls here today – Polly, who sat off-centre to his left – was interested in him and he thought he might follow it up but he couldn't be bothered that day, he had other things to think about. He stared insolently out at the class and let his mind drift beneath the studied façade.

Ben Frewer was just calling a break when the police arrived. The principal of the college had not been too happy about the disruption they would cause to his timetables but Keith Adams had assured him that they would be as unobtrusive as possible and would be checking out the male students informally. He and Fiona Walker were given the run of the Art faculty premises and were making their way through the classrooms on the ground floor when they arrived at the sculpture and ceramics studios.

"Hey, look at this – there's a life class going on," said the policewoman peering through the glass panel in the door.

"Don't tell me my luck has changed at last."

"Sorry to disappoint you but it's a male model."

"Oh well, it makes a change to see live flesh instead of a stiff on the mortuary slab." He knocked on the door and they went inside. Ben Frewer came towards them looking annoyed.

"Who the hell are you? There's a life class in progress. Didn't you read the notice on the door?"

"Police." They flashed their warrant cards at him and explained their business.

"We're having a ten-minute break. Can you make it quick before we start again? There are only five men here – if you can call these grubby little yobs men – plus our wrinkly."

"What about that one?" Adams had caught a glimpse of Jason clutching his robe round him as he retreated into the cubby-hole.

"That's our model."

"We'll speak to him too."

Six

R achel Morland was treating Gina Bonetti on a regular basis. The whiplash injury from which the woman from Moulton Manor was suffering was quite severe and Rachel insisted that she attend the physiotherapy clinic three times a week. She was a difficult patient, moody and highly strung and not at all co-operative and Rachel was sure she was not doing the exercises she had been given. She was wound up like a spring; Rachel could feel the knotted tension in her shoulders when she worked on them, and it was not helping her recovery. She had tried to put the woman at ease by chatting about her background and life before she joined the Children of Light but this had had the opposite effect. Gina either clammed up and refused to talk about her past at all or started babbling on about the baby she had lost.

She needs psychiatric help, thought Rachel as she gently massaged her patient's neck. Whatever had happened to her in the past, its effect was ticking away like a time bomb inside her and one day soon she was going to explode.

"Who is picking you up today?" she asked.

Gina was ferried backwards and forwards from Moulton Manor by a variety of people in a variety of vehicles.

"Gabriel."

"The big man himself?"

"He looks after us," said Gina proudly. "He is concerned about me."

But not concerned enough, thought Rachel, to get her the help she needed. She resolved to look out for the arrival of Gabriel and have a word with him about Gina's state of mind. She passed

Gina over to her assistant for a session of ultrasound and went into her office. She kept an eye on the car-park which was overlooked by her window whilst she sorted through her case notes but she found herself unable to concentrate as thoughts of Nick drifted through her head.

Since the evening he had come to supper the only contact she had had with him had been a message left on her answerphone in which he had told her that the ball was in her court and it was up to her to make the next move if that was what she wanted. So far she had ignored the call but she knew she must ring him before it was too late. Several times she had got as far as actually lifting the receiver to dial but had funked it at the last minute, unsure of what to say and what her reception would be. Sweet Heavens, she wanted to see him again, she longed to see him again. The glimpse of a fair-haired man in a crowded street would set her heart thudding and every time the phone trilled at home her heart would leap with anticipation, quickly dowsed as she knew it would not be him. He wouldn't ring her anymore; *she* had to make the call that would end their impasse. Before she could regret it she picked up her office phone and rang the police station. Miraculously he was there and she was put through to him immediately.

"Hello, it's me – Rachel."

There was no answer apart from the sound of a sharp, indrawn breath and she panicked, thinking he was going to hang up on her.

"Nick? Are you there?"

"I thought you'd decided you didn't want to see me again."

"No, of course not. Are you busy? Is it all right to ring you at work?"

"It's fine but rather public."

Rachel glanced at her watch. "Look, I'm taking my lunch break at twelve thirty. I thought of going to the Copper Kettle for a sandwich and coffee. Can you join me there?"

"I'll do my damndest to make it, but if I can't don't give up on me. It will be because I can't get away not because I don't want to. Are you all right?"

"Yes. Well, I hope to see you later."

As she replaced the receiver she noticed an ancient Land Rover drawing up outside. Gabriel got out. Today he was wearing a long brown robe belted at the waist with a conspicuous cross hanging from a chain round his neck. He looked like an itinerant friar. A staff and sandals would have completed the picture. She quickly got up, banging her knee on the desk, and hurried outside to intercept him. He saw her coming but made no move forward, staying beside the vehicle and watching her approach with raised eyebrows, though when she joined him he spoke first.

"Rachel. So now I see you in your other guise."

"Good morning, Gabriel. I believe you have come to collect Gina Bonetti?"

"Yes, there's nothing wrong, is there?"

"I am rather concerned about her. Perhaps we could discuss it in my office."

She went back through the swing doors and he followed her into her office. She waved him to a chair, hastily moving a pile of files from it and he seated himself and regarded her quizzically.

"Before you report on Gina's injury and your progress in treating it – or is it lack of progress? – I must tell you that there is a clash of interests here. My wife does not approve of her visits here. Gaia feels that they are not necessary, that she can heal Gina with her own skills and medicines."

"Gina was referred here from A&E as being in urgent need of physiotherapy. Having assessed her and started a course of treatment I can entirely concur with that. However, if Gina decides she wishes to forego the treatment, that is up to her. I, nor anyone, can compel her against her will."

"There is no question of that. I didn't say I agreed with Gaia. She can work wonders with her herbal knowledge but hasn't the resources that you have here in your fully equipped department. I'm sure you'll restore her to full health."

"It isn't her physical health I wished to discuss with you, but her mental state."

"Ah . . ." Gabriel folded his hands and studied them as they lay in his lap. "She has lapses, when her state of mind seems to be a little disturbed."

"Her state of mind is *very* disturbed. She needs help."

"She is getting help."

"I mean professional help. Psychiatric help."

"I think you are rather going overboard about this, if you don't mind me saying so, Rachel. I'm sure you are admirably qualified to deal with her physical hurt but I don't think her mental problems come under your remit."

"And they do yours? Are you saying *you* are qualified to deal with her mental problems?"

"How can you ask such a question? I am just an instrument and God works through me. Are you denying *his* power?"

Seeing she was getting nowhere, Rachel changed tack.

"Gina seems to be obsessed with a baby. She says that she has lost a baby, that it was taken away from her and she is very distressed. *Was* there a baby?"

Gabriel shrugged. "Who knows? I agree that something in her past has had a traumatic effect on her but I don't think there was ever a real baby. In my opinion, I think she may have had an abortion at a very young age and guilt about it is preying on her mind. Whatever one's opinions about abortion – and I'm sure you have yours and they probably differ very little from mine – you must admit that the mental after effects are far more devastating than the physical ones. I think she is yearning for the baby she never carried to term."

"I still think she needs help."

"We are working through this together. When she becomes distressed I am able to soothe her and calm her down and she soon forgets her anxieties. *You* are not helping by bringing up the subject of babies with her."

"I *don't* bring it up," said Rachel indignantly, "but it's difficult to avoid the subject as she seems to have a one-track mind."

"Forgive me for the criticism but I suggest you stick to your business and allow those who know her better to deal with her state of mind."

"I find that a strange statement coming from you, Gabriel.

You should know that the physical and mental are two halves of the whole and the well-being or ill-health of one is going to affect the other."

"Not two halves but a three-way split. What about the soul? I am fighting for her soul, Rachel, and with God's help I am going to win. Now, is my patient ready?"

"I shall send her out to you when she has finished her treatment. Perhaps whilst you're wrestling with her soul you could persuade her to do her exercises."

She walked to the door with as much dignity as she could muster, aware that Gabriel was watching her with amusement in his dark, calculating eyes.

When Rachel arrived at the Copper Kettle she found Nick already there. She had wondered how difficult this meeting would be but the awkwardness she had been anticipating vanished as soon as she came face to face with him. He greeted her warmly and made room for her at the table, which was wedged in a window alcove affording a good view of the market square outside.

"What will you have?"

"Have you ordered for yourself yet?"

"No, I thought I'd wait for you."

"A cheese and tomato baguette will be fine, please, and a coffee."

"I'll have the same. I don't suppose they have a liquor licence."

"Perhaps we should have met in a pub. I suppose that's your usual venue."

"You're broadening my horizons. At least I'm not likely to bump into any colleagues here. This is where the crimplene and pearls take afternoon tea."

"Don't knock it. I find it a change from the hospital canteen and I often pop in for a lunchtime snack. I'm sorry if you are losing face by being seen in such an establishment."

Nick caught the eye of a passing waitress and ordered. She was middle-aged and, although dressed in a stylish blue and white striped uniform, looked as if she would be more at home in the black dress and white frilly apron and cap of a bygone era. He shifted his weight on the flimsy chair and studied Rachel. Her face, framed in wispy tendrils looked pale and there were smudges under her dark, pansy eyes.

"You look tired," he commented.

"It's this heat. I can't sleep."

"Neither can I, but not for that reason." He held up his hand as she started to protest.

"Sorry, forbidden subject I know. Let me think of a nice, safe subject such as work. Are you still busy?"

"Very. There is a waiting list of patients and I can't see it ever getting smaller. Here's something that might interest you; I've just seen Gabriel from Moulton Manor."

"As a patient?" Nick leaned forward and propped his elbows on the table.

"No, I'm treating one of his flock and he came to pick her up. She's a woman called Gina Bonetti. She was involved in a car accident in the High Street recently and suffered whiplash injuries."

"I think I know who you mean. One of my mates mentioned it. Said a couple of the Children of Light were involved and the woman was a real weirdo, babbling about a lost child."

"That's my Gina Bonetti. She's suffering a real hang-up over something. I had words with Gabriel about it, suggested she had some psychiatric counselling but he didn't take kindly to my interfering in what he thought was no business of mine."

"I can believe that, I thought he was an arrogant bugger when I met him. I should have thought it would be beneath his dignity to act as chauffeur."

"I think this was the first time. Your stepsister sometimes comes."

"I didn't know she could drive."

"I don't think she does. There're usually two of them. Come to think of it, they always seem to go around in pairs – the Children of Light, I mean. Maybe Gabriel doesn't trust them out on their own."

The food arrived at this point and their talk drifted to other topics as they ate. The cafe was doing brisk business but Rachel had to admit the clientele was mostly middle-aged or older. At least they were spared gangs of teenagers and raucous background music. When he had finished eating Nick pushed back his plate and fixed his compelling grey eyes on her.

"When am I going to see you again, Rachel?"

"How about coming to a car-boot sale with me?"

She was pleased to see that she had managed to startle him.

"A car-boot? You're not serious? I shouldn't have thought it was your scene at all. Mind you, a lot of these punters could do with looking into. All manner of dicey goods and things that fell off the back of a lorry change hands at these do's."

"I'm not talking about the police point of view, leave work behind for a change. Anyway, this is a very different type of function from your usual one. It's a stately homes car-boot sale. A colleague told me about it. Apparently all the landed gentry in the area get together and put it on as a charity function. They raid their attics and sort through the family heirlooms that have been mouldering there for centuries and throw out what they don't want. I went to one in Suffolk once. It was fascinating; everything from old riding boots, brocade curtains and a sola topee to Great-Grandmama's Victorian corsets. Some of it was complete rubbish. You can't imagine how they thought anyone would buy it."

"The nobs have an inflated sense of their own importance and think we plebs should be grateful for the chance to own something that has passed through their hands."

"Hark at the poor little pauper. Anyway, are you on?"

"When and where?"

"On Sunday out at Selhampton Hall. According to the posters it's the residence of Lord and Lady Gilchrist."

"Ah, that rings a bell. They've got a priceless collection of jade and porcelain I believe."

"Which the public definitely won't get to see. I should imagine the house itself will be out of bounds and the boot sale will be somewhere in the grounds."

"I should be able to get away on Sunday but I can't guarantee it. Won't you be involved with your church on Sunday?"

"I'm on duty at eight o'clock Communion, then the rest of the day is free."

"Right, you're on. I'll pick you up at nine o'clock. It's only about half an hour's drive."

"Remember, you're going as a prospective buyer, not a policeman."

"I'm only too glad to leave work behind for the day, believe me. Are you looking for anything special?"

"The cottage is very sparsely furnished. I thought I might pick up something. Don't look alarmed, I'm not thinking about furniture. Ornaments and china or maybe a picture or two was what I had in mind."

"Well, as long as you don't get done. I suppose I'm to be the porter."

"What a good idea." Rachel checked her watch. "Help. I must fly or I'll have patients queueing up for me." She waylaid a waitress and asked for the bill.

"I'll see to that," said Nick.

"No, I asked you, it's my shout." She gathered up her handbag. "See you on Sunday, God willing."

Before he could get to his feet she had gone, wending her way between the tables and stopping briefly at the cash desk to pay the bill. Nick looked around him; at the pensioners enjoying two meals for the price of one, the matrons exchanging gossip over the table tops, the elderly man nodding over his tea in the corner, and hurriedly removed himself from the Copper Kettle.

This weather was decidedly unnatural, thought Nick as he clawed his way out of a sweaty, nightmarish sleep on the Sunday morning. Call it the greenhouse effect, global warming, El Niño or whatever, but one just shouldn't get Mays like this in England. The occasional foretaste of summer perhaps, that lasted for the odd day or two but not this continual heat, day after day, week after week as if it were the tropics and not northern Europe. It felt more like a heat wave in late August or early September, the last fling of summer before a thunderstorm brought the season to an end. It certainly felt horribly humid that morning. The sun was hazy, shimmering opaquely through a sky that shaded to almost citrus yellow where it met the rooftops and gables of Casterford.

He struggled out of bed and stood under the shower for a long time, sluicing cold water over his head and shoulders in an attempt to banish the last dregs of sleep, before shaving and dressing in light chinos and a short-sleeved polo shirt. Downstairs in his minute kitchen he made coffee, poured milk over a bowl of cereal and put a couple of slices of bread in the toaster. He browsed through the Sunday colour supplement as he ate, half expecting the phone to ring at any moment. This was the morning after the night before: Saturday night, the night of greatest activity amongst the criminal fraternity. But the phone didn't ring and he hurried to get ready before he was summoned to the station. He was very tempted to break every rule and leave his mobile behind but at the last moment he stowed it away in his pocket, collected a pair of sunglasses and went out to the garage.

He reached St James's before the service was over and sat in the car waiting for Rachel to appear. It would have been more supportive to have joined her inside and taken part, but this was a Communion service, not like Morning Prayer or Evensong where you could sit unobtrusively amongst the congregation and not appear an outsider or a fraud. The taking of the bread and the wine. *Take this, this is my body which is given for you and this is my blood which is shed for you. Take these and feed on them in your heart with thanksgiving.* He had read the Litany. Unbeknown to Rachel he had studied the prayer books and Series B and it had left him with a feeling of unease; of something beyond his grasp that he could not understand. It was meaningless and yet . . . So many people couldn't be wrong, be deluded, could they? Rachel was sincere. She lived her life by this set of tenets and that meant that she was trustworthy, truthful and of great integrity, but what about this Gabriel character? Nick was sure that he was a phoney and as for that wife of his . . . larger that life in all meanings of the word . . .

His musings were interrupted by the arrival of Rachel. She beamed at him and tossed a bag containing something black and voluminous on the back seat.

"What's that? Your Sunday morning disguise?"

"Got it in one. I got away as quickly as I could. I think there'll be a lot of people at this sale. We'll probably have to queue up to get in."

Nick looked disbelieving but found she was right as they approached the gates opening on to the driveway of Selhampton Hall. The traffic was reduced to a crawl and the single uniformed constable on duty was having trouble controlling the vehicles that converged from every direction.

"Bloody Hell! – sorry, Rachel – I didn't expect this."

"The dealers will have got here at a very early hour. All the bargains will have been snapped up."

"Then why are we here?"

"Isn't my company good enough for you or do you have to have an ulterior motive?"

"Anymore talk like that, woman, and I'll drag you off behind the nearest bush."

Part of the parkland had been cordoned off as a car-park and an officious attendant who seemed to be having an argument with his walkie-talkie signalled to them to pull in alongside the last car parked in the outer row but Nick ignored him and swung to the right, drawing in under a large beech tree.

"At least it will keep cooler here in the shade and not be like a hot tin can when we get back."

"He's coming after you." Rachel was eyeing the attendant who was striding towards them looking belligerent. Nick fished in his pocket and produced his warrant card, which he showed to the man who immediately lost his pomposity and started to look worried.

"There's nothing wrong is there, sir?"

"No, but one can't be too careful at affairs like this, can one? Don't worry, we'll just circulate and keep an eye on things generally."

He took Rachel's arm and steered her away and the man shrugged and went back to his duties.

"Nick, that was a gross abuse of your position!"

"Yes, it was, wasn't it. Come on, let's find the action."

Selhampton Hall was a beautiful old stone manor house dating from the fifteenth century. Smaller than Moulton Manor, it was far more attractive in that it appeared to have been untouched in subsequent centuries apart from a wing added in Elizabeth I's reign so that the building formed the requisite 'E' beloved of the virgin queen. Rachel would have liked to have looked over the house but although it was open to the public on certain weekends during the year this was not one of them. The boot sale was set up in a large semicircle in the parkland to the left of the building, not far from the series of formal gardens that led one from another in a fan shape that incorporated many water features. Most of the stalls and tables were positioned in shade under the massive oaks and limes that dotted the area.

As they approached it was not the hubbub from the crowds thronging the stalls that assaulted their ears but the braying voices of the stallholders.

"This must be the largest collection of Hooray Henrys I have ever come across," said Nick, looking about him.

"You're an inverted snob."

"Just listen to them. Do they think everyone is deaf or are they still harking back to the days of the Raj when the only way to make the natives understand was to bawl in English at the top of their voices?"

Rachel smiled but didn't reply. They wended their way through the crowds fascinated and amused by the variety of goods on offer.

"Yoo hoo, Clarissa!" shrieked a female voice from behind a copious pile of old magazines and books. "I thought I'd see you here. Guess what? At long last I've got rid of Great Aunt Eugenie's collection of boots!"

"My dear, how splendid for you. How was St Trop?" This speaker was a woman in her late sixties with a formidable bust and a very red face.

"Much as usual, but Henry's back was playing up and all the poor dear could do was lay on deck and let the world go by."

"Nick, your mouth is open. You're behaving like the local

yokel!" said Rachel, amused by his reaction to the conversations going on around them.

"Tell me," he said, guiding her out of the way of a gang of children who were charging in and out of the trees. "You said it was in aid of charity. What do *they* get out of it?"

"I think they pay a fee for having a stall and donate a percentage of their profits."

"Fleecing the public."

"You don't *have* to buy anything."

"True. Seen anything that's taken your fancy?"

"Not that your purse could cope with. They're certainly not giving things away."

"I'd like to buy you a present. Seriously, let me get you something."

"If I see something I really like and they're not asking a ridiculous price for it I may keep you to it. Right now I could do with an ice-cream."

There was a van parked over on the far side of the enclosure surrounded by people and Nick went over to join the queue. He returned with two dripping cones.

"Quick, take this whilst there's still some left. I overheard a group of dealers talking amongst themselves and they were over the moon. Reckoned they had made a killing over the pictures as the owners didn't realise their value."

"You don't mean long lost Constables or anything like that?"

"No, but enough Victorian artists who are becoming very collectable to keep them very happy."

At that moment Nick's mobile phone rang.

"Hell! I was afraid of this."

He moved over to a quieter spot beneath the trees and Rachel saw him talking earnestly into the receiver before ramming back the aerial and striding back towards her.

"I've got to go."

"Is something wrong?"

"There's been another break-in overnight and the van that was stolen from the Children of Light and used in another robbery has turned up. I'm sorry about this but I've got to get back to the station. We'll have to go."

"You can't help it, I understand, but I think I'll stay on."

"How will you get back?"

"It's on a bus route, I'll manage somehow."

"I hate to go off like this but I did warn you."

"I know, you're forgiven. Never let it be said I stood between you and your duty."

"Now you know why I parked away from the crush. Remember what I said. If you fall for something that's not completely over the top, buy it and I'll refund you later. I'll give you a ring this evening."

After he had gone Rachel mooched round a few more stalls and then went and sat under a tree in the shade. The atmosphere was becoming increasingly heavy and white cumulus clouds were piling up in the west. There was going to be a storm and she regretted not going back with Nick. A heat haze shimmered over the distant trees marking the boundary between parkland and the water meadows and the sun burned angrily red through the leaden atmosphere. She fanned herself with her handkerchief and decided to go in search of the Ladies. This she found round the back of the main building in what was the servants' quarters, near the stables and the outhouses. She came out of a cubicle, washed her hands and splashed water over her face and ran a comb through her tight, damp curls. As she made her way round the corner of a block of looseboxes she came face to face with Ellen Holroyd and the red-haired man called Dan. She looked startled and very put out to see Rachel and the latter was sure she would have ignored and evaded her if it had been possible.

"Hello, Ellen, looking for a bargain?"

"I . . . er . . . yes. I thought it might be amusing . . ."

"I think there is going to be a storm, don't you?"

"Yes. I . . . I hate this weather. We have got to go, haven't we, Dan?"

Rachel looked at her companion. He was tall with the very pale skin that goes with red hair and had light blue-grey eyes that reminded her momentarily of Nick. He was several years older than Ellen and appeared very mature and in control of himself. Rachel had the feeling that of all the Children of Light she had met this Dan was the only one capable of holding his own with Gabriel.

"You've just missed seeing Nick," she said to Ellen. "He was with me but was called away on police business."

"Nick is wedded to the police force, as his first wife discovered," said Ellen spitefully. "I haven't seen him for ages."

"I'm sure that can be remedied. He would love to meet up with you."

"What do you know about it? You can't tell Nick what to do as you'll soon discover."

"Ellie, we must be going," prompted her companion. She clasped his hand and after perfunctory goodbyes they went off in the direction of the park.

Rachel watched them go thoughtfully. Ellen was very hung-up over her stepbrother. Whatever had Nick done to upset her? Possibly it was jealousy. He was so much older than her that she had probably looked up to him, hero-worshipped him and resented his interest in any other woman. Rachel wondered how she had got on with his ex-wife and just why his marriage had broken up. Nick had never discussed it with her apart from remarking that she had been unable to cope with his commitment to the police.

By now the sun had disappeared, obscured by the masses of purple cloud building up in the sky, and the first rumble of thunder disturbed the thick air. It was quickly followed by another and a flash of lightning that rent the sky in a neon blaze. The stallholders hurriedly started to pack up their goods, moving out from under the trees, and the crowds drifted nearer to the house. It was then that Rachel noticed the large marquee set up on a lawn over on the far side of the house. It was a refreshment tent and she joined the people thronging towards it. The first drops of rain started falling as she reached its shelter. It was even hotter and very clammy inside and soon the rain drumming down on the roof drowned out the chatter and clatter of crockery. She queued up for a cup of tea and a ham roll and fought her way to a seat at the back of the marquee.

The storm lasted a good thirty minutes and the noise was horrific in the claustrophobic canvas interior. When it was finally over and a watery sun once more appeared through a slit in the clouds the crowd surged out through the front flaps. The smell of crushed grass was almost overpowering and globules of water glistened from every surface. Rachel noticed an opening in the canvas wall behind her and decided to make her exit that way. She slipped through the gap and found herself close to an archway that opened on to a small formal garden with a pond and stone cherub fountain in the centre. This must be part of the private gardens, she thought, but perhaps she could follow the path that led from the pond to another archway cut in a thick yew hedge and find her way back to the park.

The flagstones that made up the path were drenched and slippery and she picked her way with care, almost falling a couple of times. To her surprise the archway led, not to another garden, but to a colonnaded passage like a cloister that ran along the back of the east wing. Sure that she was trespassing and where she shouldn't be she hurried along and turned the corner. A flight of steps to her right led up to another colonnaded passage like a two-tiered cloister, one above the other. She heard footsteps going along the upper one and waited at the foot of the steps wondering if she was going to come face to face with the angry owner. The footsteps were receding and she looked upwards in time to see two figures moving between the ornate pillars. It was Ellen Holroyd and Dan. Now, what were they doing, she thought, walking along a private passage that led into the main hall?

Back in the park she met up with a work colleague and got a lift back to Melbury.

Seven

The burglary had taken place at a house situated at the end of a quiet cul-de-sac on the eastern outskirts of Casterford. The owners, a retired business couple, had been to a wedding in Swanage on the Saturday and had stayed on overnight at the hotel where the reception had been held. They returned early the next morning to find that their collection of art deco pottery had been severely depleted.

Tim Court answered the call out and Nick got back to the station in time to hear his initial report.

"The owners are a Mr and Mrs Robinson," said Court. "They're completely devastated by what they've lost but I reckon they got off lightly. The place wasn't trashed, you wouldn't know anyone had been in."

"So the thieves knew exactly what they were after and targeted that. What *was* taken?"

"They went on and on about their Clarice Cliff. Something about bizarre and *crocuses*."

"Ah . . . you're not up on the art world. Clarice Cliff was a famous potter working in the 20s and 30s. She designed a great deal of pottery in vividly coloured geometric designs."

"Yes, I saw what was left. Ugly, I thought it, not my cup of tea at all."

"How did they get in?"

"It was offered to them on a plate. An old-fashioned french window round the back that a child could have opened in a few minutes. And you won't believe this, but they hadn't even got the stuff locked away in cabinets. It was just dotted about all over the place: on the mantelpiece, on top of bureaux and tables. They were asking for trouble."

89

"So it doesn't have to be someone who knew about their collection. Anyone snooping around the place would be able to see what was on offer inside?"

"Yeah. A nice garden with a boundary hedge anyone could push through. The Robinsons are going make a list of what was taken but someone knew their stuff and creamed off the best. Apparently the choice piece that's gone missing is a vase in an early design."

"That alone would be worth several thousand. The crocus design is also highly collectable."

"Would it be easy to trace if it turns up on the market?"

"The vase might, but not the other stuff. It's valuable but not exactly rare. Go to any antique fair and you'll probably find a piece of crocus design but you'd have to pay for it. Have you interviewed the neighbours?"

"They're mostly elderly retired people who keep themselves to themselves. The couple on one side, who are deaf and doddery, heard and saw nothing and the people who live on the other side weren't there this morning when we called."

"Right. Arrange for someone to check back with them. Now, bring me up to date with the van."

"It was abandoned out at Alton Abbas. There's a lane on the edge of the village that ends in a little copse that's used by courting couples. Vehicles are often seen parked there and nobody living nearby thought anything about it at first. It's only just been reported by a . . ." Court consulted his notes. ". . . a Major Deller-Browne. He rang in complaining that a clapped-out old van – though he didn't use that expression – was lowering the tone of the area and 'why didn't the police get off their backsides and do something to earn their grossly inflated salaries'. Quote, unquote. He's a pompous little shit and if he was so upset about it spoiling his view I don't know why he didn't report it sooner. Can't have thought a couple were having it off in there all that time." He turned to look out of the window as the first streak of lightning lit the sky followed by distant thunder. "The boys are checking it over. Let's hope they finish before this little lot hits us, though I don't suppose there's a hope in hell of them finding anything. They're sure to have worn gloves or wiped their dabs off."

"I think you and I will go back and speak to this Major Browne again. If we give him the right treatment he may be able to dredge up something from his memory."

"You won't get far if you call him Browne. It's Major Deller-Browne, and don't you forget it."

"Whilst we're interviewing him get Dakin and Horner to do a house-to-house round the rest of that district. There's just a chance that someone may have noticed someone actually abandoning the van though I'm not hopeful."

As they tramped down the stairs the first rain swept against the windows and by the time they reached the car-park at the side of the building the deluge had flooded a large part of the tarmac.

Gina Bonetti cowered in the laundry, her hands over her ears, rocking backwards and forwards in distress as the storm raged and thundered overhead. She had always been scared of thunderstorms, even as a young child. One of her first memories was of being carried in her father's arms down a hillside near Fabriano in a thunderstorm just such as this. She could only have been about three at the time but she remembered being pressed against her father's chest as he slithered down the rocky path, the olive trees threshing about and snatching at her hair. She could still recall the smell of his damp shirt, a combination of sweat and rain, and the thud of his heartbeats penetrating her own little body and the mumbled curses and supplications to God as the precious olives hailed down around them.

They had left Italy soon after this episode; the failure of the crop and her English mother's desire to return to her own country prompting the move. The only other memories of her first years in Italy were of heat, intense white heat such as you never experienced in England and the scent of warm soil and aromatic shrubs.

Another crack of thunder had her cringing beside the industrial tumble-drier that thudded and throbbed in company with the noise outside. But it was not just the storm that was upsetting her now. She had seen *him*. Twice. The first time she had thought that she was hallucinating; the voices were speaking again, reminding her of things she wanted to forget. The terrible things that blurred in her memory, sometimes so distorted and horrible that she couldn't bear it, at other times so unreal and hazy that she thought she must be imagining them. But the second time she had *known* that it was him.

She had been with Jason Cunningham in the precincts of the town centre. He had been doing his juggling and conjuring act and she had been acting as his assistant. As she twirled and gestured she had seen him approaching along the alley-way. She had stumbled and then frozen in shock, unable to believe her eyes but knowing inwardly that she had always been expecting that moment. She had recovered as sheer terror had swept through her and she had snatched up their collecting bag and fought her way through the gathered crowd, desperate to escape before he saw her. Jason had been furious. He had reckoned that that day he had put on one of his best shows. The crowd had been captivated and amused and they could have made a killing. Instead, she had disappeared with the bag and the performance had fizzled out. Later he had accepted that she had been having one of her 'turns' but since then she had avoided appearing in public and now this neck injury had given her a real let-out. It was a blessing in disguise.

But he was out there. She wasn't safe and she didn't know what to do. Run away again? Where would she go? She couldn't spend the rest of her life fleeing from one place to another and she had felt safe here. Moulton Manor was in an isolated position; he wouldn't come out here and Gabriel was the only person who could soothe her when she got in one of her states. But she couldn't confide in him; although she longed to pour out all her troubles she knew he wouldn't understand. He was too aloof, too Godlike. He would tell her to trust in God but his god was not the one she had been brought up to worship. She had renounced that religion. She was an apostate and guilt still twisted her guts. She had tried to talk to Ellen. Ellen was different from the rest of the Children of Light. She still had a mind of her own and wasn't drifting along in the catatonic state most of them seemed to be in. But Ellen had not taken her seriously, she was too taken up with Dan. He was another outsider who didn't fit in here. She wanted to tell Ellen not to fall in love with him or trust him. She, Gina Bonetti, knew that love was a fool's game. It didn't last and the consequences were too dreadful to bear.

The storm had abated a little and beside her the tumble drier rumbled to a halt. She opened the door and started to take out the sheets, battling to fold them on her own, flinching as the pain shot along her neck and shoulders. Lucy or Barry should have been helping her; they were skiving as usual. A high-pitched mewling noise coming from some packing cases in the corner caught her attention. She listened intently and then crept over to where the noise was coming from. In a carton on a low shelf was a litter of kittens. Their little bodies, striped ginger and black, squirmed and wriggled in the nest of crumpled paper and rags their mother had made for them. She crooned in delight and scooped one up in her hands. The little creature was warm and soft, its mouth opening and shutting as it uttered little squeals, whilst its paws, so overlarge for its little body, kneaded the air.

"Oh, you baby. You little baby!" She cuddled it in her arms. "Baby . . . baby . . ."

Suddenly she went rigid and stared at the kitten in her arms, recoiling in shock. She hurled it violently away from her, shuddering as it hit the packing cases and slithered to the floor.

"Christ, Gina! You'll kill it! What did you do that for?" Barry had come into the laundry unnoticed by her. She pulled herself together.

"You're blaspheming. Taking the name of the Lord in vain. You'd better not let Gabriel hear you."

"What were you doing to that kitten?"

"Gabriel will drown them if he finds them."

"Well, we'd better make sure that Gaia discovers them first."

Major Deller-Browne was a wiry little man who resembled a ferocious fox terrier. He must be knocking eighty, thought Nick as he and Tim Court were shown into the Deller-Browne house, but he held himself very upright. If he suffered from arthritis or any of the usual aches and pains associated with old age he didn't show it. The major was flattered at the presence of a CID inspector and Nick played up to his vanity.

"We've come to you, Major, because as a trained observer you can probably help us. None of your neighbours noticed anything untoward."

"They wouldn't, all in their dotage." He glared at Nick as though daring him to contradict this statement. "Take no interest in preserving the status quo, not at all public spirited. Isn't that so, Audrey?" he barked at the woman beside him.

His wife was small and faded looking. She had thin hair through which her pink skull showed, and washed-out blue eyes. She looked older than her husband but this might just have been the result of years of living under his thumb. Nick doubted that she had ever crossed her husband in all the years that they had been married and she bore out this theory when she managed a meek: "Yes, dear."

"Tell me, Major, why didn't you report the presence of the van earlier?"

"Because it has happened before. At this time of year there's a car parked amongst those trees practically every night, sometimes more than one. That copse is a haven for illicit sex. The promiscuity of the youth of today . . . That piece of ground ought to be cleared. Cut the trees down and turn it into a little park with lawns and flower-beds. Far more in keeping with this district . . ."

"Yes," Nick cut him short, "but it was still there several days later. How did you account for that?"

"Thought it had broken down. Not exactly an up-to-date model, is it? I expected someone to come back, the owner or a garage mechanic, but when they didn't I realised it had been abandoned. Had it been stolen?"

"Yes. We think it was used as a getaway car in a robbery."

"Ah . . . So you're looking for evidence? Fingerprints?"

"Unfortunately that is not likely but I was hoping you might have seen something."

"The villains who did it, you mean? Are they dangerous?"

Beside him his wife was getting increasingly agitated. She pawed at his arm and he brushed her off impatiently.

"Don't interrupt, Audrey. This is important."

"But I don't think they were villains, dear."

"Mrs Deller-Browne, did *you* see the occupants?"

"Of course she didn't," snapped the major. "I don't know what has got into you, Audrey."

"But I told you . . ."

"Told me what?"

"I *did* tell you, Edwin, but you wouldn't listen . . ."

The major looked astonished at what he thought of as his wife's affrontery and Nick hastily intervened.

"Who did you see, Mrs Deller-Browne? Can you describe them to me?"

"I'm sure they weren't villains. I thought they were a courting couple."

"You saw them drive up and park the van?"

"No, I saw them get out."

"When was this?"

"I go to bed early, Inspector, but I don't sleep very well. I got up and happened to look out of the window on my way to the bathroom."

"What time would this have been?"

"After eleven. probably nearer half past. I noticed the van – you could see the back of it protruding from behind that hawthorn bush – and I saw this couple get out."

"It would have been dark."

"There was a full moon that night. It was almost as bright as daylight."

"Go on."

"Well, that's all there is really. They got out, joined hands and hurried down the road. I suppose they were almost running."

"Can you give me a description of them?"

"They were young. The girl had long hair. I remember thinking that there was something odd about her . . ."

"Yes? How were they dressed?"

"That's it. She was wearing a long dress."

"Evening dress, you mean?"

"No. It wasn't at all fancy. Just a long, straight gown and she had sandals on her feet."

Nick and Tim Court exchanged surreptitious looks and the former tried to cajole more details from the major's wife but she had nothing further to add.

"Are you sure you didn't imagine it?" snapped her husband, annoyed that she was the centre of attention.

"No, of course I didn't. I remember thinking how romantic they looked."

"Romantic!" snorted her husband. "What's romance got to do with armed robbery and violence!"

The two detectives took their leave of the Deller-Brownes and went back to their car. Court hit the steering wheel with his fist.

"But I don't understand this. The van was stolen from the Children of Light. *They* reported it missing and now it looks as if two of them actually abandoned it. It doesn't make sense."

"I'm not so sure." The glimmering of an idea was beginning to form in Nick's brain but he needed to think it through before he shot off his mouth to his sergeant.

"Do you think perhaps the two of them were having a bit of nooky behind Big Brother's back?"

"I think Gabriel may be involved in this but not in the way you think. Come on, let's get back and see if the house-to-house has produced any results."

They were in luck. One of the householders interviewed lived on the corner of Church Lane where the road out of the village joined the main road to Moulton Abbas. He had been out in the garden at about eleven thirty that night calling in his dog when he had noticed a couple answering the description given by Mrs Deller-Browne thumbing a lift in a lorry.

"So the two of them had borrowed the van for a little illicit romp, couldn't start it again, so they hitched a lift back to Moulton Manor and pretended it had been stolen."

"Hmm," said Nick, pulling at his bottom lip. "But how does that little scenario fit in with the van being used in the robbery at the jewellers?"

"It must have been another van," said Court gloomily. "We just took it for granted that it was the same van. Shouldn't trust coincidences. We have it drummed into us enough times."

"Well, try and trace the lorry driver. He's our best bet at the moment. Thank God for that man and his dog."

A dog was involved in the next piece of information that came in. Chris Hames, a young constable who formed part of the team carrying out the house-to-house involving the latest burglary had found the next-door neighbours in and struck lucky.

"They knew nothing about the actual break-in," he said, checking his notes. "They were also away last night babysitting for their daughter, but they've noticed someone hanging around the place recently. A scruffy-looking yob with a dog. The couple – whose name is Petherbury – have also got a dog; a young poodle. Spends much of its day in the garden and on three separate occasions they've heard it yapping hysterically, and when they've gone out to see what was the matter there was this youth slouching about on the pavement outside with this enormous dog in tow. Apparently this great brute was frightening the living daylights out of Tinkerbell. That's the name of the Petherburys' poodle, sir."

"Did they speak to the youth?"

"On the last occasion they asked him what he was doing and he mumbled something unintelligible and they told him to clear off, which he did and they didn't see him again."

"Were they able to give you a description of him?"

"Said he had a limp and they were sure that they had seen him before, recognised the dog." Hames and paused and Nick knew what was coming next. "Said they'd seen him begging in the town centre."

"I think I know who you mean. So the Petherburys think he was casing the joint and came back and broke in later when the coast was clear?"

"It looks fishy, you must admit."

"Rather too obvious, but we'll certainly pick him up and bring him in for questioning."

"You know where he hangs out?"

"Oh yes, he's one of the commune at Moulton Manor."

*   *   *

Before he called it a day, Nick liaised briefly with Tim Court. He was not yet ready to share his suspicions with his sergeant but he discussed their next line of enquiry.

"First thing in the morning we'll give this Gabriel a ring and ask him to come in and identify the van."

"He'll probably want to send someone else after it."

"Then we must just make sure that it's he who comes. I want his fingerprints. I don't want to ask him and risk putting him on his guard but we need to get his dabs."

"I reckon we can manage that. He'll have to touch the van and handle the documents," said Court with a grin.

"Good man. Whilst you've got Gabriel occupied here we'll pick up his beggar and see what he has to say for himself."

Before he left for home, Nick remembered that he had promised to ring Rachel. She didn't answer so he left a message on her answerphone. As he slammed out of the building he wondered if she had got home safely. She must have been caught in the storm and he reckoned he was not in high favour at the moment. At least she was adult enough not to take his abandonment of her personally. She knew the score and accepted his commitment to his job and was a valuable sounding board. He had some serious thinking to do, to sort out the jumble of ideas and suspicions that were forming in his mind, but when he had made some sense of them himself he wanted to try out his theories on her.

Policemen didn't discuss their cases with outsiders but he knew that Rachel would respect his confidences. Nothing he told her would go any further and an unbiased mind on the subject would help him sort out facts from wishful thinking.

The water in the car-park had subsided and the hot, humid atmosphere had dispersed with the rain. A welcome breeze tugged at his hair as he walked over to his car and although he welcomed the freshening air he couldn't help wondering if the storm had heralded the end of the fine weather and whether this summer might go on record as the shortest ever.

As soon as he got into the station the next morning Nick put through a call to Moulton Manor. Gaia answered and to his frustration she told him that Gabriel had gone away.

"Can I help?" Her rich, throaty voice purred down the line.

"We've found your blue van that was stolen. I need Gabriel to come and identify it and take possession."

"Couldn't someone else do that?"

"It's registered in Gabriel's name so I'm afraid it must be him," said Nick firmly. "When will he be back?"

"Not until the weekend I'm afraid. He's in London at a convention."

"Then perhaps you'll pass on the message and ask him to come in when he returns. In the meantime you'll have to manage without the van for a little longer."

"We have other vehicles. Where is it? Is it far away?"

"It is here in police possession. It has been checked for forensic evidence; fingerprints and that sort of thing."

"Did you find anything?"

"Not a whisker. By the way, there were no keys left in it. I presume you have a spare set?"

"Gabriel will know about that. I'll tell him as soon as he gets back and he will be in touch."

Nick had barely replaced the receiver when the phone rang again. He snatched it up and listened in growing incredulity, gesturing to Tim Court across the room.

"There's been another burglary – at Selhampton Hall. I don't believe this! I was there yesterday – at a car-boot sale. That was where I was when I was called back here."

"You mean someone turned the Hall over during a boot sale?"

"No, it happened later that evening or during the night. But hell, the place was swarming with people yesterday!"

"Inside the Hall?"

"No. The boot sale was in the park but the world and his wife were milling around the grounds not to mention most of the landed gentry of Dorset!"

"What was taken? The usual small-time stuff?"

"No. That was the local bobby. Lord and Lady Gilchrist – that's the owners – are doing their nut. They've got a valuable

99

collection of oriental porcelain; that wasn't touched but some very valuable glassware has disappeared."

"Surely they've got a security system?"

"Of sorts. If it's not up to scratch, and it sounds as if it isn't, they're not going to get much joy from the insurers. Let's get going."

Selhampton Hall looked very different that morning. Without the attendant crowds and the turmoil of the car-boot sale it was somehow more imposing; an architectural gem in a verdant setting. A small group of people, including two children, were working their way through the parkland disposing of the litter left behind, and when Nick and Court got out of their car the scent of crushed grass and drenched greenery assailed their nostrils. PC Taylor was waiting for them in the formal courtyard. He explained the situation as they went inside to meet Lord and Lady Gilchrist.

"What was taken?"

"A lamp and a vase."

"Just two objects?"

"That's what they reported but now Lady Gilchrist says some of her jewellery is missing plus some cash."

"We're not talking about the Gilchrist collection?"

"No. That's safely tucked away in rooms with a very sophisticated security alarm system. This stuff was taken from the east wing where the family have their living quarters. It wasn't under lock and key."

"Some people ask for trouble," said Nick, thinking of the art deco ceramics that had recently been stolen. "How did the thief get in?"

"There are no signs of a break-in, but Lord Gilchrist says there was an intruder in the grounds during the evening. A brick was chucked through a window in the entrance hall and smashed a picture."

"Didn't he report it?"

"No," said Taylor heavily, "he thought it was a local yob going in for a spot of vandalism after the boot sale and he was busy entertaining."

"Entertaining?"

"Half the County names were in and out of here during the day and some of they stayed on for supper."

"Perhaps it's an inside job," suggested Court.

"Try telling that to his lordship. He's convinced one of the Booters is responsible for the theft."

"Has he any theories as to how they got in?"

"According to him, that's our job," said Taylor woodenly. "He insists the stuff was still there when they retired for the night."

"Right, the sooner we speak to him the better."

Lord Gilchrist was a tall, ascetic-looking man in his sixties. His wife, Grace, was small, plump and volatile. The irrelevant thought that they were like Jack Sprat and his wife crossed Nick's mind as introductions were made.

"I understand two glass ornaments were taken. Can you describe them to me?" asked Nick.

"Glass? Well, yes they were –" Lord Gilchrist gave a mirthless smile – "but not any old glass. There was a Tiffany table lamp and a Lalique vase."

Nick blinked. Since getting involved with Rachel he had assimilated some knowledge of antiques, as she was interested in the subject and had dragged him to several antique fairs. He knew they were not talking peanuts.

"They would be very valuable?"

"Yes," said Lord Gilchrist briefly.

"What sort of money are we talking about?"

"I'm not sure."

"But you must have had them insured, sir? Evaluated for insurance purposes."

"They were included in the general house contents."

"You mean they weren't individually listed?" Nick was incredulous.

"Goddamn it, Inspector, have you any idea how much insurance I pay for the Gilchrist collection? The premiums are enormous, it's an albatross round my neck. The rest of our belongings get minimum cover. I know these art nouveau pieces are increasing in value but these were family pieces. The lamp was bought by my grandmother during a visit to the States and the vase on a trip to

Paris. They've been in the family ever since they were originally purchased. They've never been through an auction house or been listed in a catalogue. They were part of the furniture. We *used* them; the lamp was lit every evening. An ugly thing I've always thought. All that multi-coloured glass in the shade; rather like Venetian glass and I've always thought that very vulgar."

"The vase was rather beautiful," put in Lady Gilchrist. "It was cameo-cut in delicate shades of green and turquoise. I used it for foliage arrangements."

"Perhaps you'll show me exactly where they were?"

Lord Gilchrist led the way through the entrance hall which was a typical medieval hall with a high vaulted ceiling and a small minstrels' gallery. There was a lobby leading to a formidable oak door at the far end.

"That's where the Gilchrist Collection is housed," said Lord Gilchrist. "I don't want to de-activate the alarm system and I can assure you everything is present and correct. Our living quarters are through here."

'Here' was another door opening off the opposite end of the hall and the two detectives followed him as he unlocked the door and ushered them inside.

"Is this always kept locked?" inquired Nick.

"Yes, always. This is our private accommodation. We only use one wing for living purposes. The rest of the Hall is a showpiece, not a home! We feel more secure behind locked doors." He gave a short bark of laughter, again devoid of mirth.

"You open the house to the public?"

"Yes. Have to do something to pay for the upkeep."

"When was it last opened?"

"Easter weekend. The public is not allowed in this part of the house, it is cordoned off."

That was only about five weeks ago, thought Nick as they were shown into a sitting room that despite its generous proportions and panelled walls managed to look quite cosy. It appeared that this burglary was following the same pattern as the previous ones on stately homes. The thieves had sussed the place and then struck later.

"The lamp was on here –" Lord Gilchrist indicated the top of a grand piano – "and the vase stood on that side table."

"And you are sure they were there when you went to bed? I understand there was a disturbance earlier in the evening?"

"I'm quite sure. What happened earlier was just a piece of mindless vandalism."

"What happened exactly?"

"We were sitting in here with some friends when there was this almighty crash – about nine thirty it was. We rushed out . . ."

"Was this door locked then?"

"Yes, Inspector. I unlocked the door and we all went through into the hall. It was getting dark so I switched on the lights. There was no sign of any intruder but a picture on the wall was hanging at a tilted angle and the glass was broken. There was a piece of brick lying on the floor nearby. My first thought was the Gilchrist Collection, but of course the alarm would have gone off if that had been tampered with. We went outside but there was no sign of anyone."

"It must have been one of the people at the car-boot sale," said Lady Gilchrist. "There were some very odd people there I can assure you."

"But the boot sale took place in the park a long way from the house." Nick didn't think it politic to admit to his presence at that affair.

"But the storm," wailed Grace Gilchrist. "They rushed to the house for cover." She spoke as a medieval chatelaine facing an advancing army. "There was a marquee erected near the kitchen block and they swarmed into that and were trying to shelter in the stables and the outhouses."

Nick walked back into the entrance and looked up at the minstrels' gallery.

"Can you get into that gallery?"

"Yes, it leads off a corridor," said Gilchrist, looking surprised at the question.

"I believe you are missing some jewellery as well, Lady Gilchrist. Tell me about that."

"My engagement ring and another diamond ring and a pearl necklace and earrings."

"Where were they?"

"In my dressing room."

"Under lock and key."

"No. I was wearing them yesterday. I took them off when I retired to bed. I was *so* exhausted, Inspector, after the strains of the day – I shall never agree to be host for such an event again – that I just left them in a pile on the dressing-table. I didn't realise they had been taken until a couple of hours ago. There was some money too."

"Yes?"

"We spent much of yesterday evening counting up the profits," put in Lord Gilchrist heavily. "It was recorded and locked away in the safe but my wife overlooked one lot. It was left in a box on the dresser in the dining room. That was taken too."

Nick asked to be shown their sleeping quarters. He noted that Lord and Lady Gilchrist had separate bedrooms and their own dressing-rooms.

"Inspector, is this the work of the same gang involved in the other burglaries we've heard so much about recently?"

"It is impossible to say at this stage but it may well be. With your permission I'll get our forensic team to go over the house."

"I am convinced that everything was in place when we went to bed. Someone must have got in during the night but I don't know how."

"I think I do, Lord Gilchrist, and it was during the day. I think someone got into the hall during the afternoon and hid themselves somewhere upstairs. During the evening they moved into the minstrels' gallery and threw a brick down into the hall smashing a picture. This had the desired effect. You all streamed out of your private quarters to look for the intruder and he in turn took the opportunity to slip into this part of the house which is usually under lock and key. He secreted himself somewhere in here and during the night he helped himself to things he had probably marked out earlier. He was probably still somewhere on the premises when you arose this morning and got out later during the kerfuffle."

"This is unbelievable!" said Lord Gilchrist and his wife gave a sudden piercing shriek. "But he must have been in my bedroom! Good God, James, he may have been hiding in my wardrobe. What a ghastly thought!"

Eight

The results of the SOCO search at Selhampton Hall bore out Nick Holroyd's theory as to how the burglary had been carried out. Traces of an intruder were found in an old disused pantry in the form of a footprint in the floury dust of the floor. Traces of this deposit were also found on the floor of the minstrels' gallery. There were no fingerprints and nothing to show how the burglar had effected his exit.

"I'm not sure if this one is linked to the others," said Nick, mulling over the case with Tim Court later that week. "The stakes were much higher. Not your usual domestic appliances or small antiques and knick-knacks but two very rare collector's pieces, and it was elaborately planned."

"Surely if they are that rare they will be traceable if they turn up on the open market?"

"It is not as simple as that. There are no photographs in existence, all we have is Gilchrist's description and as they are not known pieces they could surface anywhere without anyone recognising them."

"What did the arts and antiques squad have to say about value when you contacted them?"

"The sky's the limit. The Tiffany lamp at the very lowest estimate would fetch at least twenty thousand and could top five hundred thousand if someone wanted it badly enough. I know, the mind boggles, doesn't it? The vase probably in excess of eight thousand."

"Someone knew what they were about, didn't they?"

"Yes," said Nick slowly, "almost as if they were stolen to order and the thief knocked off the cash and jewellery as an afterthought and an extra perk for himself."

"I should think Lord Gilchrist will be sick as a parrot when he learns how much they were worth. Do you really think he didn't know?"

"It looks that way. It's like those cases you see on *The Antiques Roadshow* when an old piece of pottery that has been used as a doorstop turns out to be a priceless vase. Familiarity breeds contempt. They've been lying around in full view ever since they were brought home by his grandmother and they'd become part of the furniture. No one really noticed them or thought of their value."

"So where do we go from here?"

"The descriptions have been circulated to all known dealers and auction houses in Europe and the States but if they've gone to a private unscrupulous collector they will never surface again."

"What did the Super want?"

Nick had been summoned to Tom Powell's office earlier that morning and had come out looking glum.

"Of all the cases we've been investigating this is the one to stick in his craw. Wheels within wheels. Apparently the CC is a friend of the Gilchrists, and he's screaming for action. I had quite a job persuading Powell that it just wasn't possible to interview everyone who had been at the car-boot sale and that, anyway, a massive operation like that would also involve the local aristocracy. That saved the day."

"The footprint we found is not going to be of much help either unless we get a suspect we can match it against. A popular Adidas brand, size ten – there's hundreds of them out there on the street. At least it rules out a women unless she's a giantess."

"I think there was more than one person involved."

"An accomplice keeping a look-out?"

"As I've said before, my bet is that we are talking about a well-organised network but how this latest scam fits into it I'm not yet sure." Nick refused to be drawn any more about his suppositions and Court went off disgruntled at being kept in the dark and wondering if his boss had lost it.

* * *

That afternoon, as she left the hospital, Rachel found Nick waiting for her in his car.

"Hello, we hadn't arranged to meet, had we?" she asked in puzzlement, wondering if she could possibly have forgotten a date.

"No, I was just hoping I'd catch you and you hadn't got anything planned for this evening."

"Well, no . . ."

"Good. I'd take you out for a meal but we need to talk and you can't have a private conversation in a restaurant. How about picking up a takeaway and coming back to my place?"

"This all sounds very ominous. What do we need to talk about?"

"Don't worry. This is not about us. I need to run something past you and get your views. OK?"

"Very succinct, but I've no idea what you're talking about."

"All will be revealed. Now, which would you prefer – Chinese, Indian or we could have a pizza?"

They decided on Indian and it wasn't until they had finished their meal and were relaxing and sipping coffee in Nick's living room that he broached the subject that had been exercising him for much of the last few days.

"This case I'm working on – all these local robberies and burglaries – I've got a theory but not an atom of proof."

"I was going to ask you about that. I saw in the paper that there was a break-in at Selhampton Hall the night following the car-boot sale. Are you investigating that?"

"Yes, but I'm not sure that it is the work of the same gang. That's one of the things I want to talk through with you." Nick leaned back in his chair and crossed his arms behind his head. "What would you say if I told you I thought the Children of Light may be behind these burglaries?"

Rachel considered this. "I ought to be horrified at the suggestion but I'm not," she said, looking perplexed.

"Horrified because I'm denigrating a religious community?"

"That's just it. I'm not sure how authentic it is. Don't get me wrong. Most of the people I've met from Moulton Manor seem genuine in their beliefs but I'm not happy about Gabriel's influence. He is very charismatic and I'm sure he wields great power over them but whether it's for good or evil . . . What makes you think they could be involved?"

"Apart from Selhampton Hall all the stuff nicked so far has been easily disposed of items or relatively small hauls of cash. We're not dealing with a big-time gang and there has been no violence or threat to life; just a steady spate of break-ins and larceny, but it's been highly organised. The thieves knew exactly what they wanted and when to carry out the raids. I think there is a mastermind behind it who has a network of spies."

"You think Gabriel is the mastermind and his Children of Light are the spies?"

"Why not? They are about in the community. You can't go into the town centre without falling over a couple of them busking. They're in an ideal position to suss out possible targets and to note how good or bad security arrangements are in different stores as well as noting any valuables that individuals may be carrying. We know for a fact that that crippled lout with the dog was hanging around a house that was burgled recently. We've had him in for questioning but unfortunately we couldn't pin anything on him. As for the stately homes that have been hit – it has always been just after they have been open to the public. Some of the Children of Light could have gone round for the purpose of finding out what could be taken and how it could be done."

"That's persuasive argument, but even if you accept that Gabriel is a charlatan how do you account for his followers equating stealing with their religious beliefs?"

"Because they don't look on it as stealing but rather as a redistribution of wealth? Rob the rich to help the poor? It's an idea that would appeal to the idealistic youth he has in tow."

"Are you saying that if you are correct in your assumption all the ill-gotten gains are being funnelled to charity?" said Rachel, looking thoughtful.

"Don't tell me you're sympathetic to the idea?"

"I must admit it has a certain appeal but no, you can't bend the rules of a civilized society like that or anarchy would reign. Anyway, in most cases they weren't robbing the rich, were they?

Just helping themselves to things that people like you and I could ill afford to lose."

"That's very true and I'm sure Gabriel is getting rich out of it."

"You mean his disciples think the spoils are funding good causes whilst in actual fact he is pocketing the profits?"

"Not quite. I've been putting out feelers about their charitable work and they *do* give large sums to charity. Far more than the community could possibly earn, even taking into consideration the income they get from the craftwork and market gardening side of things. Apparently when he bought Moulton Manor it was understood that the money for it came from an inheritance. Some inheritance it must have been, but I shouldn't think it is still funding the set-up. The Children of Light are having to work for their keep in other ways: busking, begging and burglary. And I bet some of the proceeds from the burglaries are helping to keep Gabriel and Gaia in the manner to which they've become accustomed."

"Why do you think the break-in at Selhampton Hall may not be connected with the other burglaries?"

"Because this time something *very* valuable was taken."

He told her about the art nouveau glass that had been stolen and its possible value.

"I could be wrong and they're moving up-market and getting more ambitious. You were there longer than me, you didn't happen to notice anyone from Moulton Manor at the boot sale, did you?"

"Yes, I did."

Nick raised his eyebrows and Rachel said slowly:

"You're not going to like this but your sister was there – with the boyfriend."

"What has the crazy girl got herself into!"

"There may be a perfectly innocent explanation for them being where they were . . ."

"But you don't really think so, do you? No, young Ellen has got some explaining to do."

"You're going to tackle her?"

"I'm going to try to get to the bottom of it. She may be able to give me the proof I need to back up my theory."

"Even if she is involved she's not going to admit it to you. From what she's said you're definitely not flavour of the month with her. What have you done to cross her?"

"It's a long story. When she was little she looked on me almost as a surrogate father. She was very possessive and didn't take kindly to my marrying. She did her damndest to cause trouble between us. Of course, that wasn't the reason our marriage broke up but she didn't make it any easier. After we separated, Ellen thought she was going to be kingpin again and didn't take kindly to me leaving the area and cutting myself off from her and her mother."

"Poor Ellen, she's certainly lacked a father figure in her life. That's probably why someone like Gabriel has so much influence over her. She's not going to take kindly to you interfering. In fact it may drive her further into his camp."

"You're right. She'll probably refuse to see me at all. I must get Clare to help. Maybe she can persuade Ellen to go home for a visit, then we can go along and meet up with her."

"We?"

"You're in on this too. I need your help. After all, you've seen more of Ellen lately than either I or Clare."

"I don't think my presence is going to exactly ease the path."

"I'm not trying to ease Ellen's path. I want to find out just what she has got herself into and try and extricate her if it is at all possible."

"And also get proof that your theory is correct?"

"There's that as well." Nick grinned and got to his feet. "I'll give Clare a ring now and she if she can fix up a meeting."

Contrary to expectations, the thunderstorm had not brought the fine weather to an end. After a couple of days when the temperature had dipped and the sun struggled to break through the clouds another anti-cyclone moved in and by the beginning of the following week the countryside was in the grip of another heatwave. Enterprising restauranteurs in Casterford set up pavement cafes and in the suburbs the domestic barbecues trailed their aromas of charcoal and charred meat late into the evening air.

People gravitated to their gardens. They ate out on their terraces and balconies and left their patio doors and windows open. At night these doors and windows remained open encouraging the cooler night air into the hothouse conditions indoors; an open invitation to intruders.

The campus at Casterford College sprawled untidily in a roughly triangular area bordered by the School of Science and the School of Art on two sides and the natural boundary of the river on the third. It had been designed in the fifties by an architect who favoured the colonial look. Long rows of chalet-like rooms with an integral verandah running from end to end made up most of the student accommodation. There had been plans afoot to update the place and provide more suitable quarters for some time, not least because of the too easy access from one room to another, but lack of funds had so far prevented any alterations or new construction.

The block nearest to the river and farthest from the faculty buildings housed some of the female Art and Design students. As befitted their calling, these students had allowed their imaginations to run riot when it came to stamping individuality on their rooms. From ethnic flamboyance to minimalist austerity, each room reflected its occupier's efforts to create something different from her neighbours. Carey Meadows occupied the end room which overlooked the ragged willows marking the curve of the river. She had only moved in a couple of weeks earlier and was in the middle of creating a setting worthy of her artistic status. She intended to make the end wall into a giant collage using scrap metal and plastic detritus and so as not to detract from this focal point she had spent much of the day painting the rest of the walls and the woodwork a pale, neutral grey.

That night the air still reeked with the smell of paint, intensified by the cloying heat. Carey opened the window as far as it would go, left the door leading on to the verandah wide open and collapsed on the bed in a tangle of sticky, naked limbs. She didn't know what woke her a couple of hours later. She turned over and wrenched her eyes open, focusing on the window. A black mass blocked the aperture, cutting off the dim light that usually filtered through from the distant street lights. As she struggled to orientate herself this black shadow loomed over her and as she opened her mouth to scream it pounced, knocking her back and pinning her to the bed.

A rubber-clad hand clamped over her mouth and as she struggled desperately with her attacker his hands moved to her throat, pressing relentlessly against her windpipe until she lost consciousness. As she spun into darkness she could feel his body grinding into hers.

"This man has got to be stopped."

DI Mark Collins glared at the men and women gathered in the incident room. "No one is safe until we get him behind bars. I repeat – no one. Not your wife or your girlfriend or your sister or your mother. This fiend thinks he is omnipotent, he's so sure of himself that he thinks any woman is there for his taking. He gets on to the campus, enters a student's room and rapes her in her own bed after half strangling her!"

"I've visited her in hospital," said Fiona Walker, "and she is in a very distressed state. Fortunately for her she blacked out, unfortunately for us she can't give us any description except that he was powerful, gloved and hooded."

"Someone must have seen or heard something," said Keith Adams, looking round for support. "I don't believe all the other students were tucked up asleep on their lonesome. It's my bet there were other sexual activities going on last night. Christ! The male student quarters are on the same site only a few hundred yards away – I bet there's a lot of coming and going!"

"In which case, those involved would have been too busy to notice and the others would think nothing of it."

"How easy is it for an outsider to get on the campus?"

"Too easy," said Collins, pointing to the plan that was pinned on the wall. "Carey Meadows's room was the end one and her attacker could have come along the towpath and through the hedge. It runs alongside the building."

"Unless it *was* one of the other students. I mean, someone could have been trying to make it with her and when she didn't respond he may have decided to screw her by pretending to be the rapist."

"No. This attack was too violent and it has all the hallmarks of the other attacks. However, our rapist *could* be one of the students. Someone whose urge is becoming so great and uncontrollable that he's now shitting on his own doorstep."

"All the male students were interviewed and re-interviewed last time and we didn't get any joy."

"I think this time we must press for DNA testing. I think on the strength of this latest rape we've got enough facts to justify it."

"It's going to take time."

"It is, and knock a huge hole in our budget but it must be done. And now . . ." Collins scowled round the room. ". . . I'd like to know which one of you blabbed to the Press? It was on the local radio early morning news bulletin almost before I knew about it!"

"It was probably one of the other female students," said Fiona Walker. "They're all terrified, and understandably so."

"Well, liaise with the college authorities about stepping up security. Presumably they have their own counselling service."

"Yes, sir."

"In view of the publicity I have called a news conference for six p.m."

"Are you going to release details of the DNA testing programme?"

"Oh yes. If we can be seen to be doing something positive at least it will keep them off our backs."

There was a message on Nick's answerphone when he arrived home at his flat. It was from Clare Holroyd and when he played it back her anxious voice spilled out into the room.

"It's Clare, Nick. I'm really worried. I did what you asked and rang Moulton Manor but they say she's not there – that she's left the community. I'm sure something's happened to her! She really *is* missing this time – you must do something! *Please* get in touch!" The message ended with a fit of coughing.

"Cut the fags, Clare," muttered Nick as he played it through again. Although he knew that Clare liked to squeeze the last ounce of drama out of a situation he could tell that she was seriously worried. He punched her number and she answered on the second ring.

"Nick? Oh, I'm so glad to hear you. Did you get my message? I'm sure something terrible has happened to Ellen. I can feel it in my bones."

"Just calm down, Clare, and tell me what's happened."

She started to gabble, her voice rising in hysteria and Nick cut her short.

"Hold on, I'll come round. I'll be with you in about thirty minutes. And Clare – try not to get in a state, I'm sure there's a perfectly simple explanation."

He put the phone down on her harangue and checked his watch, wondering if Rachel would be in. He needed her with him when he met Clare. She had spoken with Ellen several times recently and might be able to talk some sense into her stepmother. Another phone call elicited that Rachel was at home and willing to accompany him, so he made a detour and collected her.

"I was going to phone you about Ellen," said Rachel as he took the road leading back into Casterford. "Gina Bonetti came in for a session this morning and *she* told me that Ellen has left the community."

"Did she say why?"

"Only that Dan, her boyfriend, had also gone. Apparently he went first and a few days later Ellen took off. Gina thought she was upset about Dan and had decided to go after him."

"I knew there would be a logical reason for her departure. It's a pity she cleared off before we could talk to her about the pilfering."

"If she was involved in something illegal Clare should be relieved that she's now out of the way."

"Yes, but I bet Clare won't see it like that."

When Clare answered the door she brought with her the reek of stale cigarette smoke and also a whiff of alcohol. Hell, she's hit

114

the bottle, thought Nick, they'd be lucky to get any sense out of her if she was in the maudlin state that usually followed a binge. She squinted suspiciously at Rachel. Nick hurriedly introduced them to each other and she waved them into the house.

"A drink? But I suppose you don't . . ." she said to Rachel.

"Not just at the moment, thank you."

"Well, you don't mind if I do, do you?" She picked up the half full glass that stood on the drinks cabinet and added a generous slug of gin. "What about you, Nick?"

"Later. Now, what's all this about Ellen?"

"I phoned up and asked to speak to her but they said she had left."

"Who did you speak with?"

"Some young woman at first but I insisted on talking with the leader and eventually he answered. *Gabriel*! I ask you – *Gabriel*!"

"What did he say?"

"That Ellen had left the community. That everyone living there was free to come and go as they pleased and Ellen had decided to move on. He had no idea where she had gone as it was her business, not his. I could tell he was lying."

"Why should he be lying?"

"Because he's done away with her!"

"Clare, whatever do you mean?"

"It's obvious – he's got his hands on her money so he's now got rid of her!"

"Her money? What are you talking about?"

"I didn't tell you, did I? I came home from work unexpectedly one day and found Ellen here. She'd come to collect her building society and bank book. She intended giving all her savings to the Children of Light."

"Surely her savings didn't amount to much?"

"That's where you're wrong. Her grandmother left all her money to her when she died."

"What sort of sum would that be?"

"A hundred and thirty thousand!"

"Good God! I had no idea!"

"Now do you see why I'm worried?"

"But Clare, even supposing she has given all her money to the Children of Light, why should Gabriel harm her?"

"Because of us!" Clare reached blindly for her cigarette packet and shook one out. "Me, you, Rachel – we've all tried to contact her and shown an interest in the goings on at Moulton Manor. There's something fishy going on there and he can't afford to be investigated so he's murdered her and pretended that she's gone away!"

"Clare, these are crazy conjectures."

"Are they? There's something crooked going on there – I don't believe they're a religious community at all. What do *you* think?" she flashed at Rachel. "You should know."

"I have my doubts," said Rachel slowly. "Actually I've just remembered something. I forgot to tell you, Nick, but when I went over there I had quite a conversation with one of the members and she said something about all those joining the community having to bring with them a dowry. They give their savings or what they can afford to the Children of Light."

"You see! I'm right. He's got her money and he's got her out of the way so that we don't find out!"

"I think Gabriel is organising some sort of scam but I'm sure knocking off his followers is not part of it. Ellen's boyfriend has also left. I think you'll find that she's gone off with him."

"He's probably been done in too. She wouldn't go off without telling me . . . don't look like that, Nick; she promised to keep in touch – that morning when she came back here. And she said something else that I thought very strange . . ." Clare wrinkled up her brow. ". . . I was asking her where they got all the money from that they give to charity and she said . . . she said 're-member Robin Hood'."

"He robbed the rich to give to the poor," said Rachel looking at Nick.

"That bears out my theory."

"What do you mean?" asked Clare, looking puzzled.

Nick was not about to tell her. "Look, I'm sure Ellen has come to no harm but I'll go over to Moulton Manor and try and find out what has happened to her."

"You'll take a search party with you? An official one?"

"I don't think it's quite come to that, Clare, but I promise I'll have words with her friends in the community. She may have hinted to someone where she was going. What bank and building society did she use?"

Clare told him and asked why he wanted to know.

"I think it would be a good idea to check whether she has withdrawn all her savings before you start shouting that she has been murdered for her money."

"I didn't mean that – well, yes, I suppose I did, but you must admit it all seems very suspicious. What do you think?" she asked Rachel.

"I think there are some dubious activities going on at Moulton Manor and that Ellen is well out of it."

Clare accepted this and Nick distracted her from asking any more awkward questions by agreeing to a drink. By the time they left later that evening, Rachel was feeling quite well-disposed towards the older, troubled woman.

"Your stepmother is one gutsy lady," she said as they drove back to Melbury.

"She is that," he agreed. "It's not been easy for her being a one-parent family, but for all her faults she really loves Ellen."

"And she didn't love you?"

"Do you know, that's one thing I've never been sure about."

"Are you going to look into Ellen's disappearance?"

"You bet. It will give me the entrée to Moulton Manor and whilst I'm there I'm going to try my damndest to find some evidence to connect Gabriel with the burglaries."

Nick had a harder time the next morning trying to convince Superintendent Tom Powell that he had enough evidence for an official visit to Moulton Manor. His reasons were fuelled by the piece of information that had just been handed to him. Gabriel had been into the station to claim his van and a neat job had been done on lifting his fingerprints from the log book. These had been checked against the National Criminal Fingerprint Index and it turned out that Gabriel had a criminal record. Nick explained his theory and the superintendent heard him out before commenting.

"I think you may be on to something but you haven't got a shred of evidence."

"Gabriel has a record. He's done time for embezzlement, fraud, larceny."

"That's not evidence. No magistrate would give you a search warrant on such flimsy grounds."

"I have a better pretext for getting inside Moulton Manor. My stepsister was living in that community. She has disappeared and her savings with her." Nick explained about Ellen and Tom Powell looked increasingly grave.

"You really think something has happened to her?"

"My stepmother does, she is quite distraught. I had a quick check this morning into Ellen's finances. The bank wasn't very forthcoming – customer confidentiality and all that – but the building society confirmed that she had withdrawn all her savings and closed the account just before she went missing."

"She could have gone with the boyfriend. Why should this Gabriel want rid of her?"

"Because there have been too many people taking an interest in her just lately. If he is masterminding a racket the last thing he wants is the police poking around into the affairs of Moulton Manor. I want permission to go over there and try and find out what has happened to her."

"At this stage they will be just routine enquiries, do you understand? No accusations or harassment. You will be investigating a missing person and that does not give you licence to take the place to pieces searching for evidence to back up your theory."

"I can keep my eyes open."

"And your hands to yourself. Without a search warrant if you so much as open a drawer he'll have you for trespass or abuse of authority!"

Nine

Tim Court accompanied Nick Holroyd to Moulton Manor and as they drove out to Moulton Abbas Nick put him in the picture about what he knew of the Children of Light and how he thought Gabriel fitted in with their current case.

"My stepsister almost certainly left of her own accord but it gives us an excuse to have a good snoop round. If he and his followers are behind this spate of burglaries the stuff must be brought back to the Manor before it can be disposed of."

"It's not exactly going to be lying around, is it?" said Court sceptically. "A place that fucking size must have scores of attics and cellars and outbuildings. You're going to have a job explaining why you think your sister might be stashed amongst the rafters."

"OK, you've made your point. We can but try and the idea is to get her companions talking in the hope that someone will talk out of turn and give us something to go on."

A British Telecom van was parked in the courtyard when they arrived and Gabriel was talking to the driver through the open window. He straightened up and came towards them as the van pulled away. He was dressed in a linen tunic over jeans and a large crucifix hung round his neck.

"Ah, Inspector, your bush telegraph has failed you. I've already been in about the van. You've had a wasted journey."

"This is not about the van."

"Then if you've come to see your sister I'm afraid you're going to be disappointed. Ellen has left our community."

"This is not a social visit. It is an official enquiry into the whereabouts of Ellen Holroyd. She has been reported missing. This is Detective Sergeant Court."

"Welcome to Moulton Manor, Sergeant," said Gabriel gravely. "I am Gabriel, the leader of the Children of Light."

"Previously known as Garry Swain. Small-time crook and con-man," said Nick.

For a few seconds a shutter came down over Gabriel's features and his eyes went blank. He quickly recovered.

"You see before you a repentant sinner. The Lord called me and I have been saved. If you put your trust in the Lord he will forgive you."

"Cut the sermonising, Swain, and give us your version of Ellen's disappearance."

"Ellen has moved on."

"Oh? Where?"

"That I do not know. Ellen did not see fit to confide in me."

"When did she go?"

"Last Thursday – no, Wednesday."

"Did you see her go?"

"No, I was out on God's business that day and when I returned I was told that Ellen had packed and departed."

"Weren't you concerned about her?"

"Concerned? No, why should I be? Ellen was a free agent. I was disappointed that she had decided to leave us but I'm afraid the call of the loins was stronger than the call of God. Her boyfriend had moved on a few days earlier – Ellen must have decided to join him."

"Do you know where *he* went?"

"No, Inspector, but he was not a very satisfactory candidate for our simple life so I was pleased to see him go."

"I want to see Ellen's room and speak with some of those who were closest to her. I presume she had made some friends during her stay here?"

"Of course. As you wish."

Gabriel went into the house and the two detectives followed him. He led the way across the entrance hall and up the main staircase.

"Ellen did not have her own room," he threw over his shoulder, "she shared a dormitory with two others. You are quite welcome to inspect it but I don't think it will help you in finding out where Ellen has gone." He led them up a further staircase and along a corridor and threw open a door at the far end. "This is where she slept. The men are housed in another wing."

The room was long and narrow under a sloping ceiling with dormer windows set in the roof. It was divided into three cubicles by curtains on rails rather like a hospital ward. Each cubicle contained a single bed, a wooden cupboard-cum-wardrobe and a small chest of drawers and a chair. Slightly more luxurious than a nun's cell, thought Nick, but not much. Ellen's bed was stripped to the bare mattress and a blanket and quilt were folded on top. Nick looked inside the cupboard and pulled open the drawers. They were empty and he decided to waste no more time on a room that had nothing to tell him.

"I should like to speak with the other women who share this room."

Gabriel glanced at his watch. "It's coffee time. Most people will be in the refectory. You are welcome to join us."

As they descended the staircase and followed Gabriel through the house Nick looked about him in frustration at the closed doors and maze of corridors and passages. The place was a honeycomb and God knows what was hidden in those rooms let alone the numerous outbuildings. It was a hopeless task without a search warrant. Gabriel flung open a door dramatically and waved them inside. About twenty people were grouped round the long table, drinking out of earthenware beakers and chatting quietly amongst themselves. Most of them were young but there were two quite elderly men dressed in long, belted robes who only needed tonsures to make them into full-blown monks. Gabriel clapped his hands.

"Listen, everyone. This is Detective Inspector Holroyd. He is making enquiries about Ellen and needs your help."

"Ellen has been reported missing and we are anxious as to her whereabouts. I should like to know when she was last seen and if anyone witnessed her departure or knows where she has gone."

There was a silence and then a young girl piped up:

"Is she wanted by the police?" and gave an embarrassed giggle.

"We are concerned about her safety."

"Marian, Jackie? Can you help the inspector?" asked Gabriel. "They shared the dormitory," he explained to the two detectives as two women in their twenties stepped forward.

"When did you last see her?"

"Wednesday afternoon," said the taller of the women, eyeing them curiously, "about four o'clock."

"So she didn't go to bed that night?"

"Two of the children were ill. She said she was going to spend the night in the nursery and help look after them."

"And did she?"

"No," said a middle-aged woman, pausing in her task of pouring coffee from a large, brown jug. "I was expecting her to come and give me a hand but she didn't turn up."

"Did anyone see her after four o'clock? What about your evening meal? You all gather for that, don't you?"

"Ellen wasn't there," said a sullen-looking, swarthy youth and there was a murmur of agreement.

"We don't call a register, Inspector," said Gabriel smoothly, "it is quite usual for someone to be busy and miss a meal."

"But when she didn't show up the next morning and her belongings had disappeared wasn't the alarm raised?"

"We thought she had gone to join Dan," said someone else. "He went off the previous Sunday and she was very quiet and subdued after he left. Everyone took it for granted that was where she had gone."

"You see, I told you it was an affair of the heart," said Gabriel. "Ellen packed her belongings and left. She has forsaken our community and we must pray for her soul. Well, Inspector, I don't think we can give you any more help. I'm sure Ellen will get in touch with her family eventually."

"I should like to look round outside and talk with the other members of your community. If Ellen went off during Wednesday evening, how did she leave? Did someone give her a lift into Casterford? Perhaps someone forgot to tell you."

"I'm afraid I can spare you no more time, but I shall ask Gaia to show you round."

"That won't be necessary, we'll find our own way around – unless you object?" Nick challenged him.

"Why should I object? I have nothing to hide. Good hunting, Inspector!"

"He makes my skin crawl," said Court as they emerged from the house and made their way towards the stable block. "If he's not bogus then I'm a Chinaman."

"His followers don't feel like that. They seem completely under his influence. How I'd like to take the place to pieces!"

"It's hopeless, isn't it? He could have an army hidden away in there, and we're never going to find anything wandering around like this."

"Hang on, I wonder what she wants?" Nick had noticed a woman hurrying after them. As she got closer he recognised her as the younger of the two women who had shared Ellen's room. "Perhaps something has jogged her memory."

"Have you remembered something?" he asked her as she caught up with them, panting slightly.

"I . . . I think there has been a misunderstanding. I don't know why Gabriel said that . . . he must have forgotten . . ."

"Forgotten what? Have you something to tell us about Ellen?"

"Only that she didn't take anything with her. She left all her belongings behind when she went."

"You're sure of this?" asked Nick sharply.

"Yes, I couldn't understand it but Gabriel said she must have been upset and he told me to pack it all away in a trunk and he would keep it until she sent for it."

"What are we talking about?"

"Her clothes, books, personal things . . ."

"What about money, documents? Did she have a handbag?"

"She had a little canvas satchel, she took it with her."

"That's very useful information, thank you for telling us."

"I hope I've done the right thing . . . Gabriel . . .?"

"You most certainly have. Where has Gabriel gone?"

"To the chapel. I'm sure he didn't mean to . . . to . . ."

"A simple misunderstanding. We'll just speak with him again and clear it up. Where is this chapel?"

She gave them directions and the two men strode back towards the main building.

"He has deliberately misled us," said Nick looking vexed. "How is he going to talk his way out of this one?"

The found Gabriel sitting at the back of the chapel apparently lost in thought. When he saw them he got to his feet, genuflected towards the altar and walked slowly towards them.

"You're disturbing my devotions. I hope this is really necessary."

"It is," said Nick, grimly.

"Is something wrong?"

"Why did you tell me that Ellen had packed and taken her belongings with her when in actual fact she left everything behind?"

"Well, it was just a figure of speech. I presumed she went off in a highly emotional state and when she was recovered she would send for it. Is it significant?"

"What do you think, Swain? Someone deciding to leave a community and taking themselves and their belongings off is one thing; but to vanish leaving all one's personal property behind is another thing altogether. It puts a very different complexion on her disappearance."

Nick Holroyd and Tim Court returned to Moulton Manor with an official search party. There had been no difficulty in obtaining a search warrant, though the remit was to discover what had happened to Ellen Holroyd and not, as Tom Powell pointed out, to look for stolen goods. To aid the search they had the services of a dog and his handler. They received a mixed reception from the community. Gabriel feigned indifference and told them they were wasting police time and resources but Gaia was highly indignant when the detectives told her they intended carrying out a minute search of the house and grounds.

"But this is ridiculous!" she exclaimed, shaking her head and dislodging a lock of hair that snaked over her shoulder like a grey corkscrew. "What can you hope to find?"

"Evidence of what has happened to Ellen."

"But you've already asked everyone if they know where she has gone and got a negative answer."

"I have yet to find proof that she has actually *gone*."

"Not gone? What do you mean? What are you suggesting?" She grabbed at her husband's arm as realisation dawned. "You think Ellen is *dead!*" Her usual rich, throaty voice rose to a squeak.

"Don't upset yourself, Gaia." Gabriel disentangled himself from his wife's clutches and spoke disdainfully to the policemen: "I have never heard such a ridiculous statement in my life. Of course nothing has happened to Ellen. Search all you please but you'll find no trace of her alive or dead on these premises." He turned on his heel and Court called after him:

"And where will you be . . . *sir?*"

"In the chapel," said Gabriel shortly and Gaia stared after him as he strode away, her mouth puckering in distress.

"This is terrible, Inspector. What shall I tell everyone?"

"There is no need to tell them anything. I'm sure everyone is aware of our presence and why we are here. I suggest you go about your normal business and leave us to do our job."

The search party split into three. One group, which included the police dog, was sent to scour the grounds; the second group targeted the outbuildings and craft centre and Nick and Tim Court concentrated on the house itself. They moved slowly and methodically from one room to another but found no trace of Ellen's presence. It was as if she had never lived there. The various members of the community encountered during the search stood silently aside, offering no comments or suggestions. Like ghosts at the feast as Nick remarked to his sergeant later. They also found no trace of any of the stolen goods. Moulton Manor had its fair share of electrical goods, computer hardware and equipment but Nick was sure that if asked, Gabriel could produce proof of purchase for everything on show, and he refused to give him that satisfaction.

As they descended the upper stairs after a fruitless search of the attic rooms, they came across the crippled youth huddled on a window seat examining something in a box on his lap. When he saw them he looked apprehensive. He snapped the lid shut, clutched it under his arm and stumbled off in the opposite direction.

"Hey – you! What have you got there?" said Court, moving after him.

In reply the youth threw an anxious look over his shoulder and hobbled away faster. The detective grunted in annoyance and dived after him, bringing him down in a rugger tackle and catching him a glancing blow on the injured leg. The youth let out a bellow of pain that was half sob, half outrage and the box flew out of his hands, scattering its contents in a wide arc over the floor.

"Oh shit!" muttered Court shamefaced and the next second found himself pinned to the floor and held at bay by an enormous dog that appeared from nowhere and leapt at him.

"Call it off!" said Nick sharply and the youth said half-heartedly:

"Buggins, come here."

The dog growled and buried its nose in the folds of Court's shirt.

"It's all right, Buggins, leave him alone." This time the dog obeyed and Court scrambled to his feet.

"That dog is dangerous, it should be put down!"

"He looks after me. You attacked me so he went for you! You can't blame him!"

"You want to keep him under control!" Court bent down to see what had fallen out of the box. "It's playing cards!" he said in disgust, picking up a handful. "What do you want these for?"

"I'm learning card tricks and to juggle," Lonny replied with dignity.

"Oh, take them away and get lost. And make sure that dog wears a muzzle before you take him outside again."

"He's not a Rottweiler or a Dobermann."

"No, he's worse. The Hound of the Baskervilles has nothing on him."

Lonny shuffled away and his dog padded beside him casting baleful glances back at the two detectives.

"What the hell did you do that for?" asked Nick when they had disappeared round the corner.

"I thought he was a phoney – the leg I mean. You know – that he was pretending to be a cripple for his begging purposes."

"Well now you know different. If he tells Gabriel, you'll be up for aggravated assault. We've already had him in for questioning and had to let him go."

"Perhaps we didn't ask the right questions," said Court gloomily, rubbing dog saliva off his sleeve.

"Hey, look out there. It looks as if they've found something."

The two men paused at an oriel window that overlooked the stable block. Two of the outside search party were hurrying back towards the house. They saw Holroyd and Court watching them from the window and one of them raised his arm and beckoned.

"I wonder what they've turned up?" said Court.

"How do you get out of this building? It's like a maze."

As they negotiated another staircase and headed for the side door Nick Holroyd felt the first twinges of apprehension. He hadn't really thought any harm had come to Ellen. Perhaps he had been wrong.

They met in the yard and he immediately noticed the grim looks on the officers' faces.

"What's come up?"

"We've found a body, sir."

Beyond the vegetable garden and the paddocks the ground rose steeply, climbing up to a ridge crowned with stunted Scots pines. These marked the boundary between Moulton Manor and the acreage belonging to the neighbouring farm. The recent storm had caused a landslide and part of the escarpment had broken away creating a miniature ravine in the gleaming red sandstone. It was in this chasm that the police dog had made its grizzly find.

"It's a skeleton – a child's skeleton," said the officer hurriedly, seeing the look on Nick's face.

"A *skeleton*!"

"Yes. Of a baby or a very young child. There's been a landslip and it's opened up a big chunk of the hillside. The dog found it, just below the surface."

"Have you called in the team?"

"No, sir, I thought you should see it first."

They walked through the vegetable garden across to where the rest of the search party stood sentinel round the disturbed ground and the spaniel whimpered softly at his handler's side. The bones lay in a little hollow that had been exposed by the tumbling scree. Nick Holroyd felt his throat tighten as he looked at the pitiful, bleached remains. Shreds of black hair still clung to the little skull and resting beside the tiny sternum was some sort of locket or pendant, coated in red mud but still visibly attached to a fragment of chain.

"One of the inmates here has got rid of an illegitimate baby," said Tim Court shaking his head.

"The Children of Light have only been here for three years. This has to have been here longer to have been reduced to a skeleton. We can't lay this at Gabriel's door."

"There was a girls' school here before that. One of the pupils must have got rid of a baby."

"For Christ's sake, use your eyes, Tim. This is not a new-born baby – it's much too big." Nick swung round to the silent onlookers. "Well, don't stand there like a lot of zombies! Get the pathologist out here – I want him to see it *in situ*, and send for the SOCOs. When the photographer has done his stuff and the bones have been removed I want the rest of this area dug up. Pray God we don't find any more!"

"Any sign of how it died?"

"The pathologist will hopefully be able to tell us. I don't want to disturb it until he's examined it. Cordon off the area and don't let any of inmates near. I'm going back to find the high priest."

He did not have to look far. As he crossed the yard Gabriel came hurrying towards him. His white hair stood up round his head like a halo and there was a strange expression on his usually impassive face.

"Something is very wrong. I am receiving bad vibes. What have you found?"

"The skeleton of a child," said Nick brutally, wondering if Gabriel could possibly have known about the secret grave and been involved in the crime.

"An innocent babe! Sweet Lord!" Gabriel made the sign of the cross in the air. "Where is it buried? I must go there!"

"You'll do no such thing." Nick barred his way. "I suggest you go back indoors and gather your minions together so that my men can interview them. This is a very serious discovery."

"Are you saying this child was murdered?"

"When a body is discovered in a clandestine grave I think we can safely rule out natural death."

"This can have nothing to do with us. We only moved here three years ago and you say it is a skeleton you have found . . ." The man might be shocked, thought Nick, but he was still capable of arriving at the same conclusion as himself.

"At this point I have no idea how long the skeleton has been there but no doubt the pathologist will be able to oblige. In the meantime this is a full-scale murder investigation and you and your followers are involved whether you like it or not."

No more bodies were found at Moulton Manor. The landslip was thoroughly dug over revealing no evidence as to how and why the body had been buried in that particular place and the whereabouts of Ellen Holroyd remained a mystery. The autopsy on the child's skeleton revealed that the skull had been fractured by a blow to the right temple and the pathologist estimated that it was an infant of between six months to a year and that death had occurred probably four to five years before.

Nick was put in charge of the investigation, whilst the enquiry into the burglaries was put on the back burner. After much deliberation it was decided to run the story of Ellen's disappearance in the media.

"I don't think she has come to any harm," said Nick, discussing tactics with the superintendent. "I think she's just done a bunk, but if she sees her photo splashed across the papers and realises there's concern for her safety hopefully she'll make contact and we can cross *that* problem off our list."

Tom Powell was happy to agree. Anything to get the press off his back and distract them from the seeming incompetence of the police in nailing the Wessex Rapist was to be welcomed.

"Have we got a photograph?"

"My stepmother will have one. What about her boyfriend? Do you think we should run a check on him? Advertise his disappearance too?"

"For the time being, no. See what response we get to the publicity on Ellen. She may make contact but if it produces no results then we must investigate further. Our priority now is this child's death. Has Wickham any idea how the skull was fractured?"

Wickham was the pathologist and his initial autopsy report was lying on Powell's desk.

"No, but it was not necessarily caused by a blow. It could have been a fall. The child would certainly have been crawling, possibly even toddling and could have fallen down the stairs or out of a window. On the other hand, he reckons it could have been caused by the child having been violently shaken and the head banged against something."

"So, we could be talking about a mishap or manslaughter and not a cold-blooded murder?"

"Yes. It's open to speculation at the moment, but whatever happened it was covered up."

"Yes, and it's not like a new-born babe that could have been killed at birth and the birth itself concealed without anyone being the wiser. This child's birth must have been registered and it was looked after for the first months of its life. People must have noticed when it was suddenly absent."

"Not necessarily. It doesn't have to be local. It could be the child of a single mother moving from one place to another. Who is to know if she's mislaid a baby en route?"

"True. You've got a hard task ahead of you trying to establish identity. How are you getting on at Moulton Manor?"

"We're taking statements from all the community but I think they are in the clear. The body was buried there before they moved in. I think our best bet is the girls' school that occupied the place before the Children of Light. I've been in touch with the education authorities. It was a privately run school but they've put me on to the chairman of the old board of governors and he is getting me a list of past staff and pupils. It's going to be a hell of a job tracing them all. It was a boarding school and the pupils came from all over including many from overseas. When it went bankrupt they scattered to the four winds."

"We've got a human tragedy here. Any child's death, whether it's due to accident, illness or homicide is a terrible thing. How is Court taking it?"

"How do you mean?"

"He and his wife lost a child through cot death a few years back. Four months old I think it was. This must bring it all back."

"Christ! I never knew that! He's never mentioned it. I know he's got a toddler."

"Some things you don't talk about. The best thing to do is to keep him so busy he doesn't have time to brood."

"That will be no problem."

The Taj Mahal restaurant, recently opened, was attracting a good flow of customers eager to try out the cuisine of a new Indian restaurant. Situated just off the main shopping centre of Casterford it served an area where at night there were very few eating places. That evening it was filling up fast and Keith Adams, sitting in an alcove at the back of the restaurant, was aware that he was occupying a table laid for four and that if he didn't soon finish his meal he would have strangers for company. He picked through the remains of his vindaloo, assuaged his burning throat with the last dregs of his lager and ordered a coffee from a passing waiter.

Whilst he waited for it to arrive he idly studied the other customers. Most of them were in pairs and he was reminded painfully of his single status and the lonely vacuum that engulfed him when he got an evening off. As if to emphasise this the door opened and his friend Nick Holroyd entered accompanied by a woman. Lucky old sod, he hadn't been long in the area either but he'd managed to find himself a woman. A good-looker too. Nick saw him sitting there and came over.

"Are you waiting to be served or have you finished?"

"Almost finished, just waiting for a coffee. Why don't you join me? The place is very busy tonight."

"Thanks. You haven't met Rachel, have you? Rachel, this is Keith Adams, a colleague and friend of mine from the station. Keith, this is Rachel Morland. She's a physiotherapist at the hospital and an old friend."

"Not so much of the old. So you're a policeman too. Are you working on the same case?"

"No, Keith is investigating the Wessex Rapist," said Nick, pulling out a chair for her. "But you don't want us to start talking shop, do you?"

"It depends how technical it gets. Nick was just telling me about this baby's skeleton that was found at Moulton Manor," she said to Adams. "It's a shocking thing, a young life ended before it's hardly begun. I wonder if it was baptised."

"Rachel is a lay reader in the C of E," explained Nick. "She's into religion in a big way."

"You make it sound like some dubious hobby," she protested.

"You know I'm only kidding."

The waiter arrived, bringing Keith Adams' coffee and took their order.

"This set-up out at Moulton Manor is connected to some religious sect, isn't it?" asked Adams. "Have they got anything to do with this baby's death?"

"Almost certainly not. I've got a horrible feeling we may never solve this one."

"Have you no clue as to identity?"

"There was a medallion round the neck. A gold one, so it's cleaned up nicely. There's a cross engraved on one side and what appears to be the head of the Virgin Mary on the other."

"That points to Roman Catholic connections surely?" said Rachel.

"Yes, but it doesn't really help us in making an identification."

"How long do you reckon she's been there?" asked

Adams, taking a sip of coffee and choking as it went the wrong way.

"You're jumping the gun. We don't know what sex it is."

"I just thought a necklace pointed to a female."

"Do you mean you can't tell from the bones whether it is a boy or a girl?" asked Rachel, intrigued and horrified at the same time.

"Not at this age. The basic skeleton alters as it develops and the pelvis and pelvic girdle end up completely different in the two sexes at puberty but it is almost impossible to tell in such young remains."

"How sad." Rachel toyed with the condiment set and looked pensive. "Nick – this couldn't be anything to do with Gina Bonetti, could it? I mean she's got this fixation about losing her baby . . ."

"Gina Bonetti?" queried Adams.

"She belongs to the community at Moulton Abbas," said Nick and explained briefly what he knew about her.

"She's half Italian," said Rachel, "so it follows that she has Roman Catholic roots though she's certainly strayed far from them now. Have you spoken to her about the discovery?"

"She's been interviewed and was completely off the wall according to the constable who questioned her, but he was assured by the other members that this was par for the course so he didn't follow it up."

"Couldn't you do tests . . . DNA and all that?" said Rachel vaguely.

"We could certainly get Bonetti's genetic fingerprint if she was willing to cooperate but I'm not sure about extracting DNA from a skeleton. Do you know?" he asked Adams.

"It can be done but the results could take weeks, months even. I was on a case up north involving an unidentified skeleton. You're talking about Mitochondrial DNA which is passed solely through the maternal line and it is a very lengthy process getting results."

"You've lost me," said Rachel, "but have I made an absurd suggestion?"

"No, it's something I ought to have thought of myself," said

Nick. "I'll certainly interview her again. Are you going?" he asked Adams, who had pushed back his chair and got to his feet.

"Yes, I've got an appointment with my snout. It's been nice meeting you," he said to Rachel. "Enjoy your meal." He clapped Nick on the shoulder and picked his way across the crowded room.

"He's a very pleasant man," said Rachel watching him settle his bill and leave.

"Yes, he is. We've become good mates."

"Is he married?"

"Was. Another police statistic of marriage bliss biting the dust."

"There seems to be an awful lot of it in the force."

"It's an occupational hazard."

"He reminds me of Mike."

"Yes, he does. Perhaps that's why we connected. Do you keep in touch with him?"

"Yes, we correspond. What about you?"

"No. I keep meaning to give him a ring but somehow it doesn't get done . . ."

Michael Croft had been his immediate boss and colleague in his previous posting. Temporarily crippled as the result of a police operation that went wrong, Mike had been courting Rachel when he first met her. The fact that Rachel had ended the relationship and admitted her feelings for Nick hadn't assuaged the guilt he still felt about Mike.

"I believe there is a new woman in his life," said Rachel.

"Really?"

"Yes, a civilian secretary who works with him. I hope it works out. Mike deserves a break."

"He certainly does," said Nick fervently.

"I really thought we were on to something but we've drawn a blank." Mark Collins faced the rest of his team in the incident room and rapped the report in front of him. "The results of the DNA testing have come through – out rapist is not one of the college students."

There was a concerted groan from his audience and a young constable piped up from the back of the room:

"Do we spread the net wider and take in the college professors and the visiting tutors?"

"The CC is screaming about the costs of this little exercise. He's not going to back another hunch unless we've got something concrete to go on. Meanwhile, our man is out there stalking the streets and could claim another victim at any time. Has anybody any ideas?"

"He's definitely targeting the young lassies. Surely that must be significant?"

"That's bullshit, Crawford, and you know it. Unless he's seriously sick he's not going to go for the older women when there are plenty of dolly birds about. And let's face it, it's the teenagers and women in their twenties who are more likely to be out and about late at night and with the local college population we have a concentration of that age group."

"We're going to have to go back to the beginning and interview all the victims again," said Keith Adams. "One of them may have remembered something about their attacker which they'd blanked out at first."

"I like the 'we'," said Fiona Walker, raising her eyebrows. "Don't you mean *me?*"

"You've been their first contact with the police," said Collins. "You've gained their confidence and they're more likely to open up to you but you'll have backing. They should be getting over the trauma by now and able to face a male officer without having hysterics."

"So they're unreasonable and suffering from neurosis if they're *still* feeling the effects of these vicious assaults, are they," she muttered.

"What did you say, Walker?"

"You heard . . . *sir.*"

Mark Collins ignored this and moved on to discuss the locations of the attacks. Each separate incidence had been plotted on the map which took pride of place on the wall and an attempt was made to correlate these different sites

135

and try and come up with a common denominator that linked them.

In another part of the building Nick Holroyd pulled the phone towards him and punched out the extension number of the hospital physiotherapy department. Most of his team were now concentrating on tracing staff and pupils of the former girls' school that had occupied Moulton Manor; others were carrying out another search of the piece of land in which the baby's skeleton had been found and re-questioning the Children of Light. One of Rachel's colleagues answered the phone and told him that Rachel was busy with a patient but that she would get her to call back as soon as she was free. Nick fidgeted round the office and snatched up the receiver when the phone rang about five minutes later.

"Rachel, I've been thinking about what you said last night about Gina Bonetti."

"You think your skeleton could really be something to do with her?"

"It's a long shot but I want to question her. I think it would be a good idea to do it away from Moulton Manor and Gabriel's influence. Is she coming in for treatment?"

"Yes, she's got an appointment at five o'clock – my last patient."

"Good, I'll come along and catch her there."

"Are you using my clinic as an interview room?"

"Don't get alarmed. I'll grab her as she leaves the building before she meets up with whoever comes to pick her up."

"Supposing it's Gabriel?"

"I'll cross that bridge when I come to it."

But although Nick waited outside the physiotherapy department for some time that afternoon no Gina Bonetti emerged from the building and later Rachel told him that she hadn't turned up for her appointment.

Ten

The two boys were playing truant when they stumbled across the body. Instead of going to school they had cycled down to the river, hidden their bikes beneath a hedge and slid down the bank armed with home-made fishing rods and jam jars. The early-morning mist was rapidly evaporating and the moisture burned off the tops of the willows in a bronze haze like smoke. The willows themselves were heavy with curtains of green foliage, past the golden stage but not yet at the full drapery of summer.

As they slithered through the sedge and reeds a coot shot out of cover, ploughing across the water with a harsh squawk and one of the boys threw a stone at it.

"Don't do that!" said the other. "I bet it's got a nest somewhere near. Let's try and find it."

They left their fishing rods on the bank and pushed their way through the willow fronds. It was like being inside a green cave. They abandoned the hunt for the coot's nest and began to think about making a den inside the cool, hidden room beneath the branches.

One of the boys actually tripped over the body before they noticed it. He stumbled and lurched forward, colliding with a cold, marble arm and found himself looking into a distorted, bulging-eyed face. He scrambled to his feet and clutched at his companion's arm. They stared down at the figure lying on its back, one arm outstretched and the skirts bundled round the waist.

"Is she asleep?" quavered the smaller of the boys.

"Her face is all funny and her eyes are open."

"She's not wearing any knickers . . ."

Without consulting they backed away, grabbed their bikes and cycled back to school. They had no intention of admitting to where they had been or what they had seen, but a solicitous teacher, worried by their pale, alarmed faces, broke down their defences and they blurted out their find.

The local constable, alerted by the headmistress, took one look at the corpse and rang through for back-up.

"I've got a body here – a woman's body. It looks like the work of the rapist and this time he's killed her!"

"This was what we were afraid of," said Mark Collins, visually scrutinising the body, "that next time he actually would strangle his victim."

"It looks as if she put up a fight," said Keith Adams, looking around at the crushed and trampled grass, "unless the kids who found her disturbed the ground."

"They didn't touch her. Just took to their heels and fled as far as I can make out. Does anyone recognise her?"

"Isn't she one of that commune out at Moulton Abbas," said a young constable who was seeing his first murder victim and trying not to throw up. "I think I've seen her busking in the town centre – but she didn't look like this!"

"You'll get used to it, Beresford. The first is always the worst. Has the police surgeon turned up?"

"He's just coming, sir."

"Good. Get on to Wickham and get him out here too and where the hell are SOCO?"

The photographer had completed his job and the team was carrying out a fingertip search of the surrounding area by the time Dick Wickham arrived. He surveyed the scene gloomily and bent over the corpse.

"What can you tell us at this stage, Doc?"

"Well, she's been strangled – look at the congested face and there's petechial haemorrhage round the eyelids. The bruising on the neck looks like finger marks so she was manually strangled."

"How long has she been dead?"

"The old, old question." Wickham opened his case and took

out a rectal thermometer. "This will only be a rough estimate as you well know."

The woman was naked from the waist down, her long skirt twisted and caught up round her middle. As Wickham wielded his thermometer Beresford gulped and looked away. Wickham squinted at the thermometer and felt the victim's arms and legs.

"With the temperature reading combined with the state of rigor mortis I'd say she was killed some time early yesterday evening. Say between six o'clock and nine o'clock. Rigor mortis is fully developed."

"So it would still have been light. Was she raped before or after she was killed?"

"Can't tell at this stage, there appears to be no bruising in that area. When I've got her on the slab I'll be able to tell you more. Have you finished?"

"Yes. Get the mortuary van out here," Collins said to Beresford, and the young constable turned thankfully away.

"Sir, we've found something." One of the team searching the area beckoned to him and Collins and Adams went over. "There's a hair snagged on that bush and another one caught in that clump of reeds. They look like hers."

"Bag them up. Is there any sign of her underwear?"

"No. He could have chucked if in the stream."

"That will have to be searched."

Mark Collins carefully examined the bruised grass and the broken twigs on the bushes. "I reckon she was killed elsewhere and carried here afterwards."

"Why would he do that?"

"Because he panicked. He jumped her somewhere in town and when he realised he'd killed her he decided to move the body to a place where it might not be discovered for some time. It was just luck that those lads were skiving from school and stumbled over her."

"This part of the river is near to the college campus where the last rape took place."

"Yes, but I don't know if that is significant. We've already ruled out the male students."

"It's also a long way from Moulton Abbas."

"We'll have to try and trace her movements yesterday and find out where she went and what she was doing. We've got to get a formal identification too. You'd better send someone out to Moulton Manor to pick up their leader. He should be able to identify her for us and give us some background information. I wonder if she had any close relatives?"

Later that same morning Nick Holroyd was at the mortuary hoping to quiz Dick Wickham and find out more about the baby's skeleton.

"Can you really not tell whether it's a girl or a boy?" he asked the pathologist, who was having his elevenses in his office and was not pleased at being interrupted.

"This is not me being incompetent you know. It's almost impossible but I think I can pinpoint the age more exactly. I reckon nine months rather than six months or a year. You've got the medallion and there was a tiny scrap of lace embedded in the chain which could point to it being female but it's not conclusive. Fully-grown men wear medallions round their necks."

"And death was definitely caused by the blow to the head? It couldn't have been smothered, say, and the fracture caused when it was being buried?"

"Would that help you anymore in discovering who it was and who had killed it?" asked Wickham sarcastically.

"No, you're right, it wouldn't." Nick sighed and mooched round the office wondering if he was going to be offered a coffee. He paused to look out of the window. "What's *he* doing here?"

Gabriel was walking across the yard accompanied by a plain-clothes policeman.

"Who?"

"That's Gabriel, the guru from the religious commune out at Moulton Abbas."

"Ah, yes. He's been brought here to identify a body."

"Whose body?" asked Nick sharply.

"I thought you were part of this police force. Looks like the

Wessex Rapist struck again last night and this time he killed her. Your lot think this victim was a member of that commune."

"Christ! My stepsister was one of them and she's gone missing!"

"Steady on, man, it doesn't have to be her."

"Where is she?" Nick blundered to the door and jerked it open.

"Pull yourself together. I'm conducting this identification, not you."

He put his hand on Nick's shoulder and pressed him back to his side. "Let *him* do it, you're too personally involved."

"I've got to see!"

"All right, but are you OK?"

"I've done this before you know, Doc."

"But not when it's someone you may . . ." Wickham shrugged and followed the detective out into the main body of the mortuary.

The smell cut through Nick's senses delivering a body blow to his guts. The hated yet familiar smell of disinfectant, formalin and other nameless substances, and the chill. In spite of the bright lights it was deadly cold and he shivered. He had attended many autopsies in his time, had coped with them better than many of his colleagues, but it had been a academic exercise. He had not been involved with the victim apart from being the investigating officer. They were strangers who had met an untimely death. Not Ellen . . .

Gabriel stood by the police sergeant gazing about him incuriously. When he saw Nick he raised his eyebrows but did not speak. The mortuary attendant rolled out the gurney containing the body and bent to uncover the face. Nick drew in his breath sharply and Gabriel spoke.

"It's Gina Bonetti." He turned to Nick and his eyes glittered maliciously. "This must be a relief, Inspector."

Rachel Morland switched off the television and carried her dishes through into the kitchen. She had just seen Ellen Holroyd's picture on the early evening news and heard an appeal for anybody knowing her whereabouts to come forward. The same picture had appeared in the newspapers. It had made headlines in the early editions but had later been relegated, as news of the latest rape victim had taken precedence. As she washed up, heavy-hearted and uneasy she pondered the situation. Ellen Holroyd and Gina Bonetti; two women she had become involved with during the last few weeks. Now one of them was missing and the other one was dead. And what about the baby's skeleton? Was that connected with either of them?

She was still turning it over and over in her mind as she got into her car and drove to Barminster. It was her turn to read the Evening Office at St James's and she let herself into the church and sank on to a pew in the Lady Chapel letting the peace and sanctity of the place flow over her. But she could not stop the thoughts whirling around in her brain. She had been horrified when Nick had rung to tell her that Gina Bonetti had been found strangled, a victim of the Wessex Rapist. To think that while she had been waiting for Gina to turn up for her physiotherapy session she might have already been lying dead somewhere, the life squeezed out of her. She had been a sick, troubled woman – was she now at peace? And in death had she been reunited with her baby?

And what about Ellen Holroyd? Was she also dead and her body not yet discovered or had she high-tailed it with her boyfriend; now miles away and unaware of the fears her absence had engendered? If she was alive and well would she get in touch when she saw her face plastered all over the papers and TV? And if she did would she face charges of theft and how would Nick and Clare react?

Rachel sighed and let her gaze wander round the church. In the main body of the nave the old pews had been ripped out and modern seating arranged in a semicircle round the open centre, in keeping with Peter Stevenson's ideas of modern worship. The walls were hung with pictures executed by the Sunday School and Youth Group depicting their ideas of the Ascension and Whit-suntide and at the back were canteen facilities: a coffee machine, tea urn and all the paraphernalia of crockery and catering utensils. The church was a social hub, which was what it had been in medieval times, reflected Rachel, when the life of the community had revolved around the church and religion had not yet been sidelined. Here in the Lady Chapel though, Victorian values still reigned. Carved pews, stained glass window, heavy brass candlesticks and the almost overpowering scent from the tall vases of lilac and peonies.

She dropped to her knees and prayed. For Gina Bonetti, for the unknown baby, for Ellen Holroyd and for Nick. Then she opened her prayerbook and spoke the words of the Evening Office.

"Gina Bonetti was not raped." It was the next morning and Mark Collins made his announcement to the team at large and waited for the ripples to die down.

"Is that definite?" came from the back of the room.

"I have just attended the autopsy. Wickham would not be amused to hear someone questioning his expertise. There was no sign of sexual interference and he reckons she had not been sexually active for some time. Two possibilities spring to mind. Either the rapist was disturbed in the middle of his attack or, when he discovered he had throttled her, he panicked and couldn't get it up. The second option is perhaps more likely and this is borne out by the fact that she was not killed at the place where her body was found. There is inexplicable ventral lividity which suggests the body was originally laid face downwards for at least six hours and was moved and turned over later. As we know, she was found lying on her back so she was killed elsewhere and her body moved to that spot later. Keith?" He signalled to his sergeant and Keith Adams took up the tale.

"We found hairs from the victim snagged on bushes nearby and crushed grass and foliage suggesting that someone or something had tunnelled through the undergrowth recently. There were faint tyremarks behind a clump of bushes about fifty yards from the road. It looks as if the the killer drove as far off the road as he could get and then dragged the body the rest of the way and hid it under the willows. Although it is quite close to the college campus that section of road is fairly isolated. There are no houses nearby and there is unlikely to be anyone around at night to witness his actions."

"Are we sure this is the work of the rapist?" asked Fiona Walker slowly. "Suppose it's a copycat. Someone pretending to be the rapist in order to knock off Gina Bonetti and get the blame laid at his door? He removed her underwear and made it look as if she were the victim of a sexual attack."

"That is something that must be considered," said Collins. "Unfortunately the press got hold of the details about him half-throttling his earlier victims so that was common knowledge. But if Gina Bonetti was not killed by the rapist, why was she killed?" He turned to Nick Holroyd and Tim Court who were standing near the window. "I've asked Holroyd and Court to join us because the case they are working on seems to have a direct bearing on this. What can you tell us about Gina Bonetti, Nick?"

Nick strolled forward to the front of the room.

"You all know about the skeleton that was found at Moulton Manor. A child of about nine months, sex unknown, killed about four years ago. So far we've had no luck in establishing identity but there could be some connection with Gina Bonetti." Nick hitched himself on to the desk and regarded the men and women facing him. "Gina Bonetti is – or rather, was – a basket case. She was one of the Children of Light and you may have seen her busking in the town centre. She had a hang-up about babies; one baby in particular who she claimed was her own and had been stolen from her. She had a fixation about it; and her fellow members of the commune knew about this obsession and tried to sidetrack her. She told everyone who came in contact with her. In fact, she was involved in a road accident a short while ago resulting in her being taken to hospital and had half the nursing staff looking for this imaginary baby before the penny dropped and they realized she was fantasising. Then we have a baby's body turning up where she was living and I ask myself *was* she fantasising? Could this baby be hers?"

"I'm coming in here," interrupted Collins. "Wickham says that at some time she *had* borne a child."

"Well, well, that *is* interesting," said Nick. "I decided her claims needed investigating and tried to question her but I didn't catch up with her. The next thing I hear is that she has been found murdered."

"Gabriel, the guru of the commune, has been questioned about Gina Bonetti and some very interesting facts have emerged. When he took over Moulton Manor he more or less inherited Gina Bonetti. She had been living in the area and he thought she had been employed at the girls' school that occupied the manor before him."

Nick took up the tale. "I am already involved in trying to trace the staff and pupils of this school. It was a small, exclusive private school and it went bust, but judging by the age of the skeleton it must have been buried there during the time of the school's residence at Moulton Manor. The headmistress has since died and I'm still trying to contact the rest of the teachers but I have caught up with the former school bursar. She still lives nearby and she told me that Gina Bonetti was employed as a part-time drama and dance teacher."

"So she would have had qualifications that should make her easier to trace," said one of his listeners.

"Not necessarily. Don't forget we've not dealing here with the department of education. This was a private school, operating on a shoestring. They probably weren't over-scrupulous about credentials and may have got her on the cheap. However, Gabriel put these talents to good use with her busking and street theatre."

"Does this bursar know anything about her background? Whether she had a child?"

"No. She didn't live in, but in a nearby village. The bursar doesn't think she was married but says there *could* have been a child. Apparently Bonetti kept herself very much to herself and had no particular friends as far as she knew."

"Surely we can get DNA samples and prove if the child was hers or not," said Fiona Walker, scribbling in her notebook.

"Yes, that has been set in hand but to get a DNA fingerprint from a skeleton is a long, time-consuming process. We're not going to come up with a quick answer."

"Presuming the child *was* hers, where does that get us? Are we looking for someone who killed the child – possibly a kidnapping that went wrong – and now, four years later has knocked off the mother too, or has Gina Bonetti's death got nothing to do with the child's death, whether it was her baby or no, and she is perhaps just the latest random victim of the rapist?"

"I think the latter," said Mark Collins. "We have checked back and there is no record of a child going missing at that time or any suggestion of a kidnap plot. If there was one the police were kept in the dark about it. While we can't dismiss the possibility that this murder wasn't committed by the rapist but by someone else cashing in on the publicity, I think we must concentrate on the assumption that she *was* his latest victim and try and trace her movements that day."

"She went missing early afternoon," said Nick, consulting his notes. "She had a physiotherapy appointment at the hospital at five o'clock and was given a lift into Casterford after lunch by a couple of members of the commune who arranged to pick her up later, after her appointment. She was going to do some shopping before her appointment and then walk over to the hospital. She never turned up."

"So where was she from the time she went missing until she was killed?"

"Since doing the autopsy, Wickham has changed his mind about the time of death," said Collins. "He now thinks she could have been killed much earlier, possibly as early as late afternoon."

"The rapist has never struck in daylight before," said someone else.

"There's always a first time and it would explain why the body was moved. Our chappie saw her somewhere on her own and jumped her. When he realised that he had killed her he knew he couldn't leave her there where presumably she would be found immediately so he bundled her into his car – we know he has wheels – and disposed of the body later."

"Has her underwear been found?"

"No. It wasn't left in the vicinity of the river bank and it's not in the river. There is very little flow at that point so if he chucked it in it wouldn't have been carried far. That stretch has been thoroughly searched. It looks as if our man has taken it for a souvenir."

"He hasn't done that before."

"No. In the earlier attacks, what clothing was removed was left scattered around the scene, but he's never killed before. At this point it is difficult to see if the missing underwear is relevant or not. What we've got to establish is what Gina Bonetti did and where she went from the time she was dropped off until she met her killer. If we can get sightings and plot her route and find out *where* the attack took place, we'll be nearer to finding out who did it. This means all of you out on the street questioning everyone who was in town that afternoon."

Carey Meadows was slowly trying to claw her life back to normal though she felt that nothing would ever be normal again. Not for one second could she forget the violation she had experienced at the hands of the Wessex Rapist. The memory haunted every waking hour, and at night, when she did manage to sleep, she had terrible nightmares. Her friends rallied round but beyond their protective screen she was aware of the other students' eyes on her, pitying her, judging her and in the case of the men, wondering if she was an easy lay. She knew that the police suspected that the rapist might be one of the students and were conducting DNA tests and she found herself surreptitiously wondering, *Was it you? or you? or you?*

In the immediate aftermath of the attack she had fled back home, but the smothering concern of her parents had not helped. As an only child she had fought hard for the right to leave the nest and attend college; she knew that the longer she hid herself away the less chance she had of ever being independent again so she had returned to Casterford and was gradually resuming her studies.

Her student friends urged her to paint 'it' out of her system but she did not want to give reign to her imagination; she preferred the more disciplined parameters of the sculpture classes. Handling clay, moulding and shaping it to her will was more satisfactory than expressing herself in paint or attending lectures on art history. That morning there was a life class in progress and she tried to concentrate on the figure crouched on the podium in a good imitation of The Thinker. The model was Jason Cunningham. He thought he was God's gift to women and the other girls in the class seemed smitten by him and vied to catch his attention when he relaxed his pose. She was aware of him only in so much as she was now aware of all men as something alien and to be avoided. She positioned herself as far away as was practicable and ignored the chatter going on around her. Yet it was over to her that he sauntered when Ben Frewer, the tutor, called a break.

"Are my muscles really as well-developed as that?" he asked, looking at the figure that was evolving from the lump of clay she was manipulating.

"You're bracing your arm, which makes the muscles bunch up in an exaggerated way."

"You don't flatter a man, do you?" He circled her turntable examining her work and she wished he would go away. In her nervousness she dropped her scalpel and he bent and picked it up, looming over her as he handed it back.

She felt sudden horror flooding through her. Horror and panic so great that she was paralysed. It wasn't just his proximity, it was the *smell*. She thought she was going to be sick. She closed her eyes and when she opened them again Jason Cunningham had strolled across to the other side of the studio. With trembling hands she bundled up her tools and fumbled her smock over her head, backing towards the door. Her friend Polly noticed and came over.

"What's the matter? Don't you feel well?"

"No, I have to go . . ."

"You look ghastly – do you want me to come with you?"

"No. I'm sorry, look, I don't want to disturb the class. I'll just slip out."

"What about your work?"

"Wrap it up for me and put it in the damp cupboard, will you?"

"Are you sure you'll be all right on your own?"

"Yes. Please, Polly, don't make a fuss. I'll see you later."

She made it out of the door and into the cloakroom where she was violently sick in a wash basin. She splashed water over her face and hands, dried them on a paper towel and sunk on to the bench that ran along one of the walls. Had she imagined it? No, the recognition had been so stark and unbidden that she knew it was no hallucination. What was she to do? Her instinct was to put as much distance between herself and the college as possible and she snatched up her handbag and hurried out of the door.

Half running, half walking, she sped across the grounds and turned towards the town centre. By the time she reached the market square she was gasping for breath and nearly doubled up by a stitch. She felt safer there, surrounded by an anonymous crowd going about its business, but she knew she couldn't keep her discovery to herself. She had to tell someone. The police-woman who had been so kind and understanding. What was her name? Fiona something. She'd given her a card containing her name and phone number. What had she done with it? She rummaged in her handbag and found it in a back pocket and looked around for a phone booth. There were three just up from the bus stop and one of them was empty.

She found some coins and dialled the number on the card. To her great relief Fiona Walker answered almost immediately.

"This is Carey Meadows."

"Carey. Is anything wrong?"

"No . . . yes . . . I know who did it . . ."

There was a pause from the other end, then the policewoman spoke slowly and calmly.

"Where are you?"

"In a public phone box on the market square." She squinted out through the glass. "Near the Copper Kettle."

"Right. Go in there and get yourself a coffee or something and I'll join you as soon as I can. And Carey – don't panic."

There was a click as she cut the connection and Carey stared at the receiver in her hand, then replaced it and wandered out of the box. The Copper Kettle was busy but she managed to find an empty booth in a corner. The thought of eating or drinking anything filled her with nausea but she ordered a coffee and was toying with it when Fiona Walker arrived. The policewoman slipped into the seat opposite and smiled at her.

"I didn't think you'd be here so soon," said Carey, stirring her coffee so vigorously that it slopped into the saucer.

"I wasn't far away. Will you have a top-up?"

Carey stared down at her cup and then surrendered it to the waitress who was hovering by the table with the coffee pot. Fiona Walker ordered a scone and jam and sipped her coffee tranquilly.

"Don't you want to know?" burst out Carey, annoyed by the other's nonchalance.

"You've remembered something about that night?"

"Not remembered. I've *recognised* him!"

"You've seen someone who reminds you of your attacker?"

"It was *him*, I'm sure of it!"

"Calm down, and start at the beginning. You couldn't begin to identify your attacker before because it was dark and he was hooded. Now someone or something has jogged your memory – am I right?"

"You don't understand. I know it was him! And he's there in college at this moment!"

"Who?"

"Jason Cunningham! He's the model for our life class!"

Fiona Walker was all attention.

"What makes you so sure that it was him? You didn't see him properly and he never spoke during the attack."

"It was the *smell*!"

"The smell?"

"He came over and spoke to me in class this morning – just a short while ago – and he reeked of it and suddenly it all came flooding back. I remembered that same smell that night – it was overpowering. I can't think how I could have forgotten it . . ."

"What was this smell? Aftershave?"

"Incense."

"Incense? You mean joss sticks? That sort of thing?"

"Yes. He's one of that commune who call themselves the Children of Light. They're a weird religious lot, just the sort to burn joss sticks!"

"Joss sticks are not uncommon. Just because the smell seemed familiar doesn't mean this Jason Cunningham was your attacker."

"I *know* it was him," said Carey stubbornly. "He looked at me and his eyes . . . he knew I'd recognised him and he was *gloating*!"

"What did you do?"

"I panicked. I just rushed out of the class in the middle of the session."

"Is this Jason Cunningham still there?"

"Yes, he's flaunting himself on the podium and planning his next attack! Are you going to arrest him?"

"It's not as simple as that. We've got to have more proof than a remembered whiff of incense."

"You're not going to do anything!" wailed Carey, her face crumpling.

"Oh yes we are. This is valuable information and we'll act on it. Now, are you feeling better? Can you go back and carry on as usual?"

"I can't go back!"

"You must, Carey. Not to this morning's life class, but you must keep up with your other classes and behave normally."

"I'll never feel normal again!"

"You're doing fine. Just try and relax and leave us to do our job."

"But what are you going to do?"

"Follow up this lead you've given us. In the meantime, don't mention this to anyone. No discussing it amongst your girl friends or dropping hints to anyone."

"Did I do right to tell you?"

"You most certainly did."

151

Eleven

"She was convinced that this Jason Cunningham was the man who attacked her," insisted Fiona Walker, who was in the superintendent's office and trying to persuade him and Mark Collins that Carey Meadows had revealed the identity of the rapist.

"I've dealt with flimsy evidence in my time but a 'smell' beats the lot," said Collins sceptically. "Joss sticks! You can go into any gift shop or New Age craft place and they reek of incense and pot-pourri. It wouldn't stand up in court, the CPS would think we were joking."

"But surely we've got enough to arrest him and then we can get a DNA sample."

"You wouldn't get a warrant to start with and he could refuse to give a DNA sample."

"There are ways of getting round that," said Fiona mutinously. "This is our first lead and you're not taking it seriously . . . sir." She appealed to Tom Powell.

"Believe me we are, Walker," said the superintendent. "This will be followed up but we don't rush in half-cocked."

"Jason Cunningham has already been questioned," said Collins. "When we originally interviewed the male students from the Art faculty he was included as he was there modelling and we got no joy from him."

"We've got to have more concrete evidence. Carey Meadows wouldn't be able to pick him out in an identity parade because he was hooded and it was dark when he attacked her. If we arrest him he will deny everything and without further grounds we'll be unable to pin anything on him and will be forced to let him go. Once alerted he can disappear and go to ground and pop up later in another part of the country and start all over again – if he *is* the rapist."

"I believe her, sir," said Fiona firmly. "She was not imagining it. Meeting up with him again has made her physically ill, not to mention how it has affected her mentally. We've got to put him out of action and there is one obvious way to do it."

"Is there, Constable Walker?" said the superintendent sarcastically. "Perhaps you will enlighten us."

"We must trap him. Someone must act as decoy and I volunteer."

"That's a very dangerous undertaking and not to be gone into lightly."

"It wouldn't be dangerous, I'd have back-up and it's not as if he uses a knife or a gun."

"I should think it's just as unpleasant to be throttled as to be knifed," said Collins drily.

"Oh, come on, sir, it wouldn't come to that. I'd be wired up and in radio contact and we'd have the place staked out. The moment he jumped me you'd move in."

"I don't like this at all, putting one of my officers at risk." Tom Powell scratched his chin with his pen. "Even if we considered it how could we work out the logistics? He doesn't have a particular stamping ground, he's all over the place and we know he's got wheels."

"His attacks don't follow any pattern either, or not one we've sussed out," said Collins. "They don't occur at regular intervals, so he's not turned on by the full moon or the day of the week or any such nonsense. He just seems to operate on the spur of the moment – sees an opportunity and grabs it."

"I'd have to get acquainted with him, make him aware of me."

"And how do you propose to do that? Join the Children of Light?"

"No, there's another way. We know he's a model at the Art School. I shall have to join the class he sits for. If I'm taking part as a student I'm sure I'll have the opportunity to get chatting to him. I can lead him on. Get across my vulnerability and drop hints about the route I take home, etc."

"You've thought this all out, haven't you, Walker?"

"He's got to be stopped, sir, and this way could work. I'm quite willing to be the stalking horse and if it's properly planned the risks would be minimal."

"This would have to be carefully thought through. For a start the head of the Art faculty would have to be in the know. You couldn't just join in art classes in the middle of the term without some input from him. And what if Jason Cunningham recognises you?"

"He hasn't come across me in this investigation and even if he had I can promise you he wouldn't recall me, I can act the part."

"Carey Meadows knows you," pointed out Mark Collins.

"I think in her present state she can be persuaded to forego sculpture classes for a few weeks."

"That's just it," said Powell, "we're talking of weeks. Even if I agreed and got the go-ahead to set up something along these lines it could drag on for some time. It's unlikely to happen the first time you drag your tail across his path. It would mean creating the same opportunity night after night and think what that would mean in terms of manpower and costs. All those officers having to be pulled off other duties, leave cancelled, overtime pay."

"But what is the alternative, sir?"

"You are very persuasive, Constable Walker, and it is admirable of you to put yourself forward in this way but you are rather above the age of the average student."

"I'm only twenty-seven, sir, and if you look through the interview statements you'll see that there are some very mature students on those courses."

"Fiona can look the part," said Collins, who never ceased to be amazed at the difference between her private and working persona and who knew she could let her hair down with a vengeance. "But what about your artistic skills? If you're going to pretend to be an art student you've got to be able to produce something that's going to pass muster with all those arty types."

"I was very good at art at school," said Fiona, "and I'm sure I could carry it off. Besides, with modern art you can get away with anything."

"Right, but this must be planned down to the last little detail, nothing left to chance. And that means *you* must take no chances, Walker." Powell eyed her sternly. "Each move will be carefully plotted with complete back-up. There will be no heroics on your part."

"No, sir, and thank you, sir." Fiona beamed at him.

"That will be all, but keep it under your hat for now."

Fiona took this as dismissal and Collins moved to join her as she opened the door but the superintendent called him back.

"Wait, Collins, we have further things to discuss."

When the policewoman had left he waved the detective back to his seat. "Have you found out any more about this Gina Bonetti?"

"No, she's the complete mystery woman. All we know is that she is half Italian. She could have a whole tribe of relatives over in Italy but she doesn't appear to have any family in this country."

"Have you contacted the Italian authorities?"

"Yes, and they've promised to investigate but it's a common name over there so we won't get a quick return."

"What about her personal belongings?"

"She had very little in that way and nothing to help us flesh out her background. I spoke with the leader's wife – now *that's* some woman!" Collins sketched a very generous outline with his hands. "Big in every meaning of the word.

"Anyway, I questioned her about Gina Bonetti and she was very vague. She said many of their recruits were what she called 'lost souls' who came to them with problem backgrounds which they wanted to forget so it was policy for her and her husband not to enquire into their past but to help them to start a new phase of life."

"It sounds as if Bonetti certainly had a past but whether that has anything to do with her murder remains to be seen." The superintendent tapped his pen against his teeth. "Did the wife say anything about her mental state?"

"Again, she wouldn't give a straight answer. The most she would admit to was 'eccentric' and 'troubled'. In my opinion this

Gabriel thinks of himself as a healer and he failed with Bonetti and doesn't want to admit it. Out best bet is the school angle. She worked there whilst it was in residence at Moulton Manor and even if we can't make contact with her former colleagues, she is supposed to have lived nearby. Someone local must remember her and where she actually lived – if it was in lodgings or whether she had her own place. I'm working on that now but I'm not sure if I'm justified in spending too much manpower checking out her background if she's just a random victim of the rapist and her past is unimportant."

"Don't forget the baby's skeleton. If there is a link-up between them, anything you can dig up could be of the utmost importance."

Powell got up and walked over to the window. He stared out over the busy courtyard for a few seconds and then threw back over his shoulder: "What about Holroyd's sister? Has the appeal produced any results?"

"It's not looking too good, sir. If the girl did genuinely go off of her own accord with the boyfriend you'd think she would have got in touch by now."

"What about the public response?"

"The usual hundreds of calls, but once they were analysed most of them were from people who recognised her from her busking days. There were surprisingly few supposed sightings since she actually went missing and most of them were from miles away, some as far as Scotland and the Channel Isles. Probably all moonshine but they'll have to be checked out."

"How is Holroyd taking it?"

"She's not his real sister and I don't think they were ever close, but I think beneath his nonchalant manner he's a worried man."

"I just hope she's not another victim of the rapist and there's a body somewhere that we haven't yet discovered."

Fiona Walker studied her reflection in the mirror and then bent forward and applied another coat of lipstick. She had already gone to town on the eye make-up and blusher and she was satisfied that she could now pass for nineteen and pretty with it. She unpinned her blonde hair which she usually wore twisted up in a French pleat and brushed it down round her neck and shoulders and fixed a pair of large silver hoops in her ear lobes. She had given much thought to her dress and had decided on a skimpy T-shirt that displayed a bare midriff when she twisted her body or bent forward and a very short, black mini-skirt, worn with black sandals with exaggerated wedge soles which she had borrowed from a niece. She checked again in the mirror and grinned. The lads at the station wouldn't recognise her.

The superintendent had had words with the college principal and it had been arranged that she should temporarily join the life sculpture classes, ostensibly to take Carey Meadows's place whilst she cried off sick. Ben Frewer was unaware of her real identity and she hoped she could carry off the subterfuge. She gathered her belongings together and stowed them in a large shoulder bag, adding an outsize shirt to wear as a smock, and let herself out of the house.

She had deliberately planned to get there early and settle in before the other students arrived and she found Ben Frewer rattling around an empty studio. She made herself known to him and he regarded her doubtfully.

"I don't know what standard you've reached or how you'll fit in half-way through the term but the good Doc has asked me to accommodate you so we'll see what happens. This will be our second session with this pose; perhaps it would be better if you concentrated on sketching this time round."

Fiona reckoned she was more likely to get away with her dearth of artistic ability playing with clay rather than with pencils and paper and said she would prefer to work in 3D.

Frewer shrugged. "Suit yourself. Have you got any tools? No? Well you'll find all you need in that drawer over there. The clay is in that left-hand bin. Get wedging."

He mistook her look of incomprehension and gave a sarcastic cackle. "Christ! You teenagers are all alike, afraid of a little hard work. OK, the stuff in the middle bin has already been wedged. There should be a cheese-cutter in there."

To her relief he went into the little room off the studio which he used as his office and she put on the shirt and went over to the clay bins. There was a length of wire attached each end to a piece of wood lying on one of the lids and she used this to slice off a lump of clay which she put on one of the turntables standing in the corner. By this time the other students were drifting in and she got chatting, and under cover of this studied their movements and tried to copy what they were doing, hoping she wouldn't make too much of a fool of herself.

Jason Cunningham was late arriving and when he did put in an appearance he spent a good five minutes in the office arguing with Ben Frewer before shedding his clothes in his cubby-hole and taking up his pose. Fiona was immediately conscious that he was very aware of her. There was some backchat and argument amongst him and some of the other students as to whether he was in exactly the same position as last time but eventually the class settled down in silent concentration. He took no notice of her apart from fleeting glances from under lowered brows but she felt the curiosity emanating from him, combined with what she could only call animal magnetism and she felt a *frisson* go through her. He was like a cat, a large jungle cat ignoring its prey whilst being acutely responsive to every move made.

He was a handsome cat too, she thought, eyeing him curiously. Very dark hair with a hint of red in it and greenish-hazel eyes with a thick fringe of dark eyelashes. He had a good physique; slim but muscular and he looked strong. Strong enough to easily overpower most women. She studied his hands. They were large and powerful looking and she had a sudden horrifying presentiment of how they would feel round her neck, squeezing the life out of her. Was it worse knowing or not knowing who your attacker was? She took herself in hand. She'd volunteered for this job, she couldn't back out and she had to play him along, bait the trap and get him interested, and he already was. She smiled to herself and looked up to find him studying her appraisingly. She returned the stare and bent to her work.

The array of tools spread out before her was quite alarming. They looked more like instruments of torture than aides to modelling, but she carefully watched the other students and copied their actions, moulding, scraping, paring and getting thoroughly grubby in the process. Her efforts couldn't have been too disastrous. Ben Frewer stopped by and threw her a few words of criticism and advice but he obviously accepted her as a bona fide student. When he called a break she threw down her tools and stretched, displaying her legs to their best advantage. Jason Cunningham was immediately beside her, his dressing gown draped round his body.

"So we've got some new talent."

"I don't know about talent. This is harder than I thought."

"You're new to this game?" He prowled round her turntable. "Not bad at all. What made you join this class?"

"Well, it's because of my boyfriend," Fiona confided. "He's a sort of business entrepreneur. He owns this restaurant and he's got shares in an art gallery. I've always had an arty streak, used to enjoy it at school, so I thought I'd brush up on it and make myself more interesting to him . . . you know."

"You've got a boyfriend? Now that *is* bad news."

"I haven't known him long." Fiona simpered and thought, My God! If my colleagues could see me now they'd fall about.

"Do you live in Casterford?"

"No." She mentioned a village several miles away and waited for his reaction. It came quick and direct.

"How do you get here?"

"I stay on after work and come direct." She couldn't believe how smoothly it was going. "Getting home is more difficult but I've got an arrangement with my boyfriend. He leaves his restaurant – that's over near the old Buttermarket – at about ten o'clock so I walk along the tow-path from here and through Hamsey Grove and meet up with him on the corner."

"Aren't you afraid of walking on your own with this rapist at large?"

"I can look after myself and it's not far and I know my boyfriend will be waiting at the other end."

"He ought to come and meet you. What sort of boyfriend is he? I'd look after you better."

She giggled. "You don't know me, you don't even know my name."

"That can soon be put right – what is it?"

"Fiona."

"I like that, it suits you. I'm Jason."

She was suddenly aware of the scent emanating from him. It was faint but distinctive. It could have been aftershave or one of the masculine scents the young men seemed to drench themselves in nowadays but she didn't think so. It *was* incense and she remembered smelling a similar odour at Moulton Manor.

"Have you been doing this long?" She gestured at the podium and stool he had been sitting on. "You must be special to be able to do this sort of work."

"Oh, I'm special all right, they're lucky to get me. This is just one of the many strings to my bow."

"So what else do you do?" She managed to instil flattery and admiration in the question.

"I'm an entertainer and performer."

"You mean you're an out of work actor?" It slipped out before she could stop herself and he looked at her sharply.

"No. I'm a performing artiste. You may have caught my act in town."

She let comprehension dawn in her eyes. "I *have* seen you. I thought there was something familiar about your . . . face." She giggled and let her gaze linger on his body before focusing on his face. "Do you make a living out of it?"

He shrugged. "I don't have to. I belong to the Children of Light."

"You mean that weird religious group out at Moulton Abbas?"

"There's nothing weird about us, Fiona. Like most people you just don't understand our aims."

No, but perhaps you're going to enlighten me, she thought, but at that moment Ben Frewer called them to attention and Jason winked at her and deliberately brushed her with a bare leg as he got up and shed his robe.

"Are you going to be here on Thursday evening?"

"I wouldn't miss it for the world," she assured him.

*   *   *

Keith Adams slapped some coins down on the bar counter, picked up the two pints of beer and shouldered his way through the crowds to where Nick Holroyd was sitting at a table squeezed in between a giant copper cauldron filled with artificial flowers and a pool table. He was gazing morosely into space.

"You look pissed off. Any news of your stepsister?"

"Not a dicky-bird. The usual sightings and crank phone calls from all over the country but at the end of the day when they've all been checked out – nothing." He edged his stool further round the table to make room for Adams and picked up his glass.

"Thanks. Cheers. I can't believe if she's just run off with the boyfriend that she wouldn't get in touch, after all the publicity there's been. I'm not talking about coming back and facing the music; just a phone call to set her mother's mind at rest."

"Do you know something I don't know?"

"That's another story, but I really am getting concerned that something has happened to her. I want the whole grounds out there dug over."

"Christ, man, that would take a battalion!"

"I know. The Big White Chief won't hear of it, especially with all the manpower being expended on the rapist. He's back-pedalling on anything to do with Moulton Manor at the moment. Says once we've got this Jason Cunningham, who hangs out there, fingered for the attacks, then we can move in and put them through the wringer. At least there have been no more burglaries that fit the pattern of the case I was working on, which again points to the fact that there *is* a connection between them and the Children of Light. With all the police attention over the baby's skeleton and the murder of Gina Bonetti they've obviously shut up shop for the time being."

"You searched the manor thoroughly, didn't you?"

"Yes, but we *must* have missed something. At least you're getting your case wrapped up."

"With any luck in a couple of nights' time we'll have the little turd banged up. You've been pulled in for the stake-out, haven't you."

"Yep. Let's hope it's not a wild goose chase and Walker hasn't goofed up."

"You were at the briefing and heard her report. She's convinced she has hooked him but she did admit later that she couldn't understand why he had to get his sex by violence when the girls all seemed infatuated by him and ready to drop their knickers at a blink of his eye."

"Doesn't like it handed to him on a plate. He gets his kicks the other way. Want another?" Nick nodded at his friend's empty glass.

"Just a half. Christ! It's hot in here."

"We could have sat outside."

"With half the kids of the neighbourhood shrieking round the tables and man-eating midges? No thank you."

Nick fought his way to the bar and back.

"Here's to Thursday evening. Let's hope it's a successful operation."

"Amen to that. It could go on for weeks. Just because we've baited the trap doesn't mean he's going to spring it first time. We know he's an opportunist, doesn't plan his attacks. We could have half the force siting on its arse in Hamsey Grove night after night and nothing doing."

"It plays hell with your social life."

"How is Rachel?"

"Fine as far as I know. We don't exactly meet up all that often, what with the job and her commitments."

"I thought maybe you were lining her up as the second Mrs Holroyd."

"Ha, ha, very funny. She doesn't want to throw in her lot with a big, bad policeman."

"Didn't you say she was involved with the Church? Wants to be a woman priest?"

"That's what she reckons."

"So I suppose that's the sticking point."

"What do you mean?"

"You're divorced. The C of E still frowns on that. As a priest she couldn't marry a divorced man."

"Is that so? Well, let me tell you, I've never asked her and I have no intention of asking her. Once bitten twice shy. I'm not getting tied up again!"

"All right, there's no need to get your knickers in a twist!" Keith grinned knowingly, sure that Nick's contradictory feelings were the mark of a man in love. Nick saw the smirk and snapped back:

"Since we're getting personal, what about you?"

"What about me?"

"Your marriage hit the rocks, didn't it? You're divorced."

"Chance would be a fine thing."

"Shit, Keith, I thought you were. Oh hell, life's a bitch, isn't it?"

Hamsey Grove was a shallow saucer of land nestling in a hollow that was bounded on one side by the river and college perimeters and on the other by the edge of a housing estate that petered out into an open space known as Scarfe's Square. No one remembered who Scarfe was. The square had originally been built as an amenity and lung for the housing estate, but was now an area of broken paving, vandalised seats and a meeting place for the local teenage tearaways where the joyriders gathered and drugs were known to change hands.

Hamsey Grove had long been used by college students as a trysting place and a short cut into town. Since the advent of the Wessex Rapist very few people ventured there after dark, students or otherwise. Apart from the scattered trees through which the path wound there were thick clumps of bushes and plenty of ground cover from spring onwards. Nick Holroyd had been picked as one of a pair to patrol the river bank as joggers.

"We don't want him jumping her along the tow-path," said Mark Collins at the final briefing. "Once you get out from the willows it's too open. We can't get anyone under cover near enough to protect her. The two of you jogging along there should prevent him moving in before she reaches Hamsey."

Nick groaned. "Why me when there is all this young blood longing to get some action?"

"We're not talking the four minute mile, just a middle-aged bloke out for a gentle run. You'll see and hear more and won't bust your gut. Hammond will lap you. WDC Blackburn and DC Cole will be a courting couple actually inside the Grove."

There was a burst of jeers and catcalls.

"This is strictly in the line of business," said Lindsey Blackburn making a rude sign to her colleagues.

"They will be sitting on this bench here," said Collins, ignoring the interruption and pointing to the map of Hamsey Grove hanging on the wall behind him. "It's only just inside the grove but Walker will pass close by on her way along the path that comes out near Scarfe's Square. Parry, you will be out walking your dog near the hawthorn hedge that marks the boundary of the campus."

"I don't have a dog."

"You will have tonight and don't let it off its leash. We don't want the whole thing to go pear-shaped because the dog decides to cock its leg against the wrong tree. Any questions?"

"We'll be in radio contact, won't we?"

"You most certainly will. There will be two radio vehicles. Adams and I will be in the unmarked control van, which will be parked on the edge of Scarfe's Square. Walker will be fitted up with a covert radio which will operate on a UHF short range channel between her and us. There will be another vehicle parked in the trees in the bottom of the Grove which will be in radio contact with the rest of you."

"What about visibility? Once he gets in amongst the trees we won't be able to see what's going on."

"We'll be using night sights. Now, let's run through it again. Walker will leave the college building at exactly twenty-one thirty-five. She will walk across the courtyard and through the campus towards the river. She should reach the tow-path by twenty-one forty where she will be clocked by either Holroyd or Hammond. She will continue along there for a couple of hundred yards and then veer left into Hamsey Grove, taking the diagonal path across the middle. He is more likely to wait until she has passed the pond and is in amongst the bushes before he pounces."

"When do we move in?"

"You've got to leave it until he actually attacks me," said Fiona. "There must be no doubt about his intentions."

"There must be no risk of harming you," said Collins firmly.

"How can there be any risk when the place will be bristling with all you hulking brutes?"

"The minute he pounces you hit the button and shout, is that understood? Right, we will all rendez-vous here at twenty hundred hours. This will give us time to get into position. Someone will also be monitoring Cunningham's movements earlier in the evening to find out what vehicle he is using and where he parks it. Good luck, everybody."

It was a dark night. The new moon had risen and was now a thin arc in the eastern sky, shedding no light on the college grounds or the river, which was discernible by sound rather than by sight. It lapped sluggishly at the bank, slurping and popping at the muddy footings and releasing a faintly rotten smell. There was no wind; it was very still and humid, the heat of the day trapped in the sultry night air.

Fiona called out goodnight to her fellow students, slung her bag over her shoulders and walked out of the studio at nine thirty p.m. She had had no contact with Jason Cunningham that evening. He had ignored her completely but she had caught him looking at her speculatively from time to time, although he had not spoken or acknowledged her presence. She spent five minutes in the cloak-room fixing and adjusting her radio. As they were in the middle of a heatwave she couldn't wear a coat, which would have made things easier. Instead, she wore a long-sleeved shirt and tucked the radio inside the front collar where it nestled in her bra. The lead from this ran down the inside of her sleeved arm to the press-to-talk button concealed in her hand and a flesh-coloured earpiece hung from her right ear, partially hidden by her fall of hair and hopefully invisible in the dark. She left the building and walked through the college grounds and when she reached the tree cover she made radio contact with the control van, reporting her position. Once out on the tow-path she felt more exposed. She fished her torch out of her bag and switched it on, picking out the path of crushed grass that stretched ahead of her.

The thud of footsteps nearby had her heart thumping in reply, but it was one of the police joggers. Nick Holroyd detoured down the bank to allow her to pass, muttering a greeting as he trotted by. His footsteps retreated into the distance and silence closed in.

Now that the operation was underway she felt the stirrings of panic. What had she let herself in for? It was all very well in theory volunteering to be the decoy, but to be the sacrificial lamb for real was another thing altogether. She wiped a trickle of sweat off her brow. It was so dark and she felt so alone, though she knew she was under strict surveillance. Somehow the fact that there were all those hidden eyes watching her was almost as unnerving as thoughts of the rapist closing in. Was he following her or was the exercise a complete waste of time and effort?

As if in answer to her thoughts Collins came through on the radio.

"The target has left the college grounds and is now on the tow-path behind you. He has left his car over on the far side of Scarfe's Square and not in the college car-park so I think he means business. Are you OK?"

She activated the PTT button. "Yes. How far behind?"

"He's gaining on you. Get off the tow-path as soon as you can but slow down once you get inside the Grove."

She walked the last section of the tow-path quickly and then slithered down the bank and through the trees into Hamsey. It seemed even darker here but she knew her colleagues would be using light sensors and her movements would be carefully monitored. How far would she get before he jumped her? Would she be aware of him before it happened? She knew that once he got within striking distance there could be no more radio contact. She would be on her own until she herself called for assistance.

The men in the vehicle parked on the edge of the Grove had just reported to the control van that the target had passed them and was heading after Walker. He had been expected to stop once he reached the cover of the trees and don mask and dark clothing but this hadn't happened. He stepped boldly after Fiona, his white open-necked shirt lambent in the eerie green light of the night sights focused on him.

"I don't like this at all," muttered Collins, sweating in the claustrophobic enclosed van. "He's not bothered if she recognises him which means he's not going to allow her to finger him."

"If he's killed once, maybe he's found that a greater turn-on than the actual rape," said Adams.

Collins spoke urgently over the radio to Walker.

"He's coming up behind you fast. The minute he touches you give the signal and we'll move in."

As Fiona broke contact she could hear him approaching; the light footfalls and occasional crackle as he trod on a dead twig. She felt paralysed with apprehension and she forced herself to keep moving, her heart thudding so loud she thought it would burst out of her chest, her nerves screwed to breaking point. Would he spring from behind or try and head her off? Suppose he struck her unconscious before she could summon help? He did none of these things. Instead, he called out to her.

She stumbled in shock, then quickened her pace.

"Fiona, wait for me!" She ignored him and hurried on and he ran after her, closing the gap.

"*Fiona*! Hell, I'm sorry, I didn't mean to scare you." He had reached out to grab her but dropped his arm when he saw her face.

"What do you want?" She forced herself to speak, wondering just what was happening and whether she should have activated the button.

"I saw you up ahead and I thought you'd like some company. You shouldn't be walking through here on your own you know. The rapist could be lurking."

She gulped and tried to hide the tremor in her voice. "I don't want company. I told you my boyfriend will be waiting for me just up ahead."

"You think he might get the wrong idea if he saw you with me? Suit yourself."

Jason Cunningham shrugged, pushed past her and took the adjacent path that led out to Scarfe's Square.

Twelve

Rachel smiled and nodded and felt that her mouth was stretched in a permanent rictus. The inter-denominational service held at St Botolph's that evening had been a great success if numbers attending and mixed congregations had anything to do with it. The church had been packed, with most Christian groups well represented and the service had flowed smoothly from the Elim Pentecostal Gospel Choir to the address from the Roman Catholic Bishop. The social gathering after the service, now taking place in the extended church hall, was a different matter. The BBB – Botolph's Benefice Beanfeast – as Peter Stevenson called it, was supposed to lighten up the atmosphere and encourage further mingling of the various denominations but Rachel wasn't so sure it was working.

As a lay reader of the host Church of England she was helping to distribute coffee and food and as she moved around the hall she couldn't help noticing that not much actual socialising was going on. The priests and leaders were doing their best to circulate but the members of their flocks stuck mostly together in tight little clusters, looking with suspicion on any attempts to mix them up. It was an uphill job, she thought with a mental sigh, and if it was so difficult to get people to integrate at this level, Heaven help international diplomatic efforts.

"How is it going?" Peter Stevenson winked at her as he swung by clutching two trays of filled rolls.

"They're making great inroads into the refreshments but I wouldn't say people were *enjoying* themselves."

"It would have been a great help if we could have laid on some booze to oil the occasion but with some of our Christian brethren opposed to the vine it just wasn't on. Have you spoken with Father Ignatius yet? He has a terrific sense of humour. If anyone can get the party moving he can."

"I notice the Bishop has gone."

"Had a prior engagement for later this evening but I agree it gives a wrong impression."

"Are we wasting our time?"

"No, of course we're not. It's not like you to be so cynical, Rachel. A gathering like this would have been quite unthinkable a few years ago. We're definitely making progress."

"Yes, you're right. Sorry to be so pessimistic; I reckon I'm just tired."

"You've done your bit this evening. Why don't you slip away now?"

"Not yet. I promised to help with the washing-up."

Some time later, when most people had left and the clearing-up operation was almost over, Peter Stevenson poked his head round the kitchen door.

"You still at it, Rachel?"

"We've just about finished. I think we've put everything back where it belongs." She took off her apron and gathered up her handbag.

"Oh help. I've left my cassock and books in the vestry."

"Do you want me to pop over and get them?"

"No, I'll do it. The church will still be open, won't it?"

"St Botolph's prides itself on never being locked. I don't know how they get away with it. They've never even lost a candlestick to date. Are you sure you don't want me to go?"

"No, it's on my way and you look all in. I'll see you at the meeting on Friday."

She said goodbye to the other two women still stacking cups in the cupboards, slung her cardigan round her shoulders and went out through the side door. It was very dark and still very humid outside. St Botolph's Church loomed as a darker mass on the far side of the churchyard that separated it from the hall. She had hardly gone more than a few yards before she had strayed from the path and stumbled against the edge of a gravestone. Perhaps she should have taken up Peter's offer.

The trees, mostly yews, seemed solid and impenetrable and the scent of decaying lilac bloom was heavy in the air, cloying and putrid-sweet. A buzzing whine had her ducking as a May-bug zoomed over her head. She found her way back on to the path and the scrunch of her feet on the gravel masked the sounds of the footsteps following her through the long grass.

It was only when she stopped to slap at a marauding mosquito that she heard him and by then it was too late. She turned sharply and caught a glimpse of a dark figure hurtling towards her and then she was knocked to the ground, her scream cut off by hard leather fingers pressing into her throat.

"What the hell is going on?" exclaimed Mark Collins. One of the lookouts had reported that their quarry had made contact with Walker and had backed off.

"Fiona! What's happening?" His voice vibrated over the air waves.

"I don't know, sir." She sounded shaken and bewildered.

"Are you all right?"

"Yes. He didn't attempt anything. He's gone!"

"Quarry exited Hamsey Grove. Now crossing Scarfe's Square and making for his vehicle," came over the other radio circuit.

"It's blown!" snapped Collins in disgust. "Operation abandoned!"

By the time the team had gathered in the control vehicle Fiona Walker was slumped in a seat, sipping from a can of Coke and looking thoroughly fed up.

"What went wrong?" demanded Collins.

"He must have recognised me," said Fiona, "knew I was the fuzz and just strung us along."

"Tell us again what he said." She repeated what had taken place to her incredulous audience.

"You mean he actually warned you against the rapist?"

"Yes."

"He was taking the piss," said Keith Adams angrily. He knew he'd been set up and he was cocking a snook at us."

"What happens now?" asked someone.

"We'll have to have a rethink but get off home now, there's nothing more we can do tonight," said Collins resignedly. "I'll give you a lift home," he said to Fiona. "What about you, Keith?"

"I need some fresh air. I'll take a walk."

He jumped to the ground, called out goodnight to his colleagues and strode off down the road. He soon slackened his pace. Late evening but it was still as hot as midday. His denim jacket clung to his neck and shoulders and his hair was damp with sweat. There would be another storm, you could feel it in the atmosphere and at that moment he could think of nothing better than cool rain sluicing his weary body and freshening up the jaded gardens and dusty streets.

He was tired but he knew he wouldn't sleep if he returned to his lonely flat, he was too wound up. He thrust his hands in his pockets and tramped the streets, marvelling at how few other people were around. By the time he decided he had had enough he found himself in an area of Casterford he was unfamiliar with. It was residential and well-heeled. Solid Victorian houses, secure behind wall and hedge, lined the streets and any in-filling were designer houses or definitely up-market dwellings. A large church, Victorian Gothic, loomed up ahead of him, set in a churchyard that contained every sort of Victorian funereal folly imaginable from crumbling mausoleums to overblown cupids and angels petrified in stone. The ones near the road were clearly visible in the light cast from the street lamps. Further back in the churchyard the stonework and trees merged into shadow and beyond this he could just make out the hazy outline of lit windows which must belong to the church hall.

A bat swooped past him and another and he paused and strained to see their passage through the branches. The treetops were a solid mass but he thought he caught sight of movement beneath them. He suddenly remembered he still had his night vision binoculars in his pocket. He pulled them out and stepped inside the churchyard away from the streetlight, focusing in that direction, and was startled to see a woman cross his line of vision, hurrying along the gravel path that led to the church. Even as he watched, wondering what she was doing alone and in the dark, he noticed the other figure creeping along behind her. Suddenly alert, he concentrated on this figure and nearly exclaimed out loud. It was like a giant spider, crouching and scuttling between the gravestones. His binoculars picked out no sign of flesh; no hands, no face . . .

Bloody hell! It was Cunningham! He had sprung their trap and had immediately gone off to claim another victim. He was masked and gloved this time and about to spring on the unwary woman. Adams fumbled in his jacket for his radio and summoned back-up, then plunged across the churchyard as a choked-off scream rang out. He tripped over a grave kerb and almost measured his length amongst the knee-high grasses, but recovered with a curse and hurtled towards the two figures. They were on the ground, one under the other and he made a desperate effort to reach them before it was too late.

His flying tackle knocked the man to one side and there was a croaking gasp from the woman as she broke free, then her attacker recovered and went berserk. The two men rolled around the ground and Adams was astonished by the ferocity of the attack. He was taller and carried more weight but Cunningham was younger and more agile and he fought dirty. As they thrashed amongst the gravestones a kick below his ribcage momentarily winded Adams. He swayed on his hands and knees, gasping and retching and his assailant lurched to his feet and tried to blunder away. With a superhuman effort Adams flung out a hand and grabbed an ankle, bringing him down with a crash, face downwards on the bruised grass. Seizing his advantage he straddled the other man, jerking his arms back and pressing his face into the ground. Somehow he managed to extract his handcuffs from a pocket and snap them on.

As he slumped back on his heels, his breath rasping in his throat, he heard the sound of police sirens and the squeal of brakes and suddenly the churchyard was full of men bearing down on them.

*　　*　　*

Clare Holroyd was sitting in front of the television half watching a games show and knocking back gin when the phone rang. It set her heart racing. She was terrified of answering it these days, afraid it would be the police with bad news. She stared at it for a few seconds like a rodent mesmerised by a snake and then made herself pick up the receiver.

"Hello?"

"Ma?"

Clare gave a convulsive gasp and nearly dropped the receiver.

"Ma? Are you there?"

"Ellen! Oh my God, Ellen! I thought you were dead!"

"Steady on, Ma, I don't know what all the fuss is about."

"Don't you read the papers? Have you any idea what I've been through?"

"Calm down. I've just caught up with an English paper. I had no idea . . ."

"What do you mean? Ellen, where *are* you?"

"In France."

"France!" Clare's voice rose so sharply it could have shattered crystal. "What are you doing in France?" She made it sound like the most inaccessible regions of Outer Mongolia.

"I'm living here now."

"But why? Who are you with? It's that boyfriend, isn't it? You're living with *him*!"

"Yes, I'm with Dan. Please, try and understand . . ."

"Understand? How could you do this to me, Ellen? Go off without a word!"

"We didn't think it was anyone's business but our own."

"Not your mother's business? Do you realise that the entire police force of the country is looking for you?"

"Don't exaggerate. I'm sorry, I had no idea my going off with Dan would cause such a furore. I can't understand why."

"Haven't you followed the news at all? There are bodies turning up all over the place!"

"I'm sorry, Ma, I had no idea anyone was looking for me until I saw the paper. I've rung straight away to tell you I'm OK and to get them to call off the search."

"Where are you exactly? When are you coming home?"

"In the south. I'm not planning on returning in the near future."

"I just want to see you. You don't know what I've been through worrying about you, afraid you were dead!"

"When we're settled you must come out for a holiday."

"But what are you *doing* in France? How are you living?"

"We're managing fine. Look, I must go now, my change is running out."

"But, Ellen, what's your address? Give me your address, your phone number . . ."

"We're moving around at the moment. I'll let you know as soon as we've found somewhere permanent to live."

"But how can I contact you?"

"I'll keep in touch, I promise. And Ma, I've got a message for Nick. It's about Gina Bonetti."

"Gina *who*?"

"Bonetti. He'll know who I mean. Tell him she confided in me before I left. She told me she had been married and her ex-husband was out to get her. Can you remember that?"

"She's the one who was murdered by the rapist, isn't she?"

"Yes. Don't forget, will you? I . . ."

The line went dead and Clare was left staring at the receiver.

"Ellen? Ellen. Oh my God!" She jiggled the phone but the connection was cut so she put it down and fumbled for her handkerchief as the tears started to flow. Ellen was alive! These last awful days when Ellen's photo had stared out at her from paper and television screen and she had feared she would never see her again were over. Her daughter was alive and well but not coming back. She snatched up her glass and downed the contents, slopping some down the front of her blouse. She dabbed at it ineffectively and tried to pull herself together. She must ring Nick and pass on Ellen's message.

But when she dialled his number all she got was his answerphone. She left a message for him to ring her immediately he got in and wondered if she ought to ring the station and let them know about Ellen. No, let Nick do it. She wasn't sure what would happen now. Could she be prosecuted for wasting police time? Whoever said coping with one's children was easier as they grew older was off his trolley.

Rachel scrambled to her feet and backed away clutching her throat, unable to take in what was happening. As men converged from the trees, the beams from their torches lighting up the scene, Keith Adams looked up from his prisoner and saw her properly for the first time.

"Christ! Rachel! I didn't know it was *you!*"

"The rapist?" Her voice shook as she stared in horror at the black figure pressed into the ground.

"It's all over. He won't hurt anyone again."

Two patrol cars had answered Adams's SOS and diverted to St Botolph's and Mark Collins had also made it. He had called in at the station after dropping Fiona Walker off at her home and when he had heard the call he had slammed into his car and driven across the city, breaking all the speed limits and managing to arrive at the same time as the others. He led the rush across the churchyard, taking in the trembling woman leaning against a gravestone and the figure pinned under his sergeant.

"How the fucking hell did he get *here?*"

Adams told him briefly what had transpired and Collins turned to Rachel.

"Are you all right, Ma'am?"

"Y . . . yes. Lucky for me someone was around . . . Who . . . who is it?"

"Oh, we know who it is. Get him up!" he commanded and willing hands dragged the masked man to his feet. "OK, Keith, he's all yours."

Breathing heavily, Adams leaned forward and ripped off the hood. There was a stunned silence as the circle of men saw the shock of white hair emerge.

"Gabriel!" gasped Rachel and clapped her hand over her mouth as a wave of nausea swept through her. Gabriel the archangel. Gabriel the corrupt. And the smell of corruption seemed to physically emanate from him; the sickly sweet smell of incense enveloping them like a miasma. Adams and Collins recognised it too and both immediately came to the same conclusion. Carey Meadows had identified her attacker by smell but she had picked the wrong man. It was not one of the Children of Light but the leader himself who was the Wessex Rapist.

Adams quickly pulled himself together and adjusted his ideas before formally arresting Gabriel for the murder of Gina Bonetti and the rape of the other women. When he spoke the words: "You do not have to say anything. But it may harm your defence if you do not mention, when questioned, something which you later rely on in court. Anything you do say may be given in evidence," Gabriel's eyes glittered and he said forcefully:

"I did not kill Gina Bonetti. To kill is a mortal sin. I am a man of God!"

There was a hiss of outrage from the gathered policemen.

"You're not trying to deny that you were just about to claim another victim?" snarled Adams, and Gabriel swung round to face Rachel, forcing her to meet his eyes.

"Ah, Rachel. You wanted me to attend your ecumenical service. You see, I came."

She gaped at him, then gave a little cry of distress and slid to the ground in a faint.

After the aborted stake-out Nick Holroyd decided to salvage what was left of the evening by going to meet Rachel. He knew there was a social gathering after the service and he reckoned if he hurried he would catch her before she left for home. He arrived at the church hall as Peter Stevenson was leaving.

"Has Rachel gone? Have I missed her?"

"No. She left some things in the church – she's gone to collect them. Did she know you were coming?"

"No, I got away earlier than I expected so I thought I'd surprise her." At that moment the wail of a siren cut through the air and headlights arced through the trees.

"Is that your lot or an ambulance?" asked the vicar.

He got no reply as Nick had already started to run towards the churchyard. He caught up with him as Nick found his way barred by a wall.

"Follow me," said Stevenson and led the way round the back of the dustbins and through a gateway. "What is going on?"

That question also went unanswered as Nick plunged through the graves, unease turning to alarm as he registered the commotion and police presence up ahead. They reached the scene just as Rachel keeled over and he flung himself down on the ground beside her.

"Rachel! What's happened? Are you hurt?" He gathered her in his arms and glared upwards. "What the hell is going on?"

"She's OK. She hasn't been harmed and we've got him." Rachel's eyelids fluttered and she focused on Nick in wonder.

"Nick . . ."

"What has happened?"

"Gabriel . . . it was Gabriel . . ." she croaked. For the first time he noticed the black-clad figure held between the two officers, and a stunned expression crossed his face as he recognised the white hair.

"Will someone tell me what the fuck is going on?"

"Meet our rapist," said Adams, still breathing heavily. "He tried to jump Rachel but I saw him and managed to stop his little game."

"You fucking swine!" Nick lunged towards the manacled Gabriel but hands held him off.

"Cool it, Holroyd," said Collins, "he's in custody now and he'll answer for every one of his crimes, believe you me. Who is this?"

He indicated Peter Stevenson who had dropped down and was helping Rachel to her feet.

"The Reverend Peter Stevenson."

"This your church?" Collins asked him.

"No, but Rachel – Mrs Morland – and I have been at a function here this evening. This man . . ." he indicated Gabriel, ". . . is the leader of the cult out at Moulton Abbas. Are you saying *he's* the rapist?"

"Meet Garry Swain, con man, and now rapist and murderer!"

grated Nick. "We've enough on him to bang him up for life! He won't be attending any more services, religious or otherwise!"

"Take him away," said Collins and turned to Nick. "We'll need a statement from Mrs Morland but that can be taken later. I'll leave you to look after her now. She had better be seen by a doctor."

"I'm all right," protested Rachel, fingering her throat. "It's only a bruise."

She bent down and started to pick up the contents of her handbag which had scattered over the ground when she had dropped it. Nick handed her the bag and two of the other officers helped her to retrieve everything.

"This is not mine," she said, as one of them handed her a photograph.

"Are you sure? It was on the ground near your purse."

"Yes. I don't know where it's come from. It's not . . . wait a minute . . ." She took the photo and held it up to the light. "It's Gina Bonetti!"

"Gina Bonetti?" Nick snatched the photo from her and studied it. It showed a young, carefree woman, standing against a background of dazzling white buildings and dusty pines, her black hair tumbling round a smiling face. He turned it over. On the back was written a single word: *Fabriano* and the date, *May 1992.*

"Are you sure it is her?"

"Yes. She was younger when this was taken but it's definitely her."

"Let me have it." Collins took the photo and strode after his officers who were escorting Gabriel to a police car.

"You dropped a photo of the woman you murdered," he snapped at Gabriel. "Are you still going to deny you killed her?"

"I've never seen this before in my life," said Gabriel.

"You'll have to do better than that."

"It's not mine. You're trying to set me up. You've planted it!"

"Get him inside." Collins gestured to the car. "He won't talk himself out of this in a hurry.

Nick helped Rachel back to the church car-park. He was

horrified at how close she had come to being the latest victim
of the rapist but he tried not to let her see how devastated he was
for fear of making her reactions even worse.

"Come on, let's get you home. Try not to think about what
happened."

"That's impossible. Oh, Nick, you don't know how wonderful
it was to see you. I couldn't believe my eyes."

"I wish I always got that reaction," he said lightly. "It was
sheer coincidence. I came to meet you and I was talking to the
Rev when we heard all the kerfuffle in the churchyard. The rest is
history as they say. My car is over there in the corner."

"What about mine?"

"Leave it for now. We'll pick it up tomorrow."

He helped her into his car and she leaned back against the
upholstery suddenly shaken by another spasm of shivering.

"I can't believe it was Gabriel. How could he do such things
when he was supposed to have been called by God?"

"He was a charlatan, that's why. He used religion as a cover
for his activities."

"Do you think he forced himself on the young women in his
community? Ellen . . .?"

"I don't know, but we'll very soon find out," he said grimly.

"You think he killed Ellen like he did Gina Bonetti, don't you?
Although her body hasn't been found."

"I hope to God that isn't so but we've got to face the
possibility. The fiend has got a lot to answer for. I just wish I
. . ."

" 'Vengeance is mine, saith the Lord.' "

"Yes, but sometimes that just isn't good enough."

As he drove her back to Melbury he told her about the earlier
events of the evening and how the police had got the identity of
the rapist wrong.

"Do you think Gaia knows about his activities?" she asked.

"I don't know what the set-up is between them but I should
think she must have had suspicions. I wonder what else will crawl
out of the woodwork when we start investigating."

"You're thinking of your robberies?"

"Yes. I still think there is a connection. Perhaps we'll get proof now."

When they reached the cottage he went inside ahead of her, switching on the lights and drawing the curtains.

"You need a good stiff drink, have you got any brandy?"

"I think I'd rather have a hot drink. I feel all cold and shivery."

"It's shock. Sit down and I'll make us both one."

She was lying back in the chair, her eyes closed, when he carried the mugs through from the kitchen and his heart contracted when he saw how pale and vulnerable she looked.

"You really ought to see a doctor. Shall I give him a ring?"

"No, I'll be all right and you wouldn't be very popular at this time of night."

"Have you got any sleeping pills?"

"I'm not sure. I had some after Christopher died, I don't know if there are still some in the medicine cabinet. I don't think I want to take anything like that."

"I think you should. Get a good night's sleep and shut off from what happened this evening."

"If only it were so easy."

"Don't think of what might have happened; just remember that you were rescued in time and he won't ever attack anyone again."

He finished his drink and got slowly to his feet. "I don't like leaving you here on your own."

"You don't have to."

"What do you mean?"

"I'm asking you to stay, Nick."

He swallowed and got a grip on himself. "That's fine by me. I'll bed down on the sofa."

"No, I don't mean that. I'm . . . I'm asking you to share my bed . . ."

He stared at her, unable to trust his voice.

"Don't look at me like that. I know I'm doing it all wrong but I haven't had any practice in asking a man to sleep with me."

"Rachel . . ."

Suddenly she was in his arms and he was crushing her against his chest. They clung together for a few moments and then he pushed her away with a groan.

"No, Rachel . . ."

"Are you rejecting me?" Her lip trembled.

"No . . . Yes . . . I won't take advantage of you."

"You're not taking advantage of me."

"Yes, I would be. You've narrowly escaped being raped once this evening. I'm not picking up where Gabriel left off."

"For Heavens sake, Nick, it wouldn't be rape! How can you talk of Gabriel and rape in the same breath as *us!*"

"No, it wouldn't be physical rape, I can promise you that, but it would be mental rape, a violation of your moral code. You want comfort, bodily contact . . . No, let me finish . . ." as she started to protest, "and that would be fine for tonight, but tomorrow morning you wouldn't be able to forgive me. And what is worse, you wouldn't be able to forgive yourself."

"You don't want me."

"I want you more than I've ever wanted anything, I swear to that, and it is because I care for you so very much that I won't take advantage of you. For Christ's sake, Rachel, go upstairs and take a sedative and get some sleep! I'll stay down here and I'll see you in the morning."

Like a zombie she did as he said, stumbling up the stairs and suddenly feeling so exhausted she hardly had enough strength to wash her hands and face and clean her teeth. She felt she should have a bath, scrub away any last vestige of contact with Gabriel but she couldn't make the effort. She didn't want pills; she collapsed on to the bed and crashed into a deep, dreamless sleep.

When she surfaced the next morning after nine o'clock and went downstairs Nick had already gone. He had left her a note saying he would be in touch.

After a restless night during which he had frequently cursed his noble sentiments Nick had finally dragged himself up from the sofa at an early hour and had stretched his cramped aching limbs. He had crept up the stairs and looked in on Rachel and when he had seen how deeply she was sleeping he had decided not to risk waking her by brewing coffee or making breakfast. He had filched a couple of biscuits from the biscuit tin, scribbled her a note and let himself out of the door.

It was another bright, sunny morning but some of the humidity had dispersed during the night and there was a freshness about the early morning air that had been missing of late. The birds were in full voice and a cuckoo mocked unseen from behind the trees at the back of the village hall. He drove back to Casterford stopping briefly at his flat to shave and change his clothes. The light was flickering on the answerphone and when he played through his messages he heard the one from his stepmother. He sighed and looked at his watch. She wouldn't be up at this hour in the morning and anyway he didn't feel up to dealing with a hysterical Clare. He would ring her later in the day.

Finding nothing in the way of food but some stale bread and a half pint of milk that had definitely gone off he decided to get his breakfast in the police canteen. He was just finishing a large plateful of bacon, sausage and egg when Keith Adams joined him, flinging himself on to a chair and groaning.

"Shit, I feel contaminated. Our Garry Swain is a nasty piece of work."

"How is it going? He's not trying to wriggle out of it, is he?"

"He did at first but when the question of DNA came up he gave way. He knew we could tie him in to each rape."

"Who has he got as his legal adviser?"

"He hasn't. Says he doesn't want anyone, that *God* will help his defence."

"He's mad."

"Not mad, evil. I've met some bad 'uns in my time but no one like him. For most crimes you can think up some reason or excuse; poverty, deprivation, unbearable pressure that builds up until a person flips and lashes out; passion, fear – you name it, but he seems to be the very essence of evil. If I believed in the Devil I'd say he was the Devil incarnate. He shows no remorse, seems to think he is above the law and has the right to do what he pleases with his fellow men – or women, as is the case here."

"Keith, I haven't thanked you for what you did last night. If you hadn't happened to have come along when you did . . . Rachel . . ."

"There's nothing to thank me for, I just happened to be in the right place at the right time for once. How is Rachel?"

"Shaken. It all happened too quickly. I don't think she's realised yet how close she came to . . . Christ, it doesn't bear thinking about . . ."

"Then don't. Her God must have been watching over her last night."

"Yes." Nick soaked up the last smears of egg yolk on a piece of bread and popped it into his mouth; when he had swallowed it he asked: "Is he still denying Gina Bonetti's murder?"

"Yes, and he reckons he's got an alibi for the day she died."

"How come?"

"Believe it or not, he was at a conference in Poole on Alternative Living. He claims he was actually giving a paper in the afternoon." Adams tipped back his chair, balancing precariously on two legs. "We're checking it now. I presume that must be true but he could have slipped out and done it sometime during the day and got back without anyone noticing his absence."

"Yes, Poole is only about twenty-five miles from here. What about the photo?"

"Says it's not his and he's never seen it before in his life, but we'll break him down. It's not as if it's a recent one taken since she joined his community. This is a wedding photo taken several years ago."

"A *wedding* photo? How do you know that?"

Adams shrugged. "She was wearing a white dress – you saw the photo, didn't you – and she was flashing a hand wearing a wedding ring at the camera."

"So she *had* been married."

"Looks like it, and obviously that photo was a reminder of happier times, which is why she kept it on her. Gabriel must have found it when he killed her."

"And kept it as trophy. Perhaps we'll find her knickers when we search Moulton Manor."

"You're in on that?"

"You bet. It's my case too, remember? This time we're taking the place to pieces."

"Christ! Your stepsister."

"Yeah, and the baby's bones which may or may not tie in with Gina Bonetti. Hell – is that the time? I must be off."

Nick left the canteen and as he crossed the reception area, Bolton, the duty sergeant, leaned over the counter and called to him.

"I've been trying to get hold of you. Some woman has been ringing up for you and making a damned nuisance of herself. Says she's Mrs Holroyd." Bolton smirked at him. "I didn't know there *was* a Mrs Holroyd?"

"It's my stepmother," said Nick shortly. He went outside and used his mobile phone to call Clare, hoping he would catch her before she left for her shop.

"Nick! I've been trying to get you ever since yesterday evening. I left a message on your answerphone – didn't you get it?"

"I haven't been home," he lied. "What's the matter? I'm afraid there's no news of Ellen this end."

"That's what I'm ringing you about. She's all right, Nick, nothing's happened to her!" gabbled Clare down the line.

"Whoa, what do you mean? Has she turned up? Is she with you?"

"She's in France."

"France?"

"Yes, she phoned last evening. She's gone with that boy and she says she's living there with him now. She didn't know we were looking for her until she happened to read an English newspaper."

"Is she all right?"

"She sounded fine but she says she is not coming back – at least for the time being."

I'll bet she's not, thought Nick. "Have you got her address or a contact number?"

"No, she said they're on the move and she would ring again when they had a permanent address. Then we were cut off."

"Well, that's wonderful news. Now you can stop worrying."

"But she's still missing as far as I'm concerned – when will I see her again?"

"For God's sake, Clare, there *is* a difference between your daughter choosing to live a few hundred miles away or being found murdered!"

There was a little shriek from the other end. "Nick! How can you say such things!"

"Look, I've got to go now. Try and relax and get on with your life again. I'll be in touch."

He rang off and went back into the station to tell Tom Powell that not only had they nicked the rapist but Ellen Holroyd, his erstwhile sister, was alive and well and the hunt for her could be called off.

Thirteen

The superintendent heard him out in silence, shuffling papers on his desk, a frown hovering on his brow as he seemed distanced from what he was being told. When Nick had finished he snapped shut a file and looked up at his inspector.

"Good, good. That's one problem solved and a lessening of our work load. You must be very relieved, you and your step-mother. Young people today have no consideration of the feelings of other people . . . At least we are not now looking for another body at Moulton Manor though your search of the place so far seems to have been singularly unsuccessful."

"Sir?"

"You were in charge of the original search – right?"

"Yes."

"And you turned up nothing."

"The baby's skeleton," protested Nick.

"I'm talking about the buildings themselves."

"We made what we considered a thorough search at the time but in the light of what's happened now I want to go back and take the place to pieces."

"You will, Inspector, you will. And perhaps this time you'll find what you missed last time."

"I don't understand."

Powell got up and went over to the window. He settled his back against it, his hands on the sill and leaned forward.

"I was at a Rotary Club meeting when a piece of information about Moulton Manor came up in the course of idle conversation. Something that is well-known amongst the older residents of the county but that has apparently escaped the notice of

186

my entire personnel. I repeat, I was told this by a fellow Rotarian."

Nick digested this, not knowing to what Powell was referring, but picking up on one salient fact. Yesterday evening, when half the force under his command had been involved one way or another in the plot to trap the rapist, the superintendent had attended a Rotary Club meeting. It was unbelievable.

Tom Powell seemed to read his thoughts.

"This meeting was two evenings ago. I did not bring it up yesterday because other things took priority."

"I'm sorry, sir, but I'm not with you. What did we miss?"

"The fact that Moulton Manor is riddled with subterranean rooms and tunnels."

"What?"

"Officially it was taken over by the RAF in World War II. Actually it was used for some very hush hush activities including code breaking. I am reliably informed that there is an underground network of chambers leading off the old cellars. Did you search the cellars?"

"Yes. At least, there only appeared to be a couple and they were being used for wine storage. There were racks of homemade wine lining the walls and very solid floors with no sign of disturbance. We had a good look round, but hell, we must have missed something."

"Your stolen goods perhaps?"

"Has Gabriel . . . Garry Swain . . . been questioned about this?"

"No. At the moment we're concentrating on the rapes and trying to pin the murder on him. DS Adams and a team have gone to Poole to check his alibi for the day Gina Bonetti was killed. When his wife was informed of his arrest last night she apparently went to pieces and refused to believe he was involved. I suggest you get over there fast with a crew before she recovers and starts shifting evidence – always supposing that your theory about the burglaries is correct."

"I'm on my way."

* * *

Tom Powell had certainly been right about Gaia's collapse, thought Nick, when he arrived at Moulton Manor and confronted the woman. You couldn't say she had shrivelled in stature but she seemed to have crumpled inwards so that her rolls of flesh had taken on the appearance of a melting blancmange and her hair was surely greyer, resembling an untidy bird's nest rather than the towering chignon he had seen before.

"Inspector, there has been a terrible mistake," she exclaimed, tottering out of the house. "My poor Gabriel . . . May I see him?"

"That is not my domain. I am here on another matter."

"What is it you want to know?"

"For starters, your real name."

"Gaia. My name is Gaia."

"Mrs Swain – you are *Mrs* Swain I presume, or maybe you aren't married?"

"I am Gabriel's wife." She managed to inject some grandeur into the statement.

"Mrs Swain, I am sure we can discover your proper name but why not save us some time?"

"It's . . . it's Doreen."

"Right, Doreen, where is the rest of your community?"

"They are about the place," she said vaguely.

"*All* of them?"

"Those who are still here."

"What do you mean?"

"Some of our members took it into their heads to leave our community this morning. They displayed a shocking lack of faith in Gabriel."

Hell, thought Nick. Rats leaving the sinking ship. We ought to have got here sooner.

"How many exactly?"

"About six or seven . . . well, perhaps ten . . ."

"Right, will you get together the rest of them and assemble in the chapel. Two of my men will go with you. While you are there I want a list of those who have gone and their new addresses if known."

"But I don't understand – what has this to do with Gabriel?"

188

"Who said it had anything to do with Gabriel? Off you go, Doreen, and collect your flock."

She looked round at the group of policemen and made a visible effort to pull herself together.

"I am in charge here now that Gabriel is . . . absent. I am responsible for what happens and I demand to know just what this is all about!"

"I think it is time we searched the place again, don't you? And, yes, I have got a search warrant."

"You can't go meddling with our work, disturbing the animals . . ."

"Oh, I don't think we'll disturb any animals where we're going."

"That's one very worried lady," he said to Tim Court as they went into the house. "There's something she doesn't want us to find."

They headed for the kitchens, sending all the Children of Light that they met on the way over to the chapel. Nobody queried these orders or argued with them.

"They all seem very docile," said Court. "Not at all concerned about us being here – which you must admit is different to our usual reception as The Scum."

"They've all been brainwashed, they're not capable of thinking for themselves. Gabriel and Gaia have programmed them to do their bidding. I wonder myself whether he was into hypnosis."

There was no one in the kitchens. No one was preparing lunch or clearing up after breakfast which Nick thought was very strange. The cellars led off the scullery attached to the inner kitchen. They opened the door and went down the steps, switching on the light at the bottom.

"They look after themselves, don't they?" said Court looking round at the racks of wine lining the two rooms.

"They sell it along with their other produce." Nick picked out a bottle and read the label. "Parsnip 1998. Not everyone's cup of tea but this home-made stuff can pack a punch." He replaced the bottle and mooched round the cellar. It was very dry and cool and immaculately clean.

"There is no obvious opening or doorway. We would have noticed it before if there had been. We're already underground so the entrance must be through the walls rather than the floor."

"Well, thank God there's only two rooms to search. It must be here somewhere."

"I reckon it's concealed behind one of the wine racks. You must be able to move them out."

They pushed and pulled but could not budge them. The wooden racks seemed to be permanent fixtures, bolted into the walls.

"Shit, we're going to have to take all the bottles out and see what's behind them."

They ended up with a heap of bottles on the floor and bare shelves that revealed no hidden doors behind them.

"The Super must have got his facts wrong," said Court in disgust, sitting back on his heels and wiping a filthy hand across his face. "There's nothing here. These walls are all solid."

"There must be another cellar somewhere. You'd expect a house this size to have more then two. Let's go outside and see if we can find signs of any more from out there."

They went out into the back courtyard and looked around. The flagstones lining it were large and even, worn smooth by centuries of traffic, both human and animal. Two sides were enclosed by the house itself, the third side was a range of loose-boxes and the fourth was a wall built out of the same stone as the Manor with a gateway in it wide enough to take a horse and cart. Large tubs, fashioned out of half barrels and overflowing with flowering plants, dotted around near the house drew Nick's attention. He walked round them wondering why they had been put there at the back of the house where no one would see them and they would be in the shade for most of the day. Perhaps they had been put there to conceal a manhole cover or a coal chute. That was it – a coal chute. Most large houses over sixty years old had had one.

"Here, help me move these," he instructed Court.

They struck lucky on the fourth one. When pushed to one side a round trapdoor was exposed. It had an iron ring in the middle and when Nick pulled this the trapdoor came up smoothly revealing a flight of steps leading downwards.

"I think we've struck gold. Let's see where they go."

"Mind you don't slip and break an ankle. They're probably in a bad state of repair."

"They're not you know," said Nick, venturing downwards. "I'd say these steps are fairly new and in constant use." He reached the bottom and fumbled for the light switch he could dimly make out on the wall beside him. He switched it on.

"Christ! We *have* struck gold! Come down here and take a butcher's at this!"

Tim Court scrambled down the steps and joined his colleague. "You were right – the proverbial Aladdin's cave!"

They were in an underground room about four metres square that was filled with new electrical equipment, still boxed, that stood on the shelving that lined the room.

"Toasters, kettles, food processors . . ." Nick was trying to examine them without touching or disturbing them. ". . . hi-fi systems, speakers, videos . . . these are all things that have been nicked over the past two years. The Children of Light *were* behind our burglaries. Everything they took ended up here and they were stored here until they could be moved on through a fence – probably a whole network of fences across the country."

"There's more stuff through here." Court had opened the door at the far end of the room and found himself in a corridor with further doors leading off it. A quick preliminary exploration turned up a roomful of antiques, a selection of computer hardware and a smaller room at the end of the corridor that had been set up as an office. There was a computer system on a desk and a locked filing cabinet in the corner, plus piles of brochures on country estates, antiques magazines and auction catalogues.

"I think I can already tell you exactly where some of the stuff came from but it looks as if it will all be here, listed and indexed. This is a very professionally run enterprise and I reckon Gaia is the brains behind it, not Gabriel."

"What do we do now?"

"We leave it just as it is and let SOCO get to work on it."

Tom Powell was just leaving his office when a call came through from the switchboard.

"DI Holroyd has just called in, sir. He says he's found the evidence he was looking for and wants to know if he should arrest the entire Children of Light community? He says there's forty of them, give or take a few children . . ."

Keith Adams had had a satisfying trip to Poole, he and his team gathering far more information than he would have thought possible in one day. He was reporting back to Collins who had had a frustrating day trying to induce Gabriel to admit to the murder of Gina Bonetti.

"He *could* have done it," said Adams, "but it would have been difficult given the time scale. I struck lucky in Poole. The conference was held in the leisure centre and the woman who organised it lives nearby and I got to speak to her straight away. Gabriel definitely *did* give a paper that afternoon. He started speaking at about two thirty and carried on for about an hour. There was a break for tea and a further session after that when he answered questions from the audience. This takes us up to about five o'clock. After that they dispersed but gathered again at seven o'clock for dinner and an evening session of film and video. Mrs Maddock – that's the organiser – was very impressed with Gabriel and she sat next to him at dinner and during the evening session, so even if he went missing between five and seven o'clock he was definitely back there in time for dinner."

"Have you managed to contact any of the other people who were at the conference?"

"I've got all their names and addresses and we've already interviewed the local ones. Fortunately it was a very small conference as conferences go so the task is not impossible. Nobody we've spoken to so far remembers seeing Gabriel during that two hours but that doesn't necessarily mean he wasn't there. We're checking up with the other people but this could take some time. Several of them came from up north and some from Wales."

"So there are two hours unaccounted for." Collins looked pensive. "It would just have been possible I suppose."

"It's twenty-five miles to Poole, about thirty to forty minutes depending on the traffic, which means he would have had less than an hour in which to have killed her and move the body, but it could be done."

"But why?"

"Because he got horny."

"But it doesn't make sense, Keith. Why come all the way back to Casterford? Why not go for someone in Poole?"

"If he had done that and we tied it in with *our* rapes and then discovered that he had been there in Poole when it happened we'd have him, and he knew that."

"I still don't buy it. He's at a conference where he is one of the key figures – in the public eye and very busy for most of the time. I can't believe he would suddenly decide, in a free period, that he had to get back to Casterford and claim another victim – and in broad daylight too. Perhaps we're looking at it from the wrong angle."

"How do you mean?" asked Adams.

"Maybe he *did* kill her but it wasn't a rape that went wrong. Maybe he needed to silence her for some reason. He meant all along to kill her not rape her so he tried to make it look like an interrupted sexual attack."

"What motive could he have for killing her?"

"Who knows. That's what we have to find out. Maybe she discovered he was the rapist – don't ask me how – and threatened to expose him. Maybe it ties in with this baby's skeleton found in the grounds of Moulton Manor. If it *was* her baby he could have been the father. She had this fixation, hadn't she, about her baby being stolen. He could have abducted it and killed it without her knowing what became of it. When we discovered the skeleton she would have suspected what he had done so he had to silence her."

"But that skeleton was buried before he took over Moulton Manor," insisted Adams, tapping his fingers on the desk.

"Yes, but she was around before then and if he was looking for a place in which to set up his community he could well have met up with her earlier."

"Yes, but supposing it's true, how are we ever going to prove it?"

At that point there there was a great deal of noise and commotion coming from below in the station.

"What's going on?" asked Adams. "It sounds like Saturday evening on Cup Final day."

"Haven't you caught up with the rest of the day's happenings?" Collins told him about Holroyd's discoveries at Moulton Manor.

"This place is no longer a police station – it's more like a bloody prison camp. Welcome to Stalag II!"

Rachel was attending the weekly choir practice but her heart wasn't in it. She opened her mouth and sang at the appropriate moments but her thoughts were miles away. Since the evening of the attack on her when Nick had stayed the night she had not seen him. He had rung several times to check that she was OK and also to let her know that Ellen had turned up in France, for which she was profoundly thankful. He had also told her over the phone about his findings at Moulton Manor and of the arrest of Gaia and her accomplices, but there had been no personal contact. Maybe he was avoiding her? Perhaps her behaviour that night had rung warning bells and he was trying to extricate himself from a relationship he didn't want to develop? She felt very mixed-up and hurt and wished that she could sort out her feelings.

"You look very pensive tonight," said Peter Stevenson as they put away hymn books and collected up song sheets after choir practice had finished. "Are you still worrying about the attack on you or is something else bothering you?"

"I think I've come to terms with the attack. It's . . . it's my private life that seems to be in a shambles at the moment . . ."

"Want to talk about it?"

"Why not?" She sighed and sat down in a pew and looked up at him.

"You can't have a relationship based just on sexual attraction, can you? There has to be more going for it . . ."

"Are we talking about your policeman friend, Nick?"

"Well, yes."

"Are you sleeping with him?"

"Of course not," she retorted, wondering why she was discussing her sex life, or lack of it, with someone who was younger than herself and a church minister to boot. Still, he *was* married with a young family and he was a youth adviser though she certainly didn't fit into that category.

"Then I would say your relationship is already based on far more than sex. You are obviously very attracted to each other, but respect each other enough not to indulge in casual sex."

"I *want* to sleep with him, Peter, but for me that would be a complete commitment and that is something he doesn't want to accept from me or to make himself."

"Why are you so sure of that? In many ways you seem ideally suited. You are good friends and that is the most important single factor in any relationship."

"But we're not suited. I am a Christian, hoping to be ordained one day and he is not even a believer."

"He hasn't shut his mind to it, has he? He is trying to understand and is coming to it with an open mind. Believe you me, Rachel, I'm sure the good Lord is far more pleased with someone genuinely trying to understand and rationalise the whole process of faith, than with a cradle Christian who just gives lip-service and never thinks it through."

"He's divorced."

"Well, that's not the impediment it used to be. Thank Heavens the C of E is now treating its priesthood as human and not paragons on pedestals."

"Not that marriage comes into it," she continued as if he hadn't spoken. "It's once bitten, twice shy as far as he is concerned and I have never thought that anyone else could take Christopher's place."

"That's all right then, isn't it?" He grinned knowingly at her. "Let things take their course and stop worrying."

"Yes. Thanks for listening to me. It's been a help."

"To trot out an old cliché – let your heart rule your head sometimes and don't always try to rationalise everything."

"Yes, father, no, father." She grinned.

"Would you like to come over to the rectory for a drink?"

"No, thanks all the same. I must be getting home. Are Jenny and the children all right?"

"Just fine."

They switched off the lights and went out through the vestry door which he locked behind them.

"By the way," he said as he walked with her to her car, "Jenny and I slept together before we married."

"You did?"

"Yes, even though I was training for the priesthood. I think she wanted to make sure my equipment was all present and correct." And with that parting shot he grinned at her and turned back towards the rectory.

She had hardly got inside her cottage before the phone started ringing. It was Nick, wanting to meet her the following evening. She felt a stab of guilt as she heard his familiar voice. What would he say if he knew that she had just been discussing him with the Des Rev as he called Peter Stevenson. It would probably pull the plug on their friendship once and for all.

"You're not doing anything tomorrow evening, are you?"

"No," she said smiling, "do you want to come here for a meal?"

"No, you come here. I'll cook for you."

"So you cook too?"

"Don't be cheeky. I've cooked for you before."

"You haven't you know. It's always been take-aways."

"Then you have a treat in store. My coq au vin has to be seen and tasted to be believed."

"That could be taken the wrong way, Nick. Do you want me to bring anything?"

"Just yourself. We'll eat about eight o'clock. Shall I come and pick you up?"

"And interrupt your efforts in the kitchen? No way, I'll drive myself over."

"OK. I'll see you tomorrow, Rachel. Take care." And he rang off.

As she replaced the receiver she couldn't help wondering why he had insisted on her going to his flat. Was he afraid she would invite him into her bed again?

During her lunch break the next day she was window-shopping in town when she happened to pass Feathers, the boutique where Clare Holroyd worked. As she looked in through the window Clare moved into vision from behind a display of swimwear and they recognised each other at the same time. Clare beckoned her inside and Rachel stepped through the doorway, grateful for the cool air circulating from a fan set up on the counter.

"How are you, Clare?"

"So relieved now that I know that Ellen is all right. I feel as if I have just woken up from a terrible nightmare."

"I bet you do. Has she been in contact again?"

"No, and knowing Ellen she probably won't be. She's done her duty as she sees it in letting me know she's safe and God knows when I'll see her again."

"Don't be too hard on her, Clare. Her freedom has gone to her head but she'll settle down one day and you'll wonder what all the fuss was about."

"Yes, well . . . Have you seen much of Nick lately?"

"We keep in touch," said Rachel cautiously.

"That doesn't exactly sound like the height of passion," said Clare with a short, mirthless laugh. "He refuses to try and find out exactly where Ellen is living in France."

"He really can't use police resources for that. Now that she's turned up it ceases to be police business."

"I knew you'd say that. He . . ."

A customer interrupted her and whilst she dealt with her Rachel looked through the racks of clothes. Most of the dresses and skirts and tops were brightly and boldly coloured. Suitable for the South of France perhaps, but Casterford? They were too flamboyant for her, though this terracotta-coloured sundress was rather attractive . . .

"That would suit you," said Clare, coming back to her. "With your dark hair and eyes you can wear that colour."

"I don't think it would fit my lifestyle."

"More's the pity. You need glamorising – make Nick sit up and take notice. Oh my God!" She clapped her hands over her mouth and looked aghast. "Sorry, I shouldn't use that expression in front of you. But talking of Nick – I've just remembered, Ellen gave me a message to give him and I'd forgotten all about it."

"Was it important?"

"I don't know. I couldn't have thought so, could I, or I wouldn't have forgotten it. Now, what exactly did she say?"

Clare screwed up her face in concentration.

"It was about that woman – the one who was murdered."

"Gina Bonetti?"

"That's the name. She told Ellen that she'd been married and her ex-husband was after her."

"Is that all she said – are you sure?"

"Yes. I'm sure there was nothing else. I wonder what she really meant. Do you think it has any significance?"

"I think maybe the police will think so. It could shed some light on her murder," said Rachel tactfully.

"Yes, I suppose you're right. I'd better give Nick a ring and let him know. The trouble is he's never there when I phone him and he never answers his messages."

"I'm seeing him this evening, do you want me to tell him?"

"Oh, would you? It will save me bring torn off a strip for forgetting. Tell him I was so over the moon at hearing from Ellen that it slipped my memory. Would you like a cup of tea if I put the kettle on?"

"Thanks, but I've got to get back to work. And you've got some more customers."

Clare went to help them and Rachel waved goodbye and hurried back to the hospital.

The questioning of Garry Swain, alias Gabriel, continued and although he admitted to the rapes he denied the murder of Gina Bonetti.

"Why are we bothering," said Adams in disgust as he and Collins took a much needed break. "We've got him for the rapes, he'll get life over and over; he'll never come out whether we nail him for the murder or not."

"You're forgetting something. If *he* didn't kill Bonetti someone else did so the murder hunt is still on."

"Yeah. Well I sat in on Holroyd's interrogation of the wife and she insists he didn't molest any of the young women in his community so there will be no charges on that score."

"Did you believe her?"

"Yes, strangely enough I did. If Gabriel makes your skin crawl I reckon she's even worse. A real weirdo." Adams wrinkled up his nose in disgust. "She looks on him as some super being, a little god, who has sexual appetites that have to be fed. She can't satisfy him – that figures – and she forbade him to touch any of the Children of Light, which he seems to have accepted, so he looked elsewhere."

"She must have known what he was up to, realised that he was the rapist."

"She says not, but she must have suspected at the very least even if she didn't connive in it. She honestly doesn't seem to think that he has done any wrong; she thinks he's above the rules that govern us lesser mortals."

Collins shook his head. "The whole thing is fucking sick. It's at times like this that you regret that the death penalty was done away with. Society would definitely be a better place without the likes of the Swains. They need stamping underfoot like the cockroaches they are!"

"I know one thing, it's going to be a hell of a job sorting out just what went on at Moulton Manor."

That evening Nick was expressing the same thoughts to Rachel. She had arrived bursting with the news Clare had given her but he insisted that they eat first so that it wasn't until they had finished their meal and were relaxing over coffee that the subject of Moulton Manor and the Children of Light came up.

"He's evil," said Rachel with a shudder, "and I instinctively knew that the first time I met him though I tried to be rational. When he showed me over the chapel I wanted to make the sign of the cross to ward off the evil eye."

"He's a power freak. He got his kicks from domination."

"Was he the brains behind the robberies?"

"No, that was Gaia. She'd organised a real little Robin Hood scam."

"Have you really arrested the entire community?"

"We've let some of them go already; the older people who thought they were in a genuine religious commune were not involved. The others will be released on bail pending trial. She concentrated on the young ones, fired them up with the idea that they were getting their own back on a materialistic society and helping the real needy of the world."

"And were they?"

"Well, yes, they were. She kept meticulous accounts on disc. Lists of everything that was stolen, where from, how much they realised and where the money went. The Children of Light made substantial donations to Oxfam, Save the Children, War on Want, the Kosovo Appeal – you name it, they benefited according to her records."

"I'm beginning to feel sympathetic . . ."

"I was afraid you'd say that. She had a right little bunch of Artful Dodgers working for her."

"Including your stepsister?"

"There's worse to come. Selhampton Hall was targeted and Ellen and the boyfriend were the ones supposed to do it over but according to her lists nothing came of it – the burglary didn't take place and nothing was taken. What I think happened is that Ellen and Dan decided they were on to a good thing and that *they* were going to benefit rather than charity. Instead of taking the usual, easily-disposed-of goods they went for the real McCoy, having made plans to escape to France with their ill-gotten gains. He went first and she followed a few days later to throw people off the scent."

"So what you're saying is that whilst most of the Children of

Light thought they were helping their fellow men, Ellen and Dan were out for number one and were real thieves."

"I'm afraid so. Clare may bleat about wanting to see her darling daughter but if Ellen has any sense she'll stay away from these shores for a long while."

"That reminds me, I bumped into Clare yesterday and she asked me to pass on a message that Ellen had given her for you. She'd forgotten about it until then."

"What is it?"

"Now, let me get this right . . ." Rachel told him what Clare had said and he looked very pensive.

"Do you think there was a custody battle over a child and that's why she was obsessed with having lost her baby?" she asked.

"Could be. This opens up several interesting possibilities. But enough of that. I didn't ask you here to spend the entire evening discussing police business."

"What did you ask me for?" she asked sweetly, batting her eyelashes at him.

He didn't rise to it. "To enjoy the company of my favourite woman and show off my culinary skills."

"It was an excellent meal. You've kept quiet about your skills."

"It doesn't do to let people know you can cook. You get taken advantage of. Besides, I don't have the time or inclination to bother most of the while."

"Point taken. Let me help you with the washing up."

"I thought you'd never ask."

The chatted in a desultory manner as they washed and dried the dishes but Nick seemed increasingly preoccupied. He replied when she spoke to him but she was sure that he wasn't really listening to her. He was miles away.

"The moon is black and is bleeding purple ink, isn't it," she said in a conversational tone.

"Yes . . . what did you say?"

"I think I've outstayed my welcome."

"I'm sorry, Rachel, you could never do that, it's just that something has come up."

"It has? Since when?"

"Look, I have to go back to the station. I'm sorry about this; I'll make it up to you when this case is over. Do you mind?"

"Do I have any choice in the matter? I realise your work takes precedence over me."

"Oh, hell, it doesn't. It's just that I've got to get this cleared up, then I can concentrate on you."

"Is that a threat or a promise? No, don't worry, I'm not going to be awkward. I could do with an early night."

He practically pushed her out of the door and when she had gone he grabbed his jacket and drove the short distance to the Station. There were plenty of people still working and he found one of Collin's team inputing information into the computer.

"That photo that was found at the scene of Swain's arrest – is it still with Forensics?"

"No, they've finished with it. It's locked away with the other evidence."

"Can I have a look at it?"

The man shrugged and fetched it for him and Nick studied it for the second time. Yes, he supposed she could be wearing a wedding dress. Not the traditional full-blown rig with headdress and veil but it was white and decorative and she definitely *had* got a ring on the third finger of her left hand. He made a note of the writing on the back: *Fabriano, May 1992*, and handed it back to the sergeant with thanks.

Back home he consulted an atlas and looked up a map of Italy. As he had thought Fabriano was a small town about one hundred miles from Rome. Tomorrow, before he went into work he had a phone call to make.

Fourteen

After a bad night in which he was prey to a horrific night-mare, Nick finally surfaced at half past six the next morning. He had had difficulty in getting to sleep and when he had at last dropped off he had dreamt that Rachel was in danger. She was being chased by Ellen and when she ran into the station seeking help the desk sergeant changed into Gabriel who hauled her off to a cell and proceeded to sexually assault her under the pitiless gaze of Gaia who encouraged him with nods and applause.

He dragged himself out of bed, still haunted by the dream and showered, shaved and dressed. An hour and two mugs of coffee later he felt more able to face the day. He checked his watch: seven thirty, which meant it would be nine thirty in Italy. With any luck he would catch Luigi Rossi at his desk in Rome.

Ispettore Rossi was his counterpart in the Polizia Criminale. A few years ago they had worked together on a case involving both British and Italian criminals, and having discovered an instant rapport they had kept in touch ever since. He pulled the phone towards him and punched out the international code for Italy, followed by the number of the police bureau and then Luigi's extension number. In a very short time he was connected and identified himself.

"*Nico! Ciao, vecchio amico. Come stai? Come posso aiutarti?*"

"Speak English, you rogue. I know you're fluent in my lingo."

There was a chuckle from the other end. "The same old Nico – you do not change. What can I do for you?"

"I'm hoping you can get me some information. How are things in Rome?"

"I get older and the criminals get more clever and sophisticated, and that is not talking about the Mafiosi."

"At least we don't have that to contend with here. Do you have contacts in Fabriano?"

"Fabriano? It depends what you want to know."

Nick told him and Luigi listened carefully, repeating words under his breath as he made notes.

"That should be no problem. It is not police business but I can go to the right authority. When I have found out for you I will fax it through."

"No, don't do that. Phone me here."

"You don't want the poking eyes – huh?"

"Caught you out, Luigi – it's *prying* eyes, and yes, you're right; this is a little undercover investigation. When I get the information and, if it is what I think it will be, I shall decide what to do and maybe later you can fax it through as evidence. Have you got my home number?"

"I think so but I will write it down now."

Nick gave him the number and enquired after his wife.

"She is fine. We are now the grandparents."

"I don't believe it, you've left me behind."

"When are you coming over to see us? You take the holiday and come and visit us. You and your woman. You have a woman?"

"Why don't you come here and I'll show you parts of England you haven't seen."

"It is too cold. Always the rain and the cold."

"Don't you believe it. I bet it's hotter here at the moment than it is in Rome. We have a heatwave."

"When do you want this information?"

"How about today?"

There was a snort from the other end of the line.

"How is it you say? – you should be so lucky!"

The heat was searing. The countryside shrivelled before it could assume its summer canopy of foliage. Early poppies slashed the hedgerows and field edges with scarlet but quickly withered and joined the bleached, desiccated scrub that passed for grass.

Everywhere was like a tinderbox and the fire service was kept busy coping with the numerous fires started accidentally by a carelessly tossed cigarette butt or spontaneous combustion. That night Moulton Manor was torched.

Public relief that the rapist was caught and the spate of burglaries that had plagued the area brought to an end turned to rumblings of bitterness and antagonism against the Children of Light. The Press fed this animosity, referring to Moulton Manor as 'this canker in our midst, this blot on our countryside'. The knowledge that the two perpetrators were already in custody awaiting trial did little to alleviate the ill will gaining momentum amongst the inhabitants of Casterford and district.

A group of vigilantes, egged on by local opinion, drove out to Moulton Abbas and under cover of darkness set fire to the Manor. A single fiery brand tossed in through a smashed window was all that was needed to start the conflagration, which spread rapidly, devouring the ancient timbers with hungry tongues of flame and quickly reaching the barn and outbuildings, setting the entire complex ablaze.

Alerted by nearby villagers, the fire brigade and police were quickly on the scene but little could be done to quench the inferno. It was more by luck than skill that the remaining Children of Light still living there on parole got out alive. They had been sleeping in the wing farthest from the seat of the blaze and were rescued with only minutes to spare. The livestock was not so lucky, incinerated along with the craft-ware and produce and the entire contents of the tithe barn.

Nick Holroyd was part of the police presence, called out because of his involvement with the happenings at Moulton Manor. He watched with mixed feelings as the firemen tackled the flames. A part of him held a sneaking sympathy with the people who had decided to raze this place of evil connections to the ground, whilst the rest of him was horrified and disgusted by their total disregard for the safety of its inhabitants. Most of the Children of Light were as much victims of Gabriel as the members of the public that he and Gaia had preyed upon. Their ideals had been shattered and they were now paying the price for their muddled beliefs.

Ann Quinton

He mopped his sweating brow and wrinkled up his nose at the smell of burning animal flesh, unable to rid himself of the idea that he was attending some monstrous barbecue. He walked away from the glowing front façade of the building and trudged through charred debris across the courtyard towards the wing which had housed the chapel. The mighty glass windows had shattered and melted and the metal frames were bent and distorted, reminding him of photos he had seen of the Blitz.

"Don't go any nearer, sir," warned a fireman, "it's not safe. The roof girders could come down at any minute."

Nick stayed where he was and looked in. Was it his imagination or could he really distinguish the smell of incense amongst the stink of burning? The pews and carpet and wall-hangings had all been destroyed but the altar still stood, a solid slab of stone although the cross that stood on it was blackened and twisted and looked more like a swastika than an emblem of Christianity.

He turned away and went back to join his colleagues. Perhaps it was fitting that Moulton Manor had bitten the dust. It drew a line beneath the two cases that had been exercising the entire force for such a long time. Gabriel was going down for the rapes and Gaia's thieves' kitchen had been sorted. The only loose end was the murder of Gina Bonetti and he had a line on that. How long would it take Luigi Rossi to come up with the answers to his queries?

The call from Rome came the next morning as he was eating his breakfast. He listened in silence as his Italian friend told him the results of his enquiries.

"This is what you wanted to know, Nico?"

"Yes, thanks very much."

"It is what you expected? It will help with your investigation."

"It certainly will. I may need written confirmation later."

"Any time. Are you going to tell me what it is all about?"

"You shall be told everything when it is finished, I promise. And thanks for your help, I owe you."

"One day I will call it in. *Ciao*, Nico."

Nick replaced the receiver and stared out of the window unseeingly. His hunch had paid off. He was awaiting just one

206

more piece of information, then he would have to decide what he was going to do. When he reached the station a report was waiting on his desk and as he read it through the last fact slotted into place. He was very preoccupied for the rest of that day. The station was abuzz with the fire at Moulton Manor and its consequences but his mind was on other things. He knew he couldn't sit on the knowledge he had acquired; he had to act on it, but just how and when he wasn't sure.

He was still worrying about his course of action when he left the building later that day. As he crossed the car-park he bumped into Keith Adams who was also making for his car.

"You calling it a day?" asked Adams, shifting a pile of reports from one arm to another.

"Yes. You look as if you're taking work home with you."

"Shit, this can wait 'til later. How about a having a jar at The Forrester's Arms?"

"I've got a better idea. Why not come over to my place. I've been sorting out those tapes you wanted to borrow. You can pick them up and I've always got a four-pack in the fridge."

"Sounds fine to me. I'll follow you up."

A short while later they were sprawled on chairs in Nick's sitting room.

"Do you want anything to eat? I can run to biscuits and cheese."

"No, this has saved my life." Adams took a gulp out of his can and wiped the froth off his mouth with the back of his hand. "How much longer is this heatwave going to last? I never thought I'd moan about English weather being too hot."

"They talk of storms arriving by the weekend. We could do with a good downpour to dowse the embers of Moulton Manor. It's still smouldering and the fire chief is afraid it may combust again."

"Hell, that was a turn-up for the books, wasn't it. Have you got the yobs who started it? No, scrub that question, we're not going to talk shop. I need a break."

"We have things to discuss, Keith."

"Such as?" Adams raised his eyebrows and took another swig from his can.

"I've had the report on the DNA testing of the baby's skeleton today. It's definite – Gina Bonetti was the mother of that child."

Nick got to his feet and went over to the window. He stared out at the dried-up patch of garden and tossed casually over his shoulder:

"What was she called?"

"Maria Natalie . . ."

Nick spun round and the two men locked eyes.

"It was *your* baby, wasn't it?" said Nick. "Gina Bonetti was your wife. *You* killed her!"

Keith Adams groaned and buried his head in his hands.

"How do you know? How did you find out?"

"I've had my suspicions for some time. You always insisted that it was the work of the rapist and couldn't be a copycat killing and you seemed to know right from the start that the bones were those of a girl. Then, this business of the photo of Bonetti: it certainly wasn't dropped by Rachel and Gabriel has always denied having anything to do with it, but there was another person in the equation, wasn't there – you. You were there, it could have fallen from *your* pocket when you tackled Gabriel; a fact that everybody else has apparently overlooked. She was wearing a wedding ring in that photo and you claimed it was a wedding photo and that the dress that she was wearing was a wedding dress, which I thought was a strange conclusion to come to, but you were right. Because it was taken on *your* wedding day, wasn't it? I have a contact in the Rome police and I got in touch with him and asked him to investigate. He came back with some interesting facts. He had discovered that Gina Bonetti was married by the Segretario Comunale in a civil ceremony in Fabriano on the 8th May 1992 to an Englishman named Keith Adams. Yes?"

"Yes, it's true." He gazed up at his friend with anguish in his eyes. "I didn't mean to kill her. I . . . I just lost control when I learnt what had happened to my . . . to *our* daughter . . ."

"Tell me about it."

"Can I have another beer?"

Nick got another can out of the fridge and handed it to him. Keith pulled the ring-pull, splashing beer down the front of his shirt which he ignored, and took a few sips before setting it down on the table. He started to speak, staring blindly in front of him as if he were talking to himself.

"We met in 1991. I was an ambitious young constable in Wolverhampton, recently seconded to CID, and Gina was a member of the local repertory company. She was a very volatile, temperamental person and I found her exciting, unlike anyone I had known before . . . and she was beautiful – in a very Latin sort of way . . ."

"I know, I've seen the photo."

"She was passionate and impulsive and I fell heavily for her, not realising that she was already unbalanced and her moods were due to mental problems. Anyway, we fell in love and decided to get married and she wanted the wedding to be in Fabriano where her family came from. Her mother was English and after a farming disaster when Gina was a young girl the family had moved to England and she was brought up here. However, when her mother died, when Gina was a teenager, her father moved back to Fabriano where there was a large clan of Bonettis scattered around the area.

"We had a civil wedding. I should have been suspicious at the time I suppose, that the family were so willing to allow her to marry a foreigner and a non-Catholic to boot, without the full paraphernalia of the Church of Rome. But they knew she was was unstable and I realised later that they had been only too happy to off-load her on to an innocent young Englishman who was going to take her far from their midst. Anyway, things started to go wrong right from the first. She hated me being a policeman and resented the time I spent away from her. We had rows and reconciliations and then she became pregnant . . .

"I hoped this would improve things, stabilise her. That once she had the baby to love and look after she would be different. Different!" Keith's face twisted bitterly. "Hell, it seemed to push her right over the top! She couldn't cope and she seemed indifferent to the baby, no maternal feelings at all. My little Maria was a beautiful baby and so sweet and placid – no trouble at all but Gina seemed afraid of her. She would treat her roughly and take no notice of her when she cried. I was at my wits' end. I was taking time off from the job when I shouldn't have been; I was afraid to leave Gina alone with Maria. I tried to persuade her to get help but she flew into a temper and accused me of wanting to get rid of her and wanting to take Maria away from her. Then one day I came home from work and found they had gone. She'd packed up and cleared out, taking Maria with her and I had no idea where they might be.

"I searched everywhere for them. I was desperate to find Maria but none of our friends or acquaintances knew anything about her disappearance. Gina didn't really have any friends – she'd cut herself off from her theatrical background when we married – and mine seemed to think I was well rid of her, though they were sympathetic about me losing Maria. I got the idea that she'd gone back to Italy so I took leave of absence and spent two months over there looking for her. It was useless. Her father had recently died and I spent weeks tracking down various cousins and aunts and uncles but they all denied any knowledge of her. The treated me like an alien and seemed to think it was none of their business. In the end I gave up and came home. I had no idea where she had gone but I was pretty certain she was neither in Italy nor the Wolverhampton district and when a chance came for me to transfer to Preston I took it.

"But I didn't give up hope of finding them. All the while I was working in Preston I tried to keep tabs on the repertory theatres and touring companies around the country. I subscribed to all the theatrical magazines and I scoured all the regional newspapers I could lay my hands on in the hope that she had taken up her acting career and there would be some mention of her, but it was hopeless. She'd really gone to ground. Then one day I bumped into one of the members of her old Wolverhampton repertory company and he mentioned that she was now teaching down south. He seemed to know that we were separated but had no idea that we had a daughter. I pumped him all I could but he could really tell me nothing more. He had heard through the grapevine and he thought Dorset had been mentioned.

"I came down here on holiday and realised it would be impossible to trace anyone in a couple of weeks so I applied for another transfer and got it. Once I started working here I checked out all the schools, both state and private but nobody had heard of her. Then one day I thought I caught a glimpse of her here in Casterford. She was walking along the street and before I could act she had disappeared into the crowd."

He shook his head and drank some more out of his can.

"It's ironic . . . She was performing on the streets of the town and I must have been the only person in the entire force who hadn't seen her or heard about her. Anyway, I didn't know whether I was hallucinating or whether I really *had* seen her but I was extra vigilant after that. The next thing is the baby's skeleton turns up at Moulton Manor and I have this awful gut feeling . . . Then that night in the Indian restaurant where I met you and Rachel . . . you said a medallion had been found round the baby's neck . . . it was the first I had heard of it but I recognised the description. Although Gina was a lapsed Catholic she had wanted Maria to be baptised into the Roman Catholic Church and that medallion was a baptismal present – she always wore it round her neck though I was afraid it was dangerous . . . might get caught and strangle her . . . Then you started talking about Gina Bonetti and I knew that she had killed Maria and hidden her body. But I also knew that she was still living locally and now I knew where to find her.

"The next day I intended driving over to Moulton Manor and confronting her but I didn't have to. I saw her get out of a car in Bedford Street and start to walk along the pavement. I drove up alongside her and yelled at her to get in the car and she was so startled that she did. She immediately tried to get out again but I'd locked the doors . . . I drove back to my flat and dragged her out of the car and into the place. She was very scared and quite hysterical . . . I was yelling at her to tell me what she had done to Maria and she said . . . she said 'They' had stolen her and taken her away and I went mad. I said that I knew that she had killed her and then she went all quiet and started to cry . . ."

The sweat was glistening on Keith's face and his voice cracked.

211

"Take it easy," urged Nick, but Keith shook his head and plunged on with the tale.

"She said Maria wouldn't stop crying. That she cried all the time and gave her a headache. Can you believe it? My little Maria who had been the happiest baby in the world. What had she done to her? How had she treated her, neglected her?" He shook his head in anguish. "She said one day Maria was driving her crazy with her crying and she picked her up and shook her and Maria's head . . . banged against the wall. She stopped crying then and went all quiet and Gina finally realised that she was dead . . . that she had killed her . . ."

Keith raised his head and looked despairingly at Nick.

"I could have forgiven that . . . at least understood it . . . but it was what she said next . . . She said that Maria was a bad baby and didn't deserve to live . . . that it was a good thing she had died . . . I went berserk. I grabbed hold of her and got my hands round her throat and I shook her like she had shaken Maria and then she went limp and I knew she was dead . . ."

"Bloody Hell! Keith, what a terrible affair – you can hardly be blamed."

"I am a murderer," he said simply. "I've spent most of my adult life trying to bring murderers to justice and I'm no better myself."

"What did you do next?"

"I couldn't think straight. My mind went blank and I just sat in a chair for what seemed like hours and then I started to realise that I hadn't discovered how she had buried Maria's body and not been found out and I started to get mad with her again. That brought me to my senses and I tried to work out what I should do.

"I decided I might get away with it if I could make it appear that she was the victim of the rapist. I waited until it was dark and then I wrapped her body in a blanket, put it in the boot of my car and drove over to the river. There was no one about and I carried her along the river bank and hid her beneath the willows. I took off her pants and mussed her clothes so that it would look as if she had been sexually attacked. I didn't think she would be found so soon."

212

"Christ! I don't know what to say!"

"What are you going to do? Are you going to turn me in?"

Nick paced the room, blindly touching the objects with which he came into contact. He looked as haggard as his friend.

"You saved Rachel's life . . ." He came to a sudden decision. "Write it all down, just as you've told me. I'll give you some paper and leave you to it. When you've finished, sign it. I'll hang on to it until tomorrow. You'll have the rest of this evening and tonight to . . ."

"Scarper? How will you explain the delay?"

"I'll think of some way round it."

He left Keith sitting at the table scribbling away and went into the kitchen where he tackled the job of cleaning the oven; something he had not done since he moved in. As he scraped and scoured he went over in his mind what Keith had just told him. He felt an overwhelming sympathy for his friend. He had had intense provocation but what would count against him would be his efforts to deceive the police and his attempt to pin the death on another man. From time to time he glanced into the sitting room, to see that Keith was still writing furiously and the pile of written sheets growing.

Some time later Keith got to his feet and came into the kitchen clutching his confession and the two men looked at each other.

"I'm going to turn myself in."

"You're what?"

"I want her to be acknowledged. Maria. For the past four and a half years she's been lying in the ground like an animal. Nobody knew who she was – they didn't even know she was a girl when she was found. I want her to be properly buried with her name known – Maria Natalie Adams. I want her and her mother to have a Christian burial."

"When did you first suspect him?" Rachel swiped at a marauding wasp and picked up her sandwich. She and Nick were picnicking on Chesil Beach and he had been telling her about Keith Adams's confession and subsequent events.

"I suppose right from the time his daughter's body was

discovered there was this niggle at the back of my mind but I refused to acknowledge it. I didn't want to think it through, pursue the doubts I was having."

"That's understandable. I feel so sorry for him, he obviously didn't mean to kill her. What will happen to him?"

"As you say, it wasn't a planned murder, he was provoked beyond bearing. I think he'll get away with manslaughter. He was a damned fine police officer, it's a shame."

"She's to be pitied too. She was mentally ill, she wasn't responsible for her actions."

"She was aware enough to know that she had done something terrible and to be afraid of what would happen if Keith caught up with her."

"She should never have had children. She couldn't cope and it tipped her over the top."

"Talking of children . . ." Nick leaned back and tucked his arms behind his head. He addressed the sky. ". . . it's time we started thinking about a family. We're not getting any younger, we're certainly well past the first flush of youth."

"*What* did you say?" she gasped weakly. He sat up and bent over her, laying a finger over her mouth.

"Ssh, don't say anything, I haven't finished."

"I don't think I'm capable."

"Hear me out. I've got some leave due to me, quite a lot. How are you fixed – can you take some holiday?"

"Well, yes, I suppose I could . . ."

"Good. I thought we'd get married – at the end of the month." She gaped at him.

"But you don't want to get married."

"Who said?"

"Well, I've always had the impression that the last thing you would contemplate was getting married again."

"A man can change his mind. And I've had a word with the Des Rev. He said the fact that I'm divorced shouldn't affect you becoming a priest if you want to later."

"*You've* spoken to Peter?"

"Yes. He was quite in favour of it, thought it was a good idea."

"Words fail me. The all boys together act! Deciding my future between you – don't I get consulted?"

"But I've just asked you . . ."

"You didn't you know."

"Well, I'm asking you now. Will you be my wife, Rachel Morland? To have and to hold until death us do part."

"There's something you should know."

"You're not going to tell me that you're *not* a widow. That there is still a Rev Morland?"

"No, of course not. I've been thinking about us a lot recently, trying to sort out my attitude to you, to sex, to love, and I had reached a decision."

She paused and he looked at her and groaned.

"Don't do this to me, Rachel. Don't turn me down, I can't bear it."

"Actually, I was going to say that I am willing to live with you without benefit of marriage lines. So you don't have to marry me."

"God damn it, woman, I *want* to marry you, don't you understand? I *love* you and neither of us would be truly happy with less than the real thing. I know there will be a problem with the wedding ceremony – you'll want a church wedding and me being divorced."

"I've never asked you: were *you* the guilty party?"

"She left me."

"Then the problem may not be insurmountable. Peter may be able to sort something out with the Bishop."

"Am I taking it that you're saying yes?"

"I suppose I am. Yes, of course I am. I couldn't bear to lose you, Nick."

"Nor I you. The events of the last few weeks have really brought home to me how fleeting happiness can be. You mustn't let it slip through your fingers, you don't get a second chance."

"That's a lovely collection of clichés."

"I'm not used to doing this, words fail me." He rolled over and got to his feet.

"I'm just going back to the car for something. I won't be a moment."

While he was gone she wrestled with her wedding ring. It had never been off her finger since Christopher had placed it there during their wedding ceremony. At first she thought it was stuck and immovable but eventually she managed to twist it round and slip it off. She held it in her palm for a few seconds and then put it on a right hand finger. Her marriage to Christopher had been happy and successful but the time had come to move on and she was sure he would have approved. He had always insisted that she mustn't look back and even when he was dying he had urged her to go on living and try and find happiness with someone else. She had always thought that that would be impossible but now she knew that she had been wrong. She had been given a second chance and she was going to grab it. Marriage to Nick would be a challenge but it wouldn't be dull. There would have to be a great deal of give and take on both sides but they were mature enough to realise this and make a go of it.

Nick came scrunching back through the stones and slithered in a shower of pebbles down the shingle bank towards her. He held out a cool bag triumphantly.

"I've brought the champagne *and* the glasses. It won't be very cold but I hope it's OK."

"You were very sure I was going to say yes."

"It was a case of either toasting our engagement or drowning my sorrows."

"You've always got an answer, haven't you? Do you think we'll spend a lot of time arguing?"

"I'm sure we shall but life certainly won't be dull." He undid the foil and twisted the bottle in its wire cradle and the cork shot out with a satisfactory pop. He poured the foaming liquid into two glasses and handed one to her.

"To us."

"To us." She touched his glass with hers and smiled at him before drinking.

"Oh, Rachel, when you look at me like that I go to pieces. How soon can we get married?"

"Don't forget we've got a funeral first."

Fifteen

The storm had raged for two hours causing chaos on the roads and minor floods in many parts of the county. The funeral party had been drenched getting from car to church and the first part of the service had been almost drowned out as the rain beat down on the roof and the thunder cracked overhead. But now it had ceased as suddenly as it had started and a weak sun filtered in through the stained glass east window throwing coloured lozenges on the two coffins resting in the chancel.

As the small group of mourners rose to sing *The Lord is my Shepherd* Rachel looked over them. Keith Adams was in the front row sandwiched between Superintendent Powell and Mark Collins. Support, duty or escort? She didn't know which. He had been sitting bowed with his head in his hands but now he sang, eyes fixed firmly ahead, carefully avoiding looking at the coffins. Behind him was Nick and Fiona Walker and a few more men and women who she was sure were also police officers. On the other side of the aisle were two elderly men who, from their garb of brown habits and sandals, must have belonged to the Children of Light community. There appeared to be no members of Gina Bonetti's family here. Presumably they would have been reluctant to attend a C of E service even if they had been contacted. At the back of the church, keeping out of the way were half a dozen men and women who Rachel thought were Press.

A single wreath adorned each coffin. The one on Gina Bonetti's was of red and white carnations; on the child's was a simple circlet of white roses and lilies. Nick had told her that the medallion found round the baby's neck had been sealed in the coffin with the tiny skeleton. The psalm finished and she moved to the chancel steps to read the collect.

"Heavenly Father,
whose Son our Saviour
took little children into his arms and blessed them:
receive, we pray, your child Maria Natalie and
your daughter Gina in your never-failing care and love,
comfort all who have loved them on earth,
and bring us all to your everlasting Kingdom,
through Jesus Christ our Lord."

There was a mumbled 'amen' from the small congregation and Rachel proceeded with the service. This was the first time she had officiated at the funeral of a child and the tragedy surrounding the two deaths made it all the more poignant. Keith had insisted that she conduct the funeral service and Peter Stevenson had been quite willing. Mother and child were being buried here in the churchyard of St James's and the cortège moved outside for the committal.

The storm had finally departed; the trees dripped with moisture and raindrops shimmered from every blade of grass as the procession moved along the gravel path and squelched through the long grass to the graveside.

When she spoke the words of the committal: ". . . earth to earth, ashes to ashes, dust to dust . . ." two figures moved out from under the cover of a nearby yew tree and walked towards them. One of the figures limped and was accompanied by an enormous dog. Jason Cunningham and Lonny had come to pay their last respects to their ex-comrade. Mark Collins moved to intercept them but the superintendent stopped him. Lonny paused on the edge of the group and the dog subsided on to its haunches, tongue lolling out of its mouth as it surveyed the mourners, but Jason came right up to the grave and Rachel handed him the little silver trowel.

He bent down and scooped up some soil and scattered it over the coffins. As he straightened up he found himself looking directly into the eyes of Fiona Walker. Puzzlement and dawning recognition struggled across his features as he did a visible double take. Then he winked boldly at her, dropped the trowel and strolled back to his friend.